Lynn's kiss began slow but surged when a warm hand slipped beneath her knit shirt and began to trace the nipple of her bare breast. "We'd better take this inside."

They stumbled toward the house, both reluctant to release the other. They managed to lock doors and shut off lights as they went. Discarded clothes marked their progress to the bedroom. In a frantic tangle of arms and legs, they fell across the old bed that had been Lynn's childhood bed. Before that it had belonged to her grandparents. There were times when Lynn felt as though she would explode from the passion Crissy generated within her. She had never been in a relationship where the physical needs remained so intense, but then again, she had never loved anyone the way she loved Crissy.

Her lips closed around a swollen nipple and a soft sigh filled her ears. She couldn't be certain if the whisper of delight was Crissy's or her own. When Crissy's hand pushed between Lynn's thighs, the loud sounds of pleasure that followed were definitely Lynn's.

"My God." Lynn sighed, raising Crissy's damp hand to her lips. "You should insure these hands."

"Umm," Crissy chuckled as Lynn rolled over on top of her and kissed her deeply. "And you should insure those lips."

"Maybe we should examine their skill level in more detail before we decide," she said as her body inched its way down.

"I agree completely."

All thoughts of sleep were soon forgotten.

Also by Frankie J. Jones:

Voices of the Heart
For Every Season
Survival of Love
Midas Touch
Room for Love
Captive Heart
Whispers in the Wind
Rhythm Tide

Writing as Megan Carter:

Please Forgive Me
Passionate Kisses
When Love Finds a Home
On the Wings of Love

THE ROAD HOME

FRANKIE J. JONES

Bella
BOOKS
2007

Bella Books, Inc.
P.O. Box 10543
Tallahassee, FL 32302

First Edition

Editor: Christi Cassidy
Cover designer: KIARO Creative Ltd.

ISBN-10: 1-59493-110-0
ISBN-13: 978-1-59493-110-9

Martha
For all you do

ACKNOWLEDGMENTS

I'd like to thank Martha Cabrera, Peggy Herring and Carol Poynor for reading the manuscript and keeping me on track. I promise to try to have the next one finished sooner—oh, wait; you've already heard that one.

Thanks to Christi Cassidy for all the effort and attention to detail she puts into every manuscript.

In the best interest of the story, I've taken a few liberties in the actual lottery process.

About the Author

Frankie Jones is an award-winning artist and freelance nature photographer. In her spare time she likes to rummage through flea markets and junk shops in search of broken treasure in need of repair. Her hobbies include woodworking, metal detecting and genealogy.

Authors love to hear from the readers. You may contact Frankie by e-mail at FrankieJJones@aol.com.

CHAPTER ONE

Lynn Strickland secured her hold on the two bags and took a deep breath. She tried to pretend the air was filled with the sweet fragrance of fresh flowers and newly mowed grass rather than the acrid exhaust from the nearby freeway. As she pulled open the door, she braced herself for the cloying scent that she had come to associate with the slow decline into death.

After nearly ten years of coming to the Morning Sunrise nursing home every Saturday, she still couldn't get used to the smell. The building was old and the furniture had long since lost any veneer of newness that it might have once held. The heavy undercurrent of industrial cleaner gave testimony to someone's attempt at cleaning. Again, she tried to pinpoint and identify the exact cause of the slightly sweet, yet musty odor. Was it the smell of lost youth and unfulfilled dreams, or the stench of dejection and hopelessness? Morning Sunrise was nothing like those exclusive retirement centers she saw advertised on television, where members spent their time playing golf on a lush eighteen-hole course or splashing gaily in sparkling, heated pools. Here, privacy was almost nonexistent. Most of the sixty or so residents spent their days in front of a television that projected a picture with a ghastly greenish tint. A few lucky ones would be in their rooms chatting with visitors, while a dozen or so of the more socially minded would congregate in the recreation room to play cards. Some of the ones who were still physically able could occasionally be found pacing around the shoebox-size outdoor area in the back. Unfortunately, the vast majority of the populace was confined to their rooms, either due to medical problems or their own personal reasons.

Lynn seldom missed a Saturday. While it was physically impossible for her to sit with everyone, she truly believed that her time there made a difference to the few she did see.

Her first visit had come about as a high school class project. She could no longer remember exactly what the assignment had been, but it dealt with interviewing people who'd lived during World War II. She quickly discovered that she enjoyed talking to the residents. At the nursing home her differences, which seemed so prominent at school, weren't an issue. No one seemed to notice or care that she never wore makeup, or that her hair was much shorter than other teenaged girls. These people accepted her for who she was, and in turn gave her back as much as she gave them.

Over the years, she had built a deep and lasting friendship with many of these men and women. A few had been moved to other facilities and sadly some had died. When the first death happened, it had been so painful that she'd almost stopped going. Then a member of the staff had pointed out how much the residents looked forward to her visits. It still hurt to lose one, but now she couldn't imagine not going. The weekly trips had become as important to her as they were to the people she visited.

Her heart clenched as it always did when she spotted Mrs. Harmon sitting on one of the couches in the entryway. Lynn had learned from the staff that even during her more lucid times, the woman sat there the entire day waiting for relatives who never came. In fact, it was a family that was no longer living. Her husband, Herman Harmon, had died twenty ears ago and their only son, Allen, had been killed in Vietnam. Mrs. Harmon had been placed in Morning Sunrise after she had been found wandering the street, nearly dead with pneumonia.

"Good morning, Mrs. Harmon," Lynn called out cheerfully. She approached slowly to see if this would be one of the days when she would be recognized. It was always a guessing game, given the poor woman's patchwork memory.

"Hello, Lynn."

Relieved that this was one of her better days, Lynn sat down on the couch and reached into one of the bags. "Would you like an orange?" She held up the bright orange fruit. She often brought oranges, not for any source of nutritional value, but rather for their warm color and wonderful smell. They always seemed to cheer people up.

The older woman's deeply lined face lit up with a brilliant smile at the offer of the small gift. It was smiles like these that prompted Lynn to always bring some little something along on her visits. It was never much, because in truth she couldn't afford a great deal. No matter how small the gift was the gratitude in their eyes never wavered.

"I'm waiting for my son, Allen," Mrs. Harmon said as she held the orange to her nose and inhaled deeply. "He's going to come to see me and bring me a bouquet of daisies. When he was a little boy he would pick daisies from the field behind the house and bring them to me." She turned the orange slowly in her hands. "You should wait with me and meet him. He's cute and single." She smiled again.

"Now, Mrs. Harmon, you know I'm too old for him. I'm almost twenty-five."

"Are you still a lesbian?"

Lynn blinked at the sudden change of direction. She was never sure how much Mrs. Harmon would remember from visit to visit. "Yes, ma'am, I'm not likely to be changing that."

Mrs. Harmon continued to sniff the orange. "You just haven't met the right man yet. You wait until you meet my Allen. He could charm bees into giving up their honey."

"This bee won't be giving up her honey anytime soon," Lynn said. Her reply was met with a healthy swat on the knee.

"Listen to how you young girls talk now. When I was your age we didn't go around talking like that."

"No. When you were my age you were sneaking off with some handsome boy," Lynn teased back.

With a hand dusted with age spots Mrs. Harmon fussed with her sparse hair. "Well, there was a time when I could still turn a boy's head."

"You still can." Lynn leaned closer. "I saw Mr. Benavidez checking you out the other day." When the older woman smiled, Lynn continued. "Heck, if I wasn't already taken, maybe I'd even try to convert you." She quickly kissed her paper-thin cheek and was instantly rewarded with a shriek of mock indignation and another sound slap on the knee.

"Don't you have other people to go bother?" She pushed at Lynn's shoulder. "What would Allen think if he walked in and saw that?" Bright pink circles warmed her cheeks and her eyes sparkled as she shook her finger at Lynn. "I'm not that kind of woman."

"You just haven't met the right woman yet," Lynn teased as she grabbed her two bags and jumped up before the old woman could swat her again. "I'll stop by on my way out. Maybe Allen will be here by then." With a quick wave she hurried down the hallway.

4

Lynn stopped several times to pass out oranges and talk to various residents. She took time to write letters for a couple of people before she went to check on Mr. Greenberg.

"How's it going today, Mr. G?" The light pleasant scent of pipe tobacco hovered around him. She had commented on it once right after she started visiting him and learned that it was a custom blend that he special-ordered from a local shop. Due to its high price tag he used it sparingly. "I brought some oranges. Would you like one?" She glanced over quickly to see if the other occupant to the room, Mr. Cook, was there, and breathed a sigh of relief when she saw he wasn't. She had tried to like the man, but he was mean through and through. In the four years or so that she had been visiting Mr. Greenberg, she had never heard Mr. Cook say a civil word about anything or anyone.

Simon Greenberg nodded and eagerly reached for the fruit. After giving it a test sniff, he tucked it away in a nearby drawer. "I have to hide everything or someone will steal it."

Lynn glanced at the laptop that was still sitting on the table exactly where she had left it the previous weekend. Obviously theft wasn't a problem. Or perhaps the thief simply wasn't into electronics. "Have you mastered that laptop?" she asked as she placed the now nearly empty bag of fruit on the end of his bed along with the second bag that contained cookies that she had brought for her friend Beulah Mae.

The short, balding man made a rude sputtering noise as he waved her over to the table where the computer sat. "Who can make any sense of these contraptions? I tell David to call on the telephone." Again he made the noise. "He works in that fancy bank. Surely he can afford to call me once a week. Why should I have to bother with this thing?"

David Greenberg had purchased the laptop for his father, hoping they could communicate more frequently through e-mail, but unfortunately Mr. Greenberg hadn't shown much interest in adopting the new technology. She picked up the laptop and took a seat on the straight-backed chair by the window. She suspected his reluctance to do so was because he enjoyed her reading the e-mails to him.

"Let's see what David has to say." She pressed the power switch. As soon as the system was up and running she moved the chair around so he could see the screen. "Watch what I'm doing, so you can check it yourself. Then you can read David's e-mail every day, and when I visit next Saturday we'll have more time to talk."

He pulled his chair slightly closer but continued to stare at the machine as if he expected it to come to life and attack them. "There are too many buttons to push, and besides, what do I know about typing? I'm not a secretary."

After she had gone through and read each of David's messages, she typed in the elder man's reply.

"That wasn't too painful, was it?" she asked as she set the laptop on a small table. She spied a deck of playing cards lying on the table and an idea came to her. "I'm going to leave this on so you can practice." She scrolled through screens until she found the games menu and opened Solitaire. "I think you'll enjoy this, since you like to play cards."

"I have real cards that I can put in my pocket and take anywhere I want to go. Why should I want to play on that thing?"

Lynn knew that he suffered with arthritis in his hands. "Well, one reason is that when you're playing electronic solitaire you don't have to shuffle and your rows never get messed up." She chose the option to begin a new game and showed him how to play. "The bad thing is, you can't cheat," she said with a sigh when she lost the game.

"I never cheat," he insisted.

"Then you're a better person than I am." She stood. "I know you can do this."

"I'm too old to be learning about all these new fads." He leaned forward in his chair. "Pedro Garza's daughter mailed him some kind of pod or some such to listen to music."

"An iPod," Lynn said as she stretched the kinks from her back.

He made the sputtering noise again. "Whatever. She says it's better because it's portable. I told him, 'If you want portable music get a transistor radio,' but nobody listens to me anymore."

"Does he enjoy the iPod?"

Mr. Greenberg shrugged. "Who can tell? We can't hear anything on it. We pushed all the buttons but couldn't get the thing to play. It was probably made in Japan."

Lynn smiled. "He has to use the earbuds."

"Ear bugs!"

"Buds. Earbuds." She tried to remember what her mother called them. "Earphones," she clarified. "They allow him to listen to his music without disturbing others."

He threw out his hands in frustration. "Why? Who's it going to disturb? We're all half deaf anyway." He pointed and tilted his head knowingly. "You watch what I'm telling you. Those things are going to make everyone deaf. It's not healthy to go poking things in your ears."

Lynn started to speak, but he was on a roll.

"I know what I'm talking about. I worked in that engine plant for thirty years. All that noise." He pointed to his ear. "That's why I can't hear so good."

Lynn patted his shoulder. "You take care and I'll see you next week."

He tried to stand. It took him a couple of practice starts to push himself upright. As discreetly as possible she stood ready to catch him in case he started to topple. She'd learned early on that the majority of the residents were very proud people and didn't welcome unsolicited assistance. As soon as he was securely on his feet, she moved toward the door. Leaving was usually the hardest part of her visits. The residents were so starved for company that some of them tended to cling. She would have liked to spend more time with each of them, but she simply didn't have that luxury. In addition to working two jobs, she also had to keep the house together. She tried to do everything herself so that Crissy, who was working and going to college, would have more time to study. Her two indulgences were Wednesday night softball and her Saturdays at the nursing home. Crissy had one more semester before she graduated from the University of Texas at San Antonio. Hopefully, she would be able to find a teaching position quickly and their lives would start to settle down. Both of their tempers had been running too high recently.

"Do you have to leave so soon?" he asked.

"Sorry, but I promised Beulah Mae I'd help her fill out some important forms. I'll try to get here a little earlier next week so we'll have more time." She felt guilty about the promise because she knew she wouldn't be able to make it any earlier. She picked up the bags from the foot of his bed. "You practice playing solitaire and try to answer some of David's e-mails. I know you'll be able to do it if you set your mind to it."

He patted her arm and nodded. "Maybe you're right, but I still don't see what's wrong with him picking up the telephone and calling." He sighed. "I want to talk to him, not some plastic box."

She waved a final good-bye and rushed out.

CHAPTER TWO

Beulah Mae Williams was standing by the window staring out at the narrow strip of lush green grass dotted with wildflowers. A closer inspection would have revealed the tiny oasis was nothing more than the easement for an exit ramp from the interstate. The greatest advantage to the room was that it had been converted from a storage room and was too small for two people.

"You've got one of the best rooms in the place," Lynn said as she stepped inside the open doorway.

Beulah Mae slowly turned and gazed at her with eyes that seemed to hold the knowledge of the world. As always, Lynn was momentarily startled by the intensity of the look. She had been visiting Beulah Mae since she had entered Morning Sunrise a little over two years ago. During that time they had grown to be close friends.

"I'll trade my great view for that pretty girlfriend of yours,"

Beulah Mae teased.

Crissy had jokingly accused Lynn of worshiping Beulah Mae, and maybe to some extent she did, because she had never known anyone like her. It seemed as though Beulah Mae had seen and done it all. She had told Lynn stories about how she had posed as a man to secure a job on more than one occasion, and lived with more women than Lynn could keep track of. She'd traveled to places and done things most folks would only read or dream about. She was an old-school butch who, as she so often said, "walked the walk and talked the talk."

Lynn studied Beulah Mae's deeply lined ebony face and smiled as she placed the bag with its few remaining oranges on a small table by the bed. She handed the one with the cookies to her. "I'm not going to tell Crissy you made that offer. She might tell me to take you up on it. Every time she comes over here with me she spends a week talking about you."

"I've always had a way with the ladies." She ran a thumb around the waistband of her tailored men's slacks and hitched them up before smoothing the front of her black-with-white trim dress shirt. The sleeves had been neatly rolled up to mid-forearm length. Despite the slight stoop of age, she still stood a good three inches taller than Lynn's own five-foot-six-inch frame. There was a breadth to her shoulders that hinted of the strength she had once possessed. "I know how to treat a woman and make her feel like the lady she is." Beulah Mae dug into the cookies.

"I'll bet you did," Lynn said.

"Did?" Beulah Mae scowled at her. "I can still make a woman quiver with pleasure and cry out for her maker." She winked. "If you don't believe me you can ask that pretty little nurse, Janelle." She bit into the cookie with a wide smile. Whether the smile was generated by her enjoyment of the cookie or memories of the young nurse was hard to say.

Lynn thought about the cute, young, blond nurse and couldn't conceal her surprise, which simply made Beulah Mae chuckle harder.

"I don't think you're supposed to be having sex with the staff," Lynn replied without thinking.

"Well, who else would I be having sex with?" Beulah Mae leaned toward her. "It certainly couldn't be any of these old women who live here. Their hearts couldn't stand the excitement." Again she winked. "When I make love to a woman, she knows she's had the best." She shook her head sadly. "Sometimes I feel guilty. I'm afraid I've ruined their lives."

Lynn rolled her eyes. She knew where this was leading.

"Yeah," Beulah Mae lamented. "After a few hours with me, the poor things will never again be satisfied. They'll spend the rest of their lives searching in vain for what I gave them." She polished off the remainder of the cookie and set the bag aside.

"Spare me," Lynn begged.

"If you'd listen to me, I could pass all my wisdom on to you. 'Course, it wouldn't be the same. You'd never be able to truly achieve my level of expertise, you being a white girl and all." Her wicked laughter danced around the room.

Lynn had heard it all before and waved it off. "Crissy loves me just the way I am. That's enough for me. You'll have to find some other Doña Juanita to pass your skills on to."

Beulah Mae sighed. "You young people today. All you ever think about is settling down." She shook her head thoughtfully. "I don't see how anyone could spend decades with only one woman. There are too many beautiful angels out there waiting for someone to love them."

"I like married life and can't wait until Crissy is out of school and everything settles down into a nice comfortable routine." She bit her tongue. She always tried to project her home life as being perfect. As if saying so would make it real. And it wasn't as though they were having any real problems. Their difficulties could all be fixed with more time together and fewer financial problems. She turned her attention back to Beulah Mae.

"I don't understand that. What about seeing the world? Young folks' idea of seeing the world is taking one of those Olivia Cruises I keep reading about. In my day, cruising was a whole different ballgame."

Lynn caught the look of sadness that flashed across Beulah Mae's face. She quickly changed the subject. "Do you still have those forms you needed help with?"

"No. I changed my mind about that, but I do need your help," Beulah Mae said as she opened her closet door and pulled a metal file box from the back. With a key that she kept on a chain around her neck she opened the cheap metal box and removed a thick manila envelope. I need you to keep this for me. I don't feel comfortable having it here anymore."

Lynn frowned. "What's in it?"

"It's something I don't want the staff seeing or knowing anything about. I want you to keep it for me for a while until I can make other arrangements for it." She handed the envelope to Lynn. "Put it inside your shirt of something, so no one will see you with it."

Lynn hefted the rather heavy envelope. "What is this?"

"It's some personal stuff of mine that I'd rather not have anyone here know about."

Lynn stared at the envelope. "I don't feel comfortable taking this."

Beulah Mae frowned. "I thought we were friends. I've already told you it's nothing illegal. Everything that's in there was come by honestly and it all belongs to me." She shook her head again. "In my day, when a friend asked for a favor you did it. You didn't stand around agonizing over every little detail. Will you keep it for me or not?"

To appease her, Lynn unfastened a button on her shirt that was tucked neatly into her jeans and slipped the envelope inside. The bundle made an obvious bulge under her shirt. "This isn't going to work."

Beulah Mae grumbled something unintelligible under her breath before reaching over and pulling Lynn's shirt partially out. "It will if you don't tuck your shirt in so tight," she scolded. With surprisingly deft fingers she soon had a loose fold in the shirt that almost completely hid the bulge of the envelope.

"That's good enough to get you out of here without any trouble," she said as she stepped back to admire her handiwork.

Lynn glanced down at her shirt. "You seemed to have had some experience at hiding things."

"That comes from carrying a piece for so many years."

"A piece of what?" Lynn asked without thinking. Almost as quickly as the words were out she realized what Beulah Mae had meant. "You carried a gun!"

Beulah Mae locked the box and placed it back in the closet. "The world I lived in was very different from the one you know."

"You mean the Klan?"

The older woman practically snorted. "The Klan was the least of my worries. I was more concerned about jealous husbands and crazy girlfriends." She rushed on before Lynn could ask more questions. "I'd also like for you to mail a letter." She stepped over to a small dresser. On top of it sat a phone and a small stack of crossword puzzle books. She opened a drawer and removed a white business-size envelope from beneath a stack of neatly folded men's undershirts. Before handing the envelope to Lynn, she removed a money clip from her pocket and peeled off a crisp five-dollar bill. "This will cover the postage and a little something extra for your trouble." She had extracted the five quickly, but Lynn was still able to see that the next bill in the small fold was a single.

Lynn hesitantly took it from her. She didn't mind mailing the letter, but Beulah Mae had access to full mail service here at the home. Why hadn't she dropped it in the outgoing mail? She considered asking, but after the lecture she'd just received on friendship she decided it was easier to take the letter without questioning her. She was dying to look at the address on the envelope but thought it would be rude. Instead, she carefully slipped it into her hip pocket. She tried to hand the money back. "Here, keep your money. I've got stamps at home."

Beulah Mae pushed Lynn's hand away before she turned, made her way back to the window and sat in one of the two chairs that faced the window.

Knowing from previous encounters that it was useless to argue with Beulah Mae, Lynn tucked the bill into her pocket and took the other seat by the window. "If you like, I'll stop by the bakery next Saturday and bring you some of those little cinnamon rolls that you love so much," she said. Beulah Mae's love of sweets was practically legendary.

Lynn still wasn't comfortable taking the money. Since this was a state facility, all the residents had to liquidate the bulk of their assets before being admitted. Most seemed to make do with whatever the state provided. In Beulah Mae's case, Lynn suspected pride kept the older woman from admitting she was financially strapped.

Beulah Mae reached back into her pocket. "In that case let me give you some more money."

"This is enough."

Beulah Mae scoffed. "You know, the wolf isn't knocking at my door."

Lynn wasn't sure what she meant, but she interpreted it to mean that money wasn't an issue. Before she could argue more, Beulah Mae suddenly changed the subject.

"My birthday is next month. I'll be eighty-five."

"That's great. Why don't you get a pass and Crissy and I will have you over to the house for a special dinner?"

"No, thanks. I don't want to put you out none."

"It's no trouble. Crissy would love to see you again." She waited for Beulah Mae's quick volley. Instead, the older woman suddenly seemed nervous. Lynn leaned forward. "Hey. You okay?"

"I'm fine." Beulah Mae replied vaguely.

"Are you upset about this birthday?"

"Why would I be upset? Birthdays aren't exactly a new experience for me." She drummed her fingers on the chair arm.

They sat in silence as Lynn tried to puzzle out what was wrong with her friend. It wasn't like her to be so nervous.

"You know," Beulah Mae began after a long moment. "I always thought I'd go back home." She looked out the window.

"Where's home?"

"Williamstown." She hesitated a moment before adding, "Colorado."

"Where's that at? I've never heard of it."

Beulah Mae chuckled. "Not surprising. The place is so small it's not even on a map."

"Was it named after your family?"

Beulah Mae leaned back in her chair. "Not exactly. It's more like I'm named after *it*."

Lynn frowned. "What do you mean?"

"I ran away from home when I was fifteen." Beulah Mae suddenly looked older as she slid a hand lined with age over the arm of the chair. "Since then I've occasionally used other names."

Lynn tried to hide her surprise at the new information and wondered if she would ever truly know this woman. She doubted it. Beulah Mae seemed to like to play her cards close to her chest. Lynn looked at her as if seeing her for the first time.

Her closely cropped hair was completely gray. Ebony eyes only slightly dimmed with age reflected a depth that sometimes frightened Lynn. Their intense gaze missed little and revealed even less. Her handsomely lined face portrayed a strong sense of strength and determination. But her most intriguing feature was the impression that she was patiently waiting for something. Lynn couldn't pinpoint exactly what it was. It wasn't the sad sense of resignation that many of the other residents exhibited.

15

It was something deeper, something that only Beulah Mae knew.

Lynn had never really thought of Beulah Mae as being elderly. In her mind she was like a piece of well-seasoned mahogany that merely toughened and improved with age.

"What did you mean when you said you were named after the town?"

Beulah Mae continued to gaze out the window. "I was born Beulah Mae Johnson. After I went out on my own I would sometimes use Williams. I guess it sort of stuck with me over the years."

"I swear you never cease to amaze me. She started to lean forward until the envelope beneath her shirt poked her ribs. "Didn't you have to fill out paperwork when you were admitted?" She straightened back up. "I mean, how did you get in here using an assumed name?"

"Like I said, I've used Williams off and on for years. So I had a history with the name, a background, if you will."

"But how?" Lynn persisted.

"You are a persistent little cuss, aren't you?"

Lynn was beginning to think her question wasn't going to be answered, but after a moment, Beulah Mae gave in.

"I ran away in nineteen thirty-seven. In those days creating a new identity wasn't such a big deal." She quickly warmed to her subject. "There were no computers to store things and paperwork was always getting lost or misplaced. Folks were more apt to take you at face value then. If you were honest, did a full day's work and treated people right, they didn't care so much about your background." She paused. "Of course, that could have partially been due to the fact that I worked blue-collar jobs and ran with others like myself—people who weren't always eager to discuss their past."

Lynn couldn't imagine. She'd been required to show two forms of identification when she was hired at the car wash. "Why did you run away?"

Beulah Mae smiled slightly before answering. "From as far back as I can remember I was different from the other girls. Where I came from 'different' wasn't looked upon very kindly."

Lynn held her questions and waited for her to continue. Her restraint was soon rewarded.

"My father was a sharecropper." Beulah Mae reached for the cookie bag.

Lynn was about to comment that she hadn't known there was sharecropping in Colorado when Beulah Mae started in on her story again.

"Every Sunday morning, come hell or high water, Papa would put on his good suit and preside over the little congregation of the Mount Gideon Colored Church of Williamstown." Beulah Mae idly tapped her fingers on the chair arm. "That's what we were called back then—colored." She grew silent for a moment as she appeared to be considering her next statement. "Seems like somebody has always had a name for me—colored, Negro, African-American, bull dagger, dyke, muff-diver, and a lot more that's too ugly to repeat." She looked up at Lynn. "Ignorance always breeds such nastiness. Have you ever noticed that?"

Lynn nodded. She had endured her share of name-calling, but she suspected her experiences were a drop in the bucket compared to what Beulah Mae had been forced to endure.

"I was the third of ten children. Mama and Papa never had anything but kids and a hard row to hoe. I was the oldest girl. By the time I turned thirteen I was almost as big and as strong as my two older brothers. My size didn't stop some of the men from noticing me. I managed to avoid them by being careful and never putting myself into a situation I couldn't get out of fast. There were a couple of close calls but thank God, I was strong enough to wallop them a good one and get away. When I turned fifteen, I realized it would only be a matter of time before Papa started thinking about getting me married off." She smiled. "I knew I was different somehow. Back then it wasn't like it is now where you see gay people walking around holding hands and raising kids. There was no television to tell me what I was feeling was normal. I didn't have a name for what I was, but I knew I couldn't live with a man. There was plenty of work for men around home, and none at all for decent women, except maybe taking in laundry from the white folks over at Cedar Hill. I remember thinking I didn't have a way out." She paused. "That all changed one hot Sunday morning. I'll never forget it. It was August eighth, nineteen thirty-seven. We were all in church and by some lucky miracle I'd managed to snag a seat by a window. It was so hot that it didn't make much difference where you sat. It was still miserable. The window just gave me some hope of a stray breeze. I can still see Papa standing at the pulpit wearing his one good black suit and preaching about the dangers of greed and gluttony." She glanced at Lynn. "No matter how hot it got, he'd never take that jacket off. He was a tall man and wide through the shoulders, with a deep penetrating voice that made the walls of that old church rattle when he got warmed up."

Lynn could almost feel the stifling heat as Beulah Mae continued on with her story.

"As I said, on this particular Sunday I was sitting by the window. I had a perfect view of the road that ran through town. It was the only road, I might add. As I sat there trying to figure out how gluttony could exist in a town where there wasn't even enough to go around, I saw this enormous shiny black car roll into town. It was the biggest, shiniest thing I'd even seen in my life. At first, I thought it must be an angel coming to take us all to heaven in that beautiful chariot. When it finally stopped two houses down from the church, an angel of a whole other kind stepped out." She chuckled again. "And so help me God, at that very moment, after only one look at that woman, everything in my life suddenly became crystal clear. I knew that I wanted her and I knew exactly what I wanted to do to her." She fell silent.

"Well, did you?" Lynn asked when she could no longer stand the suspense.

Beulah Mae nodded. "Girl, just remembering the things that I learned in the backseat of that shiny car still makes me squirm." A look of sadness crossed her face. "I was just a kid who thought she was head-over-heels in love. To make matter worse, Rachel wasn't exactly what you'd call discreet. My brother Billy Wayne caught us making out down behind the house. He tried to drag me away from her, but I got loose from him and ran. I knew Papa would kill me when he found out. Rachel was scared too and decided it might be time for her to move on. When she drove out of Williamstown, I was hiding beneath a blanket in the backseat and I never looked back."

"So you never went back to see your family?" Lynn asked, amazed. After her own father had left, it had been just her and her mother. There was no extended family other than a distant cousin who had been living in a commune near Seattle the last time anyone had heard from him.

Beulah Mae hesitated a moment. "No. I always meant to, but I was too scared, I guess. I knew Papa would never forgive me."

Lynn detected a heavy sadness in Beulah Mae. She tried to steer the conversation back to something more pleasant. "What do you want for your birthday?"

Beulah Mae looked her square in the eye. "I want to go home."

Surprised, Lynn nodded. "I see. Do you still have family living there?"

Beulah Mae shrugged. "I don't know. I lost track of everyone. That's one of the things I want to find out."

Lynn wondered if Beulah Mae could afford the trip. She never seemed to be without money, but Morning Sunrise wasn't the sort of place where people with money chose to live. She didn't know how to ask without appearing nosy or rude.

"I'm going to need some help," Beulah Mae said at last.

Lynn cringed. Money was an issue. As much as she liked Beulah Mae, she didn't have the financial means to help her. It took everything she and Crissy had to keep Crissy in school and to pay the household bills. "I wish I could help," she began, but Beulah Mae cut her off.

"I don't need money," Beulah Mae assured her. "I have enough of that. I need your help."

"With what?"

"Getting out of here," she said in a lowered voice as she leaned forward.

"Can't you request a pass?" She and Crissy had invited Beulah Mae to dinner a couple of times and it hadn't been a big deal for her to get permission to leave for a few hours.

Beulah Mae began to fidget with the crease in her slacks. "I may need more than a pass. I'm not sure I want to come back here."

Lynn tried to hide her surprise and disappointment. She had really grown fond of Beulah Mae. "You won't need my help with checking out. The staff will assist you with that."

"Well"—she cleared her throat—"it might not be quite that simple. You see, I didn't exactly sign myself in."

"What do you mean? I though you came here of your own free will."

Beulah Mae's fidgeting increased as she glanced nervously around the room. "It was more like they made me come here."

Lynn didn't know what to say. "Oh, I thought you said you moved in here on your own—"

"I did say that," Beulah Mae interrupted, "but I lied. The truth is, I forgot and left a burner on under a pot of beans and my apartment caught on fire. It wasn't that big of a deal. I had it put out before the fire department got there, but the police were called, and that nosy old neighbor told them that it wasn't the first time it had happened."

"Was it?" Lynn asked.

Beulah Mae looked guilty. "Well, not exactly. But that old goat only told them because he didn't like the idea of having a black bull dyke living next door." She shook her head and began to mumble. "It wasn't like he had anything else to worry about from me. I mean, I wasn't interested in his wife, and I only slept with his daughter twice. How was I supposed to know she'd up and leave her crazy husband?"

"You slept with his daughter!"

Beulah Mae seemed taken aback by Lynn's outburst. "It wasn't a big deal. She was well over twenty-one and willing." She shook her head. "Whew, was she ever willing. I thought I was going to have to move to get that woman away from my front door."

Lynn held up her hand. It was easy to see where this was headed. "That's enough information about the daughter. How did you get here?"

Beulah Mae's eyes blazed. "I told you. That old goat complained. He told the cops they had to do something with me, or I'd burn the whole complex down someday. That's when some highbrow white woman who acted like she'd had a corncob stuffed up her butt showed up saying she was from adult protective services, and the next thing I know I'm stuck here with a bunch of old geezers."

Lynn stared at her in amazement. She had believed the original story that Beulah Mae told her about her checking herself in here. It had never occurred to her to ask why Beulah Mae had decided to do so.

"Look, I really need your help. I've got to get back home."

Lynn rubbed her chin to give herself time to think. She had no clue what would need to be done to get her released or if it were even possible. "I guess I could do some research and find out what you would have to do to get out of here, but I suspect that if a judge put you in here then it'll take a judge to get you out. If so, that's probably going to take some time."

21

Beulah Mae shook her head. "I don't have time for you to be doing research. Once those bureaucrats get involved, it could take weeks or even months." She looked at Lynn. "Besides, I'm about to turn eighty-five. Do you think any of them will go out on a limb and say I'm capable of living alone?"

"So what can you do?"

Beulah Mae leaned in until she was inches from Lynn's face. "I want you to help me bust out of here."

CHAPTER THREE

Certain that she had somehow misunderstood Beulah Mae, Lynn could only stare. "What did you say?"

"You heard me."

"You want me to help you break out of here," she said in amazement.

"It's the only way," Beulah Mae said. "If I wait for some bureaucrat to decide I'm capable of taking care of myself, it'll take too long."

"What's the rush?"

"I'm eighty-five. How much longer do you think I have?"

A wave of concern shot through Lynn. "Are you sick?"

"No, but I'm not exactly a spring chicken either."

"Eighty-five isn't so old anymore. People are living longer now than ever before."

"Would you listen to yourself?" Beulah Mae leaned back in

her chair. "You still don't get it. If I start making a fuss about getting out of here, they might start watching me closer." She looked into Lynn's eyes. "You know as well as I do that I can take care of myself."

Lynn's first instinct was to agree, but she made herself stop. She tried to look at her friend in an objective way, as a caseworker might see her. Physically, Beulah Mae could get around well enough. It took her longer than a younger person, but that was to be expected. Whenever she came to their house for dinner, she managed fine. She admitted to being on medication for her blood pressure, but that was probably true of a large portion of the city's population. She was too vain to wear her glasses, which at times caused her problems with her sight. When she'd finally break down and put them on, she could still see well enough to read and work on the crossword puzzles she seemed to enjoy.

As for her mental capacity, she never seemed disoriented or overly forgetful. Although there were times when she would repeat a story that she had told the previous weekend, but Lynn knew plenty of much younger people who were guilty of story repetition, herself included. She realized Beulah Mae was still waiting for her answer. "Yeah, I think you could make it on your own."

"Then you'll help me?"

Lynn rubbed her chin again. "I'm not sure this is a good idea. What if you get back to Williamstown and all of your family has moved? What would you do then?"

"I can always come back here," Beulah Mae replied rationally.

"I think there's some kind of law against walking out of a nursing home, and I'm sure there's one against me sneaking you out."

"Look, if you're too scared to help, forget about it. I can handle this alone." Her spine stiffened as she turned to gaze out the window. "I've been taking care of myself for more than twice the number of years that you've been around."

Lynn knew she was being played, but the comment still irritated her. "I'm not scared. And I never said I didn't want to help you. I just don't think this is the right way to go about it." She thought for a moment. "Even if I could sneak you out of here and get you to the airport, who's to say they won't track you down and meet the plane when it lands—" She stopped. She didn't even know which airport was the closest to Williamstown, Colorado. Before she could ask, Beulah Mae waved off her protest.

"I've already thought about all those things. That's why you have to drive me," Beulah Mae said.

Lynn stared at her, even more surprised. "Beulah Mae, my old car barely gets me around town. There's no way it could get us all the way to Colorado."

"So, we'll rent one."

"I can't afford to rent a car."

"I can. I told you I have money," Beulah Mae replied, clearly growing more frustrated.

Lynn knew she was treading on shaky ground, but she had to ask. "This place is funded by the state. I thought you had to be . . . ah . . . what I mean is . . . I thought you had to liquidate your assets before they would allow you to stay here."

Beulah Mae gave a small smile. "Beulah Mae Williams might have given up all her assets. Beulah Mae Johnson did not."

"Johnson?" Lynn's head was beginning to hurt. Beulah Mae's story was beginning to run together. "Johnson is your birth name, right? Or, Williams was you real name and you used Johnson."

Beulah Mae stared at her as if she had suddenly sprouted horns. "That's the problem with you kids today. Nobody listens. My birth name was Johnson. There was a time when it was . . . more convenient for me to assume a different name. That's when I chose to use Williams. Are you with me now?"

"Yes. I think so." In truth, she had no idea how anyone changed their name and became someone else.

"That's why I need you to take care of that." She pointed toward the envelope hidden beneath Lynn's shirt. "No one here can know about it."

"What is this?"

"That's my life's savings."

Horrified, Lynn jumped up and snatched the envelope from its hiding place. "You can't do that. It's not right." She cringed at how much she sounded like Crissy.

"Why not?"

"Because it's wrong. You shouldn't trust me or anyone else with your money."

Beulah Mae's breath exploded in a loud exclamation. "Bull! If I want to trust you with my money I will. You're my friend. You aren't going to rip me off."

"How do you know?" Lynn demanded, her own frustration growing. "What do you really know about me?"

Beulah Mae took a deep breath and motioned for Lynn to sit back down. "Don't get your drawers in a wad. If you don't want to help, fine. I'll find someone else."

"Who?" Lynn was beginning to have second thoughts about Beulah Mae's sanity.

Beulah Mae shrugged and looked away. "Don't worry about it. There are other people I can turn to."

Lynn felt torn. "It's not that I don't want to help you. You're my friend. I'm worried that you may be making a mistake."

Beulah Mae sighed and shook her head. "What's the worst that could happen if I left here and then found out that I shouldn't have?"

"You could get hurt," Lynn blurted.

"Lynn, I've lived on the edge my entire life. Nothing can be worse than sitting here day in and day out watching the grass grow. It's killing me to be locked away with all these old people.

I need to get out of here." She glanced away as if embarrassed by the passion of her words.

Irked that she had been placed in this position, Lynn lashed out. "You apparently weren't watching the grass grow when you were chasing Nurse Janette."

"That was a short-term diversion."

"Please take this. I can't be responsible for it." Lynn held out the envelope, and after a moment Beulah Mae took it.

"You aren't going to rat me out to the staff, are you?"

"No. I wouldn't do that." She had to do something that would prevent Beulah Mae from doing anything foolish. She used Beulah Mae's strong sense of loyalty and honor. "I want you to promise me that you won't take off in the middle of the night. Maybe there's another way to go about this. I'll check around and see what I can find out." When Beulah Mae didn't respond, Lynn leaned closer. "Promise you won't do anything until I see you next Saturday and we have another chance to talk."

Still Beulah Mae sat quietly.

"Please promise me. I'll be as discreet as I possibly can. I won't use your name or tell anyone anything that could lead them back to you."

"I promise," Beulah Mae said, clearly not happy about doing so. "Will you still mail my letter?"

The envelope in her hip pocket was too thin to be much more than a couple of sheets of paper. "As long as you promise it's only a letter and not some other wild idea of yours."

Beulah Mae met her gaze. "I swear it's only a letter."

CHAPTER FOUR

Lynn left Beulah Mae sitting at the window and continued with her visits. She tried to give each person her full attention as she chatted or read to them or helped them with some minor chore, but her thoughts kept returning to Beulah Mae. If she refused to help Beulah Mae leave, would the stubborn old cuss attempt to go by herself? Then there was the matter of the money. Why did she have her life savings tucked away in an envelope? Would she try to give it to someone else? And what about the letter she had given her? Curiosity had finally gotten the better of her and she'd peeked at the addressee, a Miss Celine Thompson of Little Rock, Arkansas. What was the story behind it, and why did Beulah Mae feel uncomfortable about mailing it from the nursing home?

Lynn told herself to stop worrying. Surely there was some legal way that wouldn't take forever that would allow Beulah

Mae to return home, at least for a visit. If she had family there then it might be possible for them to assume some type of guardianship of her or maybe she could transfer to a nursing home near them. Heck, there was a chance that once she went back she wouldn't want to stay. After all, she had run away from the small town once before.

It was after two before Lynn finally made her way back to the lobby. Mrs. Harmon was still sitting on the couch, but she was now asleep. Lynn stepped into the sunshine and inhaled deeply. Despite being laced with car exhaust, the warm April air smelled wonderful, as it always did when she first left the nursing home. As she walked to her car she kept wondering what she could do for Beulah Mae. An underlying streak of guilt plagued her. She and Crissy should have taken Beulah Mae out more, even if it was only to their house for a simple meal or to take a ride to the country. Anything that would have gotten her away from that place for a few hours would've been a blessing.

Lynn rarely thought about growing old herself. She thought about age in connection with her mother, who was forty-four, or with Crissy's parents, who were nearly ten years older than her mom was, but she never really thought about it for herself. Who would take care of her and Crissy when they could no longer fend for themselves? Since they had no legal status as a couple, would they be separated? The thoughts were too frightening for her to think about so she shrugged them off. There was plenty of time left before they had to start worrying about growing old. Right now, she needed to be thinking about Beulah Mae.

After leaving the nursing home she drove to a Laundromat and did their laundry. While the clothes washed she devoured the peanut butter and jelly sandwich she had packed that morning and considered the problem with Beulah Mae. When no answers came, she decided she would wait and discuss it with Crissy. She would know what to do.

After the clothes were dried and folded back into the basket, she drove to the trailer park where she and her mom had finally settled after having lived in a long line of low-rent houses. Lynn had been twelve when they moved into the trailer, and at the time it had seemed like a mansion to her.

Lynn knew her mother would be home waiting for her, because since Crissy had started working late at Taco Hut on Saturdays, Lynn and her mother had dinner together every Saturday night. She parked on the roadside in front of the trailer and retrieved a table lamp from the trunk of her car. For weeks, she had watched her mom fiddle with the lamp switch until it would eventually catch and turn on. She had finally convinced her mom to let her take it home and rewire it. She made her way up the sidewalk with the lamp and a small bag of cookies, part of the batch that Crissy's mom had made for them.

"Your timing is perfect. I just put the bread in the oven," her mother said as she held open the door for her.

"It smells good in here." She gave her mom a quick peck on the cheek.

"I made spaghetti."

Lynn loved her mother's spaghetti. She made the sauce from scratch rather than the stuff from a jar that she and Crissy used. "I brought some cookies that Mrs. Anderson made. They're chocolate chip and raisin."

"Why don't you tell her you don't like raisins?" Her mom took the bag from her.

"Because Crissy likes them, but her mom gives us so many that Crissy can't eat them all. Besides, she's been giving them to us for so long that if I tell her now it'll hurt her feelings." She held up the lamp.

"Were you able to fix it?"

Lynn smiled. "We'll find out in a minute." She had already tested the lamp several times, but she loved to tease her mom. She took the lamp to the living room, placed it in its usual spot by her mother's chair and plugged it into a wall socket.

"It works," her mom said as Lynn turned the switch.

"Did you have a doubt?"

"Of course not. You've always been good at fixing things like that. I don't know where you picked it up." She stopped for a moment and tilted her head. "Maybe you got it from your granddad. He was like that. Give him a piece of baling wire and a couple of nails and he could repair anything."

"I prefer duct tape myself," Lynn said as she adjusted the lampshade to the slight angle her mom preferred for reading.

Lynn had only the vaguest memories of her grandfather. About all she remembered was that he had been a tall, thin, white-haired man who was always busy. There were times when she wasn't sure if she actually remembered those things or she had pulled them from photos and the stories her mom told. She had no memories of her grandmother.

The trailer's open floor plan allowed Lynn to watch as her mom fussed with arranging the cookies on a small plate in the kitchen. There was no one she admired more than her mother, who despite the fact that life hadn't been kind to her refused to let it make her bitter.

She had heard the story of her mother's life many times. Violet Ann Wade Strickland had been a miracle child, conceived long after the doctors had given up all hopes of James and Alice Wade ever producing a child. Alice's health problems had begun early in her life and age had done nothing to improve her health. She was thirty-nine when she realized she was pregnant. The pregnancy was plagued with problems and a long difficult birth that finally ended when the doctor ordered an emergency Cesarean. Afterward, Alice was never the same. She began to have bad days in which she couldn't get out of bed. As time passed, the number of bad days increased.

By the time Violet was in junior high, her mother was bedridden. During the summer before she entered high school, Violet could only stand by and watch as her mother gave up the exhaustive battle and died peacefully in her sleep. Twelve years later, her father, James, died of a heart attack while trying to change a tire on his truck. As if she hadn't suffered enough, two weeks after her father's death, Violet's husband walked out on her and their seven-year-old child.

A timer dinged. "Oh dear, the bread is ready and I haven't set the table yet."

"I'll do that while you get the bread." Lynn took plates from the cabinet as she had a thousand times before. Soon they were enjoying the spaghetti. The sandwich she had eaten at the Laundromat had done little to dull her appetite. While they ate, Lynn told her mother about her morning at the nursing home. She decided not to mention Beulah Mae's request because she was certain her mother wouldn't approve of her busting anyone out of the home.

After they ate, Lynn quickly did the dishes while her mom cleared the table. Then they made their way to the living room.

"How's Crissy doing in school?" her mom asked as they sat down. Her mom placed the plate of cookies on the table next to her.

Lynn stretched her legs out on the couch. "Good. She's really looking forward to having a few days off when school lets out next month."

"Is she going to summer school?"

"No. She has decided to work full-time and then finish in the fall rather than split it up. She needs fifteen more hours. That's too much for her to take in the summer and still work."

Her mother glanced up. "Does she have to work? I mean, is money that tight?"

Lynn felt her neck burning. She hated discussing money, and she certainly didn't want to admit that things were less than perfect at home. It embarrassed her that she was almost twenty-five and still struggling. She shrugged. "We're doing okay."

"I could help out a little now and then."

"No, Mom. You're saving for your retirement."

Shortly after Lynn's father left, her mom had gone to work as a seamstress for Tykes, a manufacturer of children's clothing. She had worked there for six years when without warning the company closed its doors in San Antonio and moved its operations to an overseas location where they could find cheaper labor. Her mom had finally gotten work as a waitress and for the next three years she worked in several different restaurants until she got a job as a hostess for one of Billy Bob's Steakhouses. The large chain offered a moderate pension program along with decent pay.

Her mom leaned forward in her chair. "I guess I might as well tell you now," she began in a tone that made Lynn's stomach clench.

"What's wrong?" She swung her feet to the floor and scooted to the end of the couch closer to her mother's chair.

Her mom rolled her eyes. "I swear I don't know where you get that doomsday outlook of yours. Why does anything have to be wrong?"

"I don't know," Lynn declared defensively. "It was the tone of your voice, I guess."

"It's actually good news. Do you remember Jaime Treviño?"

Lynn watched as her mom began to fuss with her hair. A regular maintenance of a popular hair product hid any signs of gray in her short, warm brown curls, although her mom would be quick to deny such accusations. "Sure. He worked at Tykes with you," she replied.

Her mother nodded. "He was a line supervisor. About a month before the plant closed, his father had a stroke and died. His parents owned a restaurant in Laredo. Jaime went back there to help his mom. He ended up staying there after things got complicated. We've sort of kept in touch. Anyway, his mom died recently and he sold the restaurant and moved back here." She took a deep breath and looked at Lynn. "I've quit my job. Jaime and I are going to open a restaurant."

33

"You quit your job!" Lynn blurted. She was on the verge of asking if her mother had lost her mind but caught herself.

"I've been able to save a decent amount and I've made a couple of small investments that have done fairly well. Do you remember where the Yellow Rose restaurant was on Main?"

Lynn didn't but found herself nodding anyway.

"When they closed a couple of years ago they never sold off any of the equipment. The owner was looking to sell, but Jaime convinced him to lease it to us. We signed a two-year lease on the building yesterday. At the end of the lease we'll have the option of buying the place if we still want it."

Lynn was glad she was sitting because she doubted her legs would have supported her. "You did what?" This time common-sense didn't prevail. "Are you out of your mind?" The spaghetti she had so enjoyed was now forming a large knot in her stomach.

Her mother frowned. "Don't use that tone of voice with me. You may be grown, but I won't have you speaking to me like that."

Sorry for her outburst, Lynn apologized. "You took me by surprise." She couldn't shake the feeling that both her mother and Beulah Mae had taken leave of their senses. She struggled to find something positive to say. All she could manage was, "Why didn't you say something?"

Her mother looked at her knowingly. "Lynn, you know I love you, but, honey, you tend to be a little overly protective of me."

"I can't help it if I worry. You quit your job and—"

Her mom held up a hand to stop the tirade Lynn was gearing up for. "This is exactly the reason I didn't say anything."

"But—"

"I'm forty-four years old. I may not be a threat to Einstein, but I've managed to take care of myself—and you, I might add." Her mother picked up a cookie and broke it in half. "I've made my share of mistakes in life. I can't honestly say that this isn't another one. All I'm sure of is that I have to do this. Maybe it won't succeed, but for once in my life I feel like I have to take a

34

chance to do something for myself. I have to try. I wish you could understand that."

Ashamed, Lynn lowered her head. "I'm sorry. I didn't mean to suggest you couldn't make it." She shrugged. "I worry about you."

Her mother reached over and patted her hand. "Oh, honey, I worry about you, too."

"Me? Why are you worried about me? I'm fine."

Her mom dodged the question. "It's nothing."

"No. I want to know. Why are you worried about me? Crissy and I are doing okay."

"Doing okay is fine when you're young, but what about ten years from now?"

Lynn started to respond but realized she didn't really have an answer. "I've got a job," she replied lamely.

"You have two jobs and are still barely getting by. Do you want to wash cars for the rest of your life?"

"I can find something better once Crissy is working and everything settles down. Then someday we'll buy the ranch and start to raise quarter horses."

Her mom exhaled heavily and leaned back in her chair. "I know that has been a lifelong dream of yours, but all of that takes money. Ranches and horses aren't cheap." When Lynn didn't respond she continued. "Dreams are wonderful things, but sometimes you have to be realistic. Even with Crissy teaching, it'll take years before you'll have enough to buy even a small ranch. And if you do manage to scrape the money together to buy it, how are you going to keep working to make the payment and run the ranch? You'll need money for horses and supplies—"

"All right, Mom, I get it. I'm a big loser and the ranch is a stupid idea."

"Lynn Marie Strickland, you stop that right now. I've never thought you were a loser, and having a dream isn't a stupid idea." She grabbed Lynn's hand. "I would never suggest that you give up your dream. I'm only saying that maybe it's time you started thinking about doing something that will help you attain it."

"Like what?" Lynn tried to hide the hurt her mom's words had caused. She wished she had the courage to get up and walk out. What gave her mom the right to question her decisions when she had just dumped her retirement savings into a restaurant? What had set her mom off on this crusade anyway? Between the two of them, Lynn felt she was being the more responsible one. After all, she hadn't quit her job to go chasing some dream. Her mom would be fortunate if her venture paid off. There was a strong possibility that she could lose every penny she had worked so hard for.

"Now that Crissy is about to graduate, maybe it's time you thought about going back to school."

Lynn gaped at her mom, unable to believe what she had heard. "Hello. Have you forgotten that I barely made it through high school?"

"That was then. You're a lot more disciplined now and Crissy could help you. I never was able to help you much."

"Forget it, Mom. I'm not college material."

"Bull hockey. You did badly in high school because you wouldn't apply yourself. You can do anything you set your mind to."

Lynn stood up. "Mom, I don't want to argue. I need to go. I have a lot of errands to run still, and I'd like to get home before dark." She only needed to stop for a few groceries, but she wanted to get away from her mom before she said too much.

"Now you're angry with me."

"No, I'm not angry," Lynn lied. "I don't see where you get these crazy ideas."

Her mom stood. "I'm sorry if I went too far, but I meant every word of it." She slipped her arm around Lynn. "Will you at least think about what I said?"

"Sure." Lynn resisted the childish impulse to twist away. Instead, she gave her mom a quick hug and rushed out.

CHAPTER FIVE

Lynn stopped at the grocery store on her way home. Once inside she grabbed a handbasket and began to make her way down the crowded aisles. As usual the store was packed with tired women pushing overflowing carts while tying to corral the kids. A sprinkling of men rushed around filling their grocery carts with snacks and beer. As she maneuvered her way through the store grabbing the few items she needed, she fought the impulse to take out her frustrations on them. Matters didn't improve when she reached the express checkout lane and found an older man with a full cart. She bit back her irritation and moved to another line where there was only one person.

"You can use the self-service aisle," the young female checker called.

Lynn shook her head. "No, thanks. I'll wait." She refused to use the self-checking aisle. She would stand in line an extra twenty minutes rather than use them. They were another management ploy to cut some poor slob from the payroll.

The woman gave a gigantic sigh as if she were carrying the weight of the world on her shoulders. "It's simple to use."

The woman's theatrics were the last straw, or maybe it was the fact that Lynn had heard the unspoken "even you can do it" dig—either way, Lynn's patience snapped. "Yeah, they're so easy to use that soon management won't need you. In fact, they won't need to hire checkers at all. And while losing you from the workforce obviously wouldn't be great loss, there are probably a few people working here who actually need a job." She slammed the basket onto the conveyor belt. "So if you don't mind, I'll wait."

The young woman's eyes had grown large and she gulped before nodding. "Uh, okay. Sure."

Lynn felt like an ass. The clerk was only a kid. She knew she should apologize, but doing so had never come easy for her. Instead, she stared at the register screen while the checker rang up her purchases. As soon as the items were paid for and bagged, Lynn rushed out of the store.

She hated being angry, especially when it was with Crissy or her mom, but this time her mom had gone too far. "I work hard," Lynn muttered as she swung the last grocery bag into the trunk and slammed the lid. "I'm not a loser."

As she pulled out of the parking lot she considered driving by the ball field to see if anyone was out practicing, but then remembered the milk and other perishables in the trunk.

She and Crissy played on a slow-pitch softball league every Wednesday night. The team practiced Sunday mornings and then a group of them gathered at their house for a barbecue. Softball was essentially their only joint social outing. Her mom simply didn't understand how things were between her and Crissy. A lack of funds could certainly hamper a lifestyle, but they were more or less used to it. They both realized it was only a temporary problem. Sure, things between them might be slightly rocky now, but it would get better as soon as Crissy found a job. Once she was teaching, her salary would more than cover their frugal living expenses, allowing them to save everything Lynn earned. A thought came to her so suddenly she hit her brakes. Thankfully there was no one behind her or she would have been rear-ended for sure. That was what this was about. Her mom must have sensed that things weren't as rosy as Lynn pretended. She was worried that the relationship wouldn't last and that Lynn would be left with nothing. It all made sense now. She was sure it stemmed back to her father walking out on them.

Lynn had been seven when her father left to buy a pack of cigarettes and never returned. After he walked out there had been plenty of rough times for her and her mom. Even after her mom got a job working at Tykes things didn't improve for a long time. Her father had left behind a hefty chunk of debt that her mom had to pay off. It had taken her almost five years and endless hours of overtime, but she had finally paid every penny they owed. Despite the fact that it had been just the two of them, Lynn had never felt alone. Even after the debts were paid off, her mother had continued to work long hours to make a decent life for them.

For as long as she could remember she had loved horses. From the time she was in high school her dream had been to have a place of her own to raise and train quarter horses. If asked, she couldn't have explained where the dream came from, because she had no real hands-on experience with horses. In fact, the only one she'd ever ridden had been on her tenth birthday when her mother had taken her to ride on the less than active nags at Brackenridge Stables. But the dream was a vital part of her. Whenever the real world became too much to handle, she would throw herself into planning her dream ranch.

Her mother had obviously forgotten that she had barely managed to make it through high school. College wasn't an option.

Besides, she didn't really need to go to college to raise horses. She'd decided long ago to teach herself. She had read every available book on quarter horses in the local branch library and scores more through interlibrary loans. The dream became even more ingrained when she met Crissy and discovered that she too dreamed of one day moving to the country and teaching school in a small rural community. She had encouraged Lynn's dream.

When Lynn arrived home, she put the groceries away before she noticed the blinking light on the answering machine. She pressed the button and listened to a message from her mom. "Lynn, I'm sorry I upset you." Her voice sounded hollow and crackly when replayed on the cheap machine. "I only said what I did because I love you and I worry about you. I know that probably doesn't qualify as a valid reason. I suppose it's more of an excuse. Please don't think I want you to give up your dream. That's not what I meant at all." The doorbell could be heard in the background of the tape. "Oh dear, that's probably Lea. She's picking me up for bingo. I'll talk to you soon, sweetie."

Lynn listened to the series of clicks as her mom hung up and the answering machine shut off. Suddenly she wondered what her mom's dreams had been. Had she harbored secret dreams when she was twenty-five? Lynn did some quick math. Her mom would have been twenty-six when her husband walked out on her, leaving her with a young child and no means of financial support. From that time until after Lynn graduated, her mom had worked hard to provide for them.

The proverbial light came on when she thought about how each year a few weeks before Lynn's birthday and Christmas her mom would start working long hours of overtime. She realized it had been to pay for the new bike, skateboard or a dozen other things she had wanted.

She had always been grateful for the gifts and she was certain that she had let her mom know how appreciative she was of them, but she had never really thanked her mom for all the extra

40

effort she had put in to get them. It was way beyond time she did, and even though she still didn't think it was a good idea, she would do whatever she could to help with her mom's new venture. She glanced at the clock. Her mom wouldn't be home from her weekly bingo game for hours. She reached for the phone but stopped. She would call her in the morning before they left for softball practice and apologize directly rather than leave a message.

She found a stamp, put it on Beulah Mae's letter and placed it on the table. Rather than leave it for the postman she would drop it off at the post office on her way to work Monday morning. She put away the laundry and tried not to notice how empty the house felt whenever Crissy wasn't there. On Saturdays Crissy worked a double shift at the Taco Hut. She wouldn't be home until nearly ten that night. The job wasn't the greatest, but the owner was good about letting Crissy adjust her hours to work around her school schedule.

To fill the empty hours, Lynn cleaned the house before sitting down with her latest library book on horse training. She was still reading when Crissy arrived home. As soon as Lynn heard the key in the lock she rushed into the living room to greet her.

"What a nice welcome." Crissy rested her head against Lynn's shoulder.

"You sound tired." Lynn relaxed slightly. Despite being exhausted, Crissy seemed to be in a good mood. This would be a good night. Recently Crissy had become extremely critical of everything Lynn did. Lynn had tried to blame Crissy's exhaustion, but sometimes she worried there might be bigger problems.

"I am tired. We had four big groups tonight and they all had kids." Crissy pulled away and dropped her purse onto the chair by the door. "I'll never understand why people allow their kids to shred their food onto the floor or plaster it on the walls."

"Come on. I'll run a hot bath and we can talk." She would

wait before she told Crissy about the fight with her mom.

Crissy kissed her cheek. "I don't think I could keep doing this without you."

Lynn hugged her closer. "Sure you could. You're one of the strongest people I've ever known."

"Having met your mother, I'll take that as a compliment."

"As you should," Lynn said as she led Crissy into the bathroom. Crissy was usually worn out when she came home from work, so Lynn always tried to give her time to decompress before she shared her own problems or accomplishments of the day.

A few minutes later, they were both in the tub with Crissy sitting between Lynn's legs. The large tub and enormous backyard were the only two decent things about the house. Other than those amenities it was merely a small, poorly constructed one-bedroom home located in an older, lower-income neighborhood.

"How was your day?"

Crissy groaned. "Jason was in one of his moods. Mr. Salazar came by this morning and they were in the office for a long time."

Jason was the nephew of the owner, Hector Salazar, and had a tendency to try to bully the employees. He had taken over the management of the morning crew a few months earlier and was making everyone's life miserable.

"Do you think Mr. Salazar will cut him loose?"

"I don't know. Jason isn't really a bad manager. He's just young and insecure in his abilities. I think with time and some more experience he'll be fine."

"Hang in there. If anybody can make this work, it's you. How about customers? Did you have any crazy encounters today?"

"Too many to think about," Crissy said. "I want to forget about work. Tell me about your day." She settled back into Lynn's arms.

"I got into an argument with Mom."

"Oh, no. What happened?" She started to sit up, but Lynn pulled her back.

"I was an asshole." She quickly filled her in on what had occurred.

"She's opening a restaurant. Wow," Crissy said. "That's awfully brave of her."

"Do you really think so?"

"Don't you?"

"I don't know. It seems sort of irresponsible to me. I mean, we didn't talk about numbers or anything, but I'm sure she has put a lot of her retirement savings into this place." She sighed heavily. "Maybe that wouldn't bother me so, if she hadn't quit her job. She had a retirement package and benefits with them."

Crissy absently trailed her hands through the water. "I don't know. That's a good location, and the place used to get a lot of business. The only thing that might be a drawback is that it's a huge building. They're probably paying for space they can't fill. What are they going to name the place?"

Lynn shrugged. "I don't know. I forgot to ask."

"Well, the good thing is the guy she's going into partnership with has experience running a restaurant and the previous restaurant did well there."

"If the place was so great, why did it close?"

"Failure isn't the only reason businesses close. Maybe the owner died or retired."

"I guess." Lynn wasn't convinced.

"The important question is, who is this Jaime Treviño?"

"He worked at Tykes when mom did. They dated, but it was sort of on the sly. I think it had something to do with him being a manager and her working the production line. He used to come to dinner occasionally. He'd take us to baseball games and museums."

"Museums?"

"Yeah, he loved art."

"They've kept in touch all these years. That's interesting."

"Crissy, don't start. Apparently they didn't click. They're just good friends."

"Good friends make the best partners."

"Stop it. I worry enough about her as it is. Don't throw a man into the mix."

"Why not? Your mom is still young. She's funny and sweet. She's very attractive. I've always wondered why she didn't date more." Crissy, the natural-born matchmaker, was warming to her subject. "I've always suspected that she simply doesn't tell you about her dates."

"Stop it. That's my mom you're talking about."

"So?"

"So. Nothing. She doesn't date."

Crissy tried to twist around to face her, but again Lynn leaned forward enough to stop her from doing so.

"Lynn, I don't believe you. Don't you want your mother to be happy?"

"Of course I do."

"Then why don't you want her to meet someone nice?"

"I didn't say I didn't want her to meet someone. I just said that she doesn't date."

Crissy laughed slightly. "I don't believe it. You're jealous."

Lynn started to scramble up but lost her footing on the slippery porcelain and slid back into the water, causing it to slosh onto the floor. "That's disgusting."

"Sit still. You're making a mess." Crissy pulled Lynn's leg back alongside her. "I didn't mean you were jealous sexually. I meant you're jealous of someone else taking your mother's attention."

"Please. I'm not a five-year-old."

"It's understandable that you feel that way. It was just the two of you for all those years and you both really depend on and support each other."

If given any encouragement, Crissy would keep this conversation going for hours, and Lynn thought it had already gone well beyond her comfort level. Rather than take a chance of starting an argument or having to listen to Crissy's matchmaking for another hour, Lynn cut the discussion short. "I'll call her tomorrow and see what I can do to help out with the restaurant." She pretended not to notice when Crissy made her little *I told you so* sound.

They settled into a comfortable silence as Lynn absentmindedly stroked Crissy's arm. The warm water was making her sleepy. She was on the verge of dozing when she remembered her talk with Beulah Mae.

"I had a rather interesting conversation with Beulah Mae."

"Really. What about?" Crissy sounded as though she were about to doze off as well.

"Her eighty-fifth birthday is coming up."

"We'll have to do something special for her," Crissy mumbled.

"Did you know that the state had her placed at Morning Sunrise?"

"No."

"She wants me to help her break out of the nursing home and take her back to Colorado." Lynn waited for the words to seep through Crissy's grogginess. When they did Crissy sat up so swiftly it startled her.

"You can't do that," Crissy said. "Not if the state had her placed in the nursing home. You'll get in trouble."

Lynn shoved down her irritation and pulled her back into her arms. "I'm not a moron. I didn't say I was going to do it."

"Sorry. I didn't think you were a moron, but sometimes you're too nice and get in over your head."

Lynn leaned her head against the wall. "I have to do something, though. She really wants to go home."

"I'm sure it wouldn't be a problem if they thought she was capable, which obviously they didn't since she was sent there by a court order. There must be health issues that you don't know anything about. Still, she might be able to get her case reviewed."

Her tone made Lynn want to defend Beulah Mae, but to maintain peace she gave in. "I guess so, but she says it'll take too long."

"I'm sure it will. That's a state-operated facility, and you know how slowly the government works. It'll probably take months."

"I think she's worried she'll die before they give her permission."

"Is she sick?"

Lynn was touched by the sound of genuine concern in her voice. "I don't think so, but she is about to turn eighty-five."

"That doesn't mean anything. If she's as healthy as she looks, she could easily live for another decade or more."

"I told her that. It's as though she's driven to get back. When she was growing up there she couldn't wait to get away, and now she can't wait to get back."

"I don't think that's so unusual. I've noticed that Grandma and Grandpa Anderson talk a lot about when they were younger, much more than my parents do."

Since she had never really known any of her grandparents, Lynn had no point of reference as a comparison. "What about your mom's parents? I've never really noticed if they do or not."

Crissy snorted. "Please. All they ever talk about is the last Caribbean cruise they took or how hard they're working to spend Mom's inheritance."

Lynn smiled. She knew Crissy didn't begrudge her grandparents' fun. The truth was that the Smiths had taken the joke of spending their daughter's inheritance to such a point that even Lynn was sick of hearing it. Both bumpers of their vehicle were plastered with a wide collection of cutesy stickers announcing their intention. In addition, they had quite an array of neon T-shirts and caps bearing the same message.

"What are you going to do?" Crissy asked.

"I promised her I'd check into it and see what she has to do. I guess I'll start with adult protective services.

"You know this could turn into a major project. Do you have the time to deal with this?"

"I have to do what I can. It's important to her."

"What if it starts dragging out and she's not willing to wait?"

Lynn didn't want to think about that. "You know how much I like her, but I can't break her out. If the state put her there, they must have had a good reason." Even as she spoke, a wave of guilt hit her.

Crissy squeezed Lynn's hand. "Good. I'm glad you're doing the right thing and not going to get yourself into trouble."

"I'm not going to get myself into trouble." She tried not to let Crissy's words get to her, but there were times when she wanted to scream that doing the right thing wasn't always right.

"Maybe not, but I want you to promise me that no matter what happens, you won't do anything drastic without calling me first."

"I'm not going to do anything stupid. I can take care of myself." She wondered why she had deliberately not made Crissy a promise. Was she considering helping Beulah Mae?

"Listen to you." Crissy's voice took on a welcomed, teasing tone. "Trying to sound all huffy and mean." She snuggled closer to Lynn. "Sometimes that big heart of yours gets you into trouble."

"I have no idea what you're talking about."

"Don't get all defensive. That was one of the reasons I fell in love with you."

Somewhat sorry that she had even started the conversation, Lynn ran her hand across Crissy's abdomen in an effort to distract her. "All this time I thought it was my nimble fingers and bedroom skills."

"Those were merely added bonuses."

Lynn kissed the top of her lover's bare shoulder and felt a gentle shudder race through Crissy's body. "Are you cold?"

"The water is getting cool."

"I can fix that." Lynn flipped the drain lever open with her toe. "Come on. Let's get dried off and into bed where I can warm you up."

CHAPTER SIX

"Watch out," Lynn scolded as the red Frisbee bearing the call numbers of a local radio station bounced off the battered barbecue grill.

"Sorry, babe," Crissy apologized as she scooped up the offending plastic disk and gave Lynn a quick kiss. "Obviously, my athletic prowess is no match for my opponent, the great Karen Winchester." The afternoon sun had warmed up considerably, causing Crissy's shoulder-length brown hair to curl into damp ringlets around her neck. As was often the case, Lynn found herself wondering what she would have done without this dynamic woman in her life. Their relationship hadn't been without its rough spots. As with many couples, most of their problems revolved around the lack of money. Lynn sometimes wondered if there had ever been a time in her life when money hadn't been a problem. Recently, they seemed to be arguing more frequently over smaller issues. She tried to tell herself that everything would get better once Crissy graduated, but in her weaker moments, she sometimes wondered if that was true.

Karen ran up to join them. At five-eleven, she possessed the body of a natural athlete. "Are you sure you don't need any help, Lynn?"

"No, thanks. It's under control." She pointed to the Frisbee. "Or it will be if you two ever learn to control that thing."

"Hey," Karen said. "Talk to your woman. She's the one who can't catch."

"I can too," Crissy said. "Who caught that pop-up out over third base last week?"

"Oh, please. My four-year-old niece could have caught that," Karen teased. "You were standing out there looking at your nails when the ball accidentally dropped into your glove."

"See, that shows how much you know," Crissy replied. "If I had been looking at my nails it would have been physically impossible for the ball to fall into my glove."

"Oh. She has a point," Erica called out.

Karen immediately started trying to defend her statement.

"If you kids are going to argue, go somewhere else and do it," Lynn said.

As Crissy and Karen raced off to continue their banter, Lynn went into the small house she and Crissy had shared for most of the five years they'd been together. She set the barbecue fork and mitt on the cracked and stained Formica table. The piece had been purchased at a garage sale and Lynn prayed for the day when she would be able to toss it out with the trash.

She had called her mother earlier and apologized. She had even offered to help in any way she could with the restaurant, which she had learned was to be named La Paloma Blanca. It would serve authentic Mexican dishes. All during the conversation she had been dying to ask about Jaime Treviño. Was there something other than friendship between them? Crissy had been wrong about the jealousy issue. She simply didn't want to see her mother get hurt again. She could still remember the endless nights after her father left when she had listened to her mom pace the floor crying. After her mom met Jaime she had laughed a lot more and there had been a new vitality about her whenever he was around. She made up her mind that she would talk to her mom about him next Saturday when they had dinner.

Her thoughts turned from her mom to Beulah Mae. Despite her conversation with Crissy the previous evening she still felt uneasy. Beulah Mae was stubborn enough to try going on her own. Once again, she wondered if she should warn someone at the nursing home. If she stood by and Beulah Mae took off alone and something happened, she would never forgive herself, but the idea of squealing on her wasn't appealing either. She rubbed her chin. The legal system wasn't likely to let the old woman leave by herself. At best, they might let her go if there was a suitable guardian to travel with her. But who would that be? She knew it couldn't be her. She couldn't afford to take off work and go to Colorado, but if she didn't, who would? Beulah Mae didn't seem to know anyone else in San Antonio. How was it possible that a person could have led a life as full as Beulah Mae's and there not be anyone around to turn to for help?

Lynn looked across the yard at her friends. She could turn to any of them for help. Would they still be around in fifty or sixty years? It wasn't likely, she admitted. After college they would probably leave to return to their hometowns or on to careers. They might stay in touch for a few years, but those communications would gradually grow fewer and less frequent until they eventually lost track of one another.

Her thoughts were interrupted by a sharp slap against the window. She was greeted by Crissy's wide, somewhat apologetic smile. Lynn studied her lover's sea-blue eyes and delicate nose with the sprinkling of freckles. Crissy hated the freckles, but Lynn thought they were cute. The warmth of the tremendous love she felt for this woman suddenly rushed over her. For the briefest moment she wished everyone would go home, so that they could spend the day together alone.

"Sorry," Crissy said through the open window.

"Are you ever going to learn to catch that thing?" Lynn shook her head to clear away the fantasies that were beginning.

"Probably not," Crissy replied before she raced off.

Lynn stood at the window and continued to study the young women. She and Crissy had met them through the softball team sponsored by LT's, a women's bar where Lynn had once worked as a bartender. A strong bond had developed within the group almost immediately. At twenty-five Lynn was the oldest, and she was also the only one of them not in college. They all worked hard during the week but religiously guarded their Wednesday nights for softball and Sundays for practice and the barbecue.

Lynn worked each weeknight, except Wednesday, busing tables at the LaCasita Mexican Restaurant. She held down a full-time day position at the Diamond T Complete Car Wash and Detail shop Monday through Friday. The salary wasn't great, but the tips were and she was putting in her time until she could be moved to the Tuesday through Saturday shift. Saturdays were where the real money in tips lay.

Crissy attended the University of Texas at San Antonio full time and still managed to put in at least twenty-four hours at the Taco Hut each week. Their schedules made for long days, and there were times when it seemed as though they never saw each other, but they were young and in love, and nothing else mattered.

Her gaze drifted to the tall, powerful form of Karen Winchester. Karen was a junior at Our Lady of the Lake University. She excelled at softball, basketball, swimming and track. Her dream was to coach a professional women's basketball team someday. Lynn smiled as Karen swept the front of her short brown hair back in a habitual gesture. Her hair wasn't long enough to get anywhere near her eyes, but she constantly pushed it back, making it stick straight up in the front.

Tina Garcia, Karen's lover of three years, walked by Karen and reached out to smooth down the damp hair that Karen had pushed up. Karen's free arm slid around Tina's waist as she caught the Frisbee with casual ease and tossed it back to Crissy. Tina was also a student at OLLU, majoring in chemistry. She hoped to pursue a career in medical research. As soon as Karen released the Frisbee, Tina wrapped her shorter wiry frame around Karen and they were soon on the ground scuffling.

Deb Jaworski's lanky frame was stretched out in the shade on an old blanket with her head resting in the ample lap of her lover, Erica Bonner. They were talking to Joann Keller.

Joann tossed her head and the sun's rays caught her bright red mass of curls. She was the youngest member of the group. At nineteen she was in a constant state of anxiety over being single.

Lynn began to set out the side dishes everyone had brought. Since the inception of the Sunday barbecues neither rain, blazing sun nor final exams had been enough to cancel the weekly get-together.

As she passed by the window, Mr. Larson, one of their neighbors, came out and said something to the group on the blanket that made them all laugh. His hair was completely white, and he walked with a cane, but his mind was as sharp as ever. He and his wife, Edith, had taught in a nearby public school for a combined total of nearly sixty years. Lynn could listen to them talk for hours. His knowledge of Texas history was amazing. She and Crissy often sat in their backyard enjoying a tall cold glass of Edith's special spiced sun tea.

Lynn liked her neighborhood that was made up of predominantly older African-Americans with a sprinkling of Anglos and Hispanics. She and Crissy rented the house right after they'd gotten together. At first they hoped to be able to move into a larger house eventually, but there never seemed to be enough money. At the first glimpse of the tired and rundown neighborhood most people would probably lock their car doors as they drove through, but in truth, the crime rate here wasn't much higher than in a lot of the other areas of San Antonio.

They liked their neighbors and got along well with them. They had never tried to hide their relationship, but they didn't aggressively flaunt it. Their neighbors had gradually grown accustomed to them and were tolerant of, if not completely in agreement with their lifestyle.

"Need any help?" Deb Jaworski asked in her flat Midwestern drawl.

"You can take the beans out." Lynn turned and nodded toward the dark blue CrockPot on the cracked and stained countertop.

"I wonder what Joann tells her mother about this weekly crock of beans," Deb said as she gathered up the pot.

Lynn shrugged. "Joann told her she belongs to a youth group that meets after church."

"Well, they are mighty fine beans to be sure," Deb agreed. "What do you suppose she'd do if she knew where Joann was actually taking them?"

Lynn stopped puttering with the silverware she was gathering. "Do you think she'd really mind? You've met her and seen how she dotes on Joann."

"She is right fond of that girl."

Lynn smiled at Deb's quaint speech. It was misleading to anyone who didn't know her. She was a third year pre-med student at the University of Texas at San Antonio and considered a grade point average that was below a perfect four-point-zero as unacceptable. She might sound like a country bumpkin but behind the façade was a brilliant mind.

"You must have heard from your family today," Lynn teased.

Deb stopped at the end of the table and grinned a wide smile that lit up her rather plain oval face. "My mom sent me a long e-mail telling me all about the picnic they had yesterday." She began repeating the events.

Lynn listened with real interest as Deb related the hilarious details of the adventures of her four brothers and two sisters. Deb was somewhere in the middle of the clan and was the first person in her family to attend college. Her father was an Ohio farmer and hadn't been able to provide much financial assistance. Deb was fighting her way through on scholarships, student loans and part-time jobs. Her older siblings sent her a few dollars whenever they could.

Crissy rapped on the window and interrupted them. "The burgers are ready."

A moment later, the rest of the gang made a noisy entrance to help carry things out to the makeshift picnic table that Lynn and Karen had made from an old discarded door and four empty five-gallon paint buckets they had scavenged from a construction worksite dump.

The first few minutes were filled with silence as they stuffed themselves with food. When the hunger pangs began to fade, it was time for serious conversation.

"Hey," Tina began. "Did you all hear that the government recently allocated forty million dollars so that a group of guys can study the breeding habit of frogs."

"No way," Deb protested.

"It's true. I read an article about it," Crissy said as she speared another pickle.

"Heck, they should go over to the stream behind Mom's trailer," Lynn joked. "There are plenty of frogs there for them to watch. It wouldn't take them long to figure out how it's done, and they'd save the taxpayers a lot of money."

"I'd sure like to land one of those cushy jobs," Erica said with a sigh.

"So what do you think will become of us after we've graduated and become famous?" Joann asked the question that never failed to come up, in some version, at every Sunday gathering.

"The first thing I'm going to buy is a new picnic table with benches," Erica said, shifting her sturdy frame on a rickety chair that someone had found by a garbage can. "I'm never sure if this thing is going to hold me."

"Darling, you know I'd catch you," Deb assured her.

"Yeah, right. You'd be so busy working on that ear of corn you wouldn't even notice unless I knocked the table over," Erica said.

"I've never known anyone who could eat so much and stay so skinny," Tina said, shaking her head as she studied Deb's lanky form.

"It's my superior intelligence," Deb said as she started putting together another hamburger. "My brain stays so busy it consumes an extraordinary amount of energy."

"It's not your brain that burns energy," Lynn teased. "It's your mouth and the bull you're always spouting." The group broke into gales of laughter as Deb and Lynn continued their good-natured teasing.

CHAPTER SEVEN

After everyone had left, Lynn locked the front door and turned to find Crissy watching her.

"You look tired," Crissy said as she went to stand by Lynn.

"Karen wore me out chasing that Frisbee," she admitted. "At least I burned off all that lunch I ate." With a grin, she pulled Crissy to her. "I can't believe you volunteered me as her next victim."

"Hey, I had to chase that thing while you were barbecuing. It was your turn. Besides, you were the last choice. The rest of us were busy cleaning up."

"Okay. I guess that's fair."

"I found a beer in the back of the refrigerator," Crissy said. "Why don't we sit out in the backyard and share it."

"Sounds good."

Together they made their way to the kitchen, where Crissy

retrieved the beer, before heading out into the darkness and settling into their dilapidated lawn chairs. They passed the cold beer between them in comfortable silence. A police car sped down a nearby street with its siren blaring. A few seconds later a second one began to wail.

"I can't wait until we're able to buy some land in the country and build our house," Crissy said. She leaned her head against the back of the chair. "I want a place that's quiet and dark. I hate the way the city lights wash the stars away." A small sigh escaped her. "I wish we didn't have to wait so long to get it."

Lynn nodded. "Maybe we should have listened to Joann."

Crissy frowned. "What do you mean?"

"Didn't you hear her talking about the lottery?"

"Oh. No. I missed that."

"She went on for at least five minutes. The jackpot is up to thirty-two million," Lynn said. "Joann bought a ticket and is absolutely sure she's going to win. She's already making a list of everything she's going to buy." She squeezed Crissy's hand.

"Joann's a dreamer. Her money would be better off in the bank."

Lynn tried not to roll her eyes, but sometimes Crissy was too practical. "Don't you ever think about winning the lottery?"

"No. It's a waste of time. Do you know what the odds of ever winning are?"

She dropped Crissy's hand and leaned forward. "What's wrong with dreaming sometimes?"

"Hey, don't run off." Crissy pulled her back. "I'm sorry. You know what an old fuddy-duddy I am. What would you do with that kind of money?"

Lynn knew Crissy was merely humoring her, but she played along. "The first thing we'd do is quit all those pissant jobs. Then we'd call every real estate agent in town and get them busy looking for the perfect ranch."

"Would you still want a ranch if you had that much money?"

"Sure I would. Money isn't the main goal behind the ranch." She looked at Crissy. "I don't want to train horses just for the money, although having more than we do now would be nice. I really want to work with them." She released Crissy's hand and waved vaguely. "You're right. It's silly to waste time dreaming like this."

"I never said it was silly to dream. I simply believe that dreams should be realistic. To me, winning the lottery isn't realistic. Dreams are accomplished through hard work and determination."

Lynn wasn't sure she agreed with her completely. It wasn't as though she had actually ever known anyone who was rich, but from what she saw on television and read in the newspaper it seemed like the richer you were the less you worked. "Joann sure wouldn't agree with you." She stifled a yawn. "By the way, you'll be happy to know our ranch was on her list."

"Joann's a sweetheart. I wish she could meet someone. She's such a good person."

"Don't start," Lynn warned.

"What?"

"You know you've got a matchmaking streak a mile wide running through you."

"What's wrong with introducing her to someone?" Crissy asked.

"She'll find someone when she's ready."

"It doesn't matter anyway. I don't know anyone who's single that she'd be interested in."

Lynn caressed Crissy's bare thigh. "I sure like these shorts on you," she said, running her hand slowly up the wide leg opening.

"Don't start something you're too tired to finish," Crissy cooed.

"I'm never too tired for this." She leaned over to brush her lips across Crissy's arm.

"I have to get up at five thirty tomorrow morning. I have a

paper to finish."

"Then I'd better get you to bed early." Her lips caressed Crissy's ear.

"Umm, I think you're absolutely right."

Lynn heard Crissy's breath catch when her hand inched its way higher up her leg.

"I love you," Crissy said, hugging Lynn to her in a tight embrace.

Lynn's kiss began slow but surged when a warm hand slipped beneath her knit shirt and began to trace the nipple of her bare breast. "We'd better take this inside."

They stumbled toward the house, both reluctant to release the other. They managed to lock doors and shut off lights as they went. Discarded clothes marked their progress to the bedroom. In a frantic tangle of arms and legs, they fell across the old bed that had been Lynn's childhood bed. Before that it had belonged to her grandparents. There were times when Lynn felt as though she would explode from the passion Crissy generated within her. She had never been in a relationship where the physical needs remained so intense, but then again, she had never loved anyone the way she loved Crissy.

Her lips closed around a swollen nipple and a soft sigh filled her ears. She couldn't be certain if the whisper of delight was Crissy's or her own. When Crissy's hand pushed between Lynn's thighs, the loud sounds of pleasure that followed were definitely Lynn's.

"My God." Lynn sighed, raising Crissy's damp hand to her lips. "You should insure these hands."

"Umm," Crissy chuckled as Lynn rolled over on top of her and kissed her deeply. "And you should insure those lips."

"Maybe we should examine their skill level in more detail before we decide," she said as her body inched its way down.

"I agree completely."

All thoughts of sleep were soon forgotten.

CHAPTER EIGHT

On Monday morning, Lynn called adult protective services during her early break at the car wash and quickly discovered that no one could provide her any answers with the vague details she felt comfortable sharing with them about Beulah Mae. Not willing to give up on the first try, she called a couple of different sections. In the end she knew no more than she had when she started. The case would have to be reviewed and possibly taken before a judge.

As she flipped through the ragged phone book searching for the name of any other agency that provided legal advice to the elderly, her boss, Ed Nevils, reached over and slammed the book shut.

"I'm not paying you to learn to read," he said as he glared down at her.

Lynn ignored his rudeness and glanced at the clock on the

wall behind him. "I still have four minutes before my break is over."

"It'll take you that long to walk back out to the line."

Knowing it was useless to argue with him she kept silent and headed back out to work. As she reached the door she met a coworker, Deon Williams. They left the break area together in silence.

As soon as they were out of earshot of Nevils, Deon nudged her with his elbow. "Don't let that bastard get you down."

Lynn shrugged. "He doesn't bother me too much. I actually sort of feel sorry for him."

Deon gawked at her. "No fuckin' way. Why?"

"Can you imagine waking up every morning and having to glue that god-awful rug to your scalp?" Lynn said, referring to the cheaply made hairpiece Nevils wore. The toupee was the butt of scores of jokes. It was bad enough that Nevils wore the thing, but he tried to pass it off as his real hair. So far the only person he had fooled was himself.

Deon snorted. "Or worse, being his wife and having to wake up to him every morning."

Lynn shuddered. "Yuck. You win."

As promised, Lynn called Beulah Mae after work that afternoon. She knew her lack of good news wouldn't be welcomed so she tried to delay the admission as long as possible. "I dropped your letter off at the post office," she said.

"Thanks. I appreciate you taking care of that for me." It was obvious that Beulah Mae wasn't going to be any help in her diversionary tactics.

Lynn took a deep breath and explained that the folks at adult protective services wouldn't commit to anything until they knew more details.

"I didn't feel comfortable giving them your name," Lynn said.

"I'm glad you didn't. It might make them watch me closer, and we don't want that if we have to make a run for it."

"Beulah Mae, we're not going to make a run for it." Lynn glanced at her watch. She only had an hour to get to LaCasita and start busing tables. "There has to be a way for you to do this legally. I left a message for a lawyer who does a lot of work with guardianships. His secretary promised he would call me back tomorrow morning."

She tried to sound more positive than she felt. She had called three law offices at lunch, after having picked them from dozens of other firms. She had chosen them because their ads stated that they dealt with nursing home issues and that their initial consultation was free. It hadn't surprised her that she had gotten no further than the secretaries, but she'd been slightly taken aback that they all seemed to lose interest as soon as she assured them that no patient abuse was involved. Only one had bothered to take her home number and told her someone would contact her soon. She couldn't tell Beulah Mae that she didn't have much hope of hearing from him.

"If he doesn't return my call by noon tomorrow, I'll find someone else," Lynn said.

"I know you won't be satisfied until you contact every lawyer in the phone book," Beulah Mae said. "How long do you think it'll take?"

Lynn ignored the thick sarcasm in the older woman's voice. "A little while, I guess, but we have to try."

"Why?" Beulah Mae lowered her voice. "All you have to do is pretend like you're taking me out to dinner and we take off. It'll be hours before they even start looking for me."

"And what happens then? How far do you think we'll get before we get caught?" She took a deep breath to control her irritation. "Look, I'm going to do all I can to help you, but you have to do this legally. I have no burning desire to go to jail."

"I never should have asked you to help. I can do this on my

own just fine. I don't—"

Lynn's last nerve frayed. "Beulah Mae, stop it. I told you I would help and I will. If I hear one more word about you taking off, so help me I'll call over there and talk to the front office." Again she took a deep breath. "Look, I'm sorry I snapped, but it scares me when you talk about running off."

"Stop talking to me like I'm four years old."

"Then stop acting like you're four."

Silence filled the phone line. Beulah Mae broke it first. "Okay, I'll wait two weeks."

"Nothing is going to get accomplished in two weeks. You know how slow these things work."

"No matter. That's all I'm waiting."

Lynn heard the determination in her voice. She also knew Beulah Mae well enough to realize she was lying to her. She wouldn't take a chance on the time dwindling away and allowing Lynn an opportunity to warn the nursing home. She knew at best she had a week before Beulah Mae headed out on her own.

"Give me three weeks," Lynn said.

"No. Two weeks. That's all you get."

"Will you give me more time if I can at least get things started?"

Beulah Mae hesitated a moment before replying. "Maybe."

Lynn couldn't help but grin at the crafty older woman's response. There was no way she would sit around and wait. Rather than argue she decided to play along. She had a week to think of some way to keep her from running off on her own. She would talk it over with Crissy again. Together they could come up with something.

CHAPTER NINE

On Wednesday night the LT Hornets beat the Alamo Ladies in the ninth inning when Lynn slammed a fly ball into deep right field. She ran full out, half expecting the right fielder to catch the ball. As she drove toward second base, the screaming of her teammates told her that by some miracle the ball had not connected with the fielder's glove. The woman at second base was screaming and waving her arms madly as Lynn approached. Lynn hit the bag without breaking stride and raced toward third, where Coach Ames was motioning for her to keep running. Her lungs burned as she poured every ounce of willpower she had left and powered her way toward home plate. From the intense look on the catcher's face, she knew the ball was headed in the same direction. She tore her gaze away and focused on the plate, willing it closer. Somewhere above all the clatter, she heard Crissy's voice screaming at her to slide. Without hesitation, she went belly down, creating a cloud of dust and confusion. Her right hand frantically groped for the plate. She touched it a fraction of a second before the catcher's mitt slammed into her back.

"S-a-a-fe," the umpire yelled, sending the crowd and players into a pandemonium of cheers and boos.

"Lynn, that was a heck of slide," Deb complimented later as the team walked across the field.

"There was so much dust, I didn't think I'd ever find the plate," she admitted as she placed an arm around Crissy's shoulders.

"I think that winning a game over the best team in the league is cause for celebration," Karen said. "Who's up for pizza?"

Lynn stiffened. She hated this part of the weekly game. She and Crissy wouldn't be able to go. Crissy's car had been acting up again. Crissy's father had told them the starter was going out. They would have to cut back even further to get it fixed. It was possible for them to get by with only one car in a crunch, but with their schedules it made things much harder. It didn't help matters that Lynn's car was running on borrowed time.

"I have to study for a test," Crissy said.

Lynn pushed the toe of her shoe into the dirt. She knew Crissy was lying. What was worse was that she knew she was doing so to try to ease Lynn's discomfort. Not having money bothered Lynn much more than it seemed to worry Crissy.

"Yeah, I've got a paper I need to work on," Deb replied. "Do you want to go?" she asked, turning to Erica.

"Are you really going to study?" Erica asked, wrapping herself around Deb's lanky frame.

"I really need to study," Deb replied, with more than a little regret in her voice.

Erica sighed and tiptoed to kiss her quickly. "Okay. I know there's no changing your mind. I'll see you tomorrow."

Deb pulled her closer and kissed her deeply. "I promise some-day it'll be different," she whispered.

"I'm not complaining," Lynn heard Erica whisper.

The group continued to plod toward the parking lot as Erica and Deb held back. They both lived in the dorm at St. Mary's but had never been able to get a room together.

"Sure you two won't join us?" Karen asked, directing her question to Crissy and Lynn. "My treat."

"Maybe next time," Lynn said, pulling away from Crissy to begin the ritual round of hugs.

"Where's your car?" Tina asked, looking around the lot.

"We walked over," Crissy said. "It's only a few blocks and we wanted to take advantage of the mild temperatures while they last."

Joann slapped at a mosquito. "These little beggars are already out and biting. Summer isn't too far off."

"I'll drop you two off, if you'd like," Tina offered.

"No, thanks," Crissy said. "I'd rather walk."

They waved a last good-bye and headed home.

"That was a great slide," Crissy said as her arm settled comfortably around Lynn's waist. They were cutting across a vacant lot that would bring them out directly behind the convenience store. It was dark and a dog barked somewhere in the distance.

Lynn's foot hit a discarded soda can and sent it rolling through the sparse grass. "I heard you screaming, telling me to slide, and I did it."

"That really got everyone fired up. You gave us the extra momentum we needed to win the game." She gave Lynn's waist a gentle squeeze. A win was especially nice, since the team had not played well so far that season.

They were nearing the lights from the convenience store and they reluctantly released their embrace.

"Do we have enough to buy a beer?" Lynn asked.

Crissy hesitated a second too long.

"Damn. We work our asses off and can't even afford a fucking beer." Lynn's shoulders tightened as her steps grew faster. She didn't normally complain so much, but lately it seemed as though nothing had gone right.

"We can buy a beer if you want one," Crissy replied.

Lynn shook her head, knowing they really couldn't afford it. She didn't know what they would do if the car's starter went out before they managed to save enough to replace it.

As they reached the back of the convenience store, Lynn stopped. "I'm sorry," she said. "I didn't mean to snap at you."

Crissy ran a hand over Lynn's hair. "It won't be forever," she promised. "As soon as I get out of college I can get a decent job and we can really start saving for the ranch."

"I know I'm being a bitch. I don't need a beer anyway." She patted her stomach.

Crissy laughed. "You're right. A beer is liable to turn you into a ninety-nine-pound weakling, as opposed to your current ninety-eight-pound status."

"Weakling." Lynn gave a mock growl. "Who are you calling a weakling?" She grabbed for Crissy, but they had played this game often enough that Crissy was already on the move, avoiding her.

They dodged and lunged at each other until Crissy raised her hands in surrender. "I can't run anymore. I give up."

"Come on," Lynn said, gasping for breath. "Let's get home. I need a shower. I swear an acre of dirt buried itself in my pants when I slid."

"Lucky dirt." Crissy leered.

Lynn draped her arm across her lover's shoulders as they walked around the side of the store. A few seconds later, the bell on the store's door dinged. She automatically dropped her arm and stepped slightly away.

The obese man leaving the convenience store was of medium height with a heavy beard and a vast potbelly. He was slurping from an enormous drink that looked large enough to quench the thirst of a family of four. Lynn watched him fumble with the drink, a large bag of chips and a candy bar as he searched for his car keys. He finally set the drink on the roof of the car. As he pulled the keys from his pocket a piece of paper came out with them and fluttered, unnoticed by him, to the ground.

"Hey, buddy, you dropped something," she yelled.

He flipped her off before he reached for his drink and climbed into the car.

"What a butt-head," Crissy mumbled.

Lynn shook her head as she eyed the car. It was an older model Lincoln Continental. One of those gas-guzzling monstrosities. As the car turned sharply and sped out of the parking lot she noticed the personalized plate. "Mr. Big." She snorted. "Can you imagine what his gas bill must be? Why do people waste money on personalized tags?"

"It's a fad."

"It's ego," she countered.

Crissy shrugged and they continued on.

A gust of wind caught the paper that had fallen from the man's pocket and swept it toward them. Lynn snatched it up as it rolled by. "I hate it when people think the world is their personal garbage can." She crumpled up the paper and started to toss it into a trash can by the gas pumps when she spied the orange border. "Hey, it's a lottery ticket."

Crissy stopped and sighed. "Talk about a waste of money. Let's take it inside to the clerk. The guy will probably come back looking for it."

Lynn shook her head. "You are so weird."

"Why?" Crissy asked in a slightly hurt tone.

Lynn bumped her with a shoulder to take the sting out of her words. "That guy isn't going to come back looking for this ticket. He has probably already forgotten he bought it." She straightened out the paper. "Heck, it's only one set of numbers.

He's not coming back for a buck." She folded the ticket in half.

"What are you going to do with it?"

"I'm going to keep it. Who knows? Maybe it—what is it that the psychic says?"

"What are you talking about?"

"That woman psychic who's on television late at night." Lynn bit her lip. "Oh, now I remember. She calls it 'the hand of fate.' That's what it was. The hand of fate blew this ticket to me."

"It was the wind that blew it to you, but more importantly, it's not your ticket."

Lynn sighed. "I swear, sometimes you are so—"

Crissy suddenly turned and planted her hands on her hips. "Don't you dare call me another name."

"Sweet." Lynn pulled an innocent face. "I was going to say you are so sweet." She tilted her head to the side and smiled.

"Bull." Crissy tried to sound angry, but Lynn knew she could make her laugh.

"Scout's honor," Lynn said and flashed the Boy Scout sign.

"You were never a Scout," Crissy reminded her.

"Maybe not in reality, but I was at heart."

Crissy ignored her. "We should turn that ticket in. It doesn't belong to us."

"I'm telling you that guy isn't going to come back here looking for this. Besides, why do you care? You didn't think Joann had a chance at beating the odds. If the odds are really that much against winning, I'm doing the guy a favor by keeping it."

"How do you think you're doing him a favor?"

"Simple. If I take this ticket into the store, the clerk will probably know who this Mr. Big is. He'll call him and the poor slob will have to turn that big gas-guzzling monstrosity around to come back over here to get it. *Bam*. Right there he has wasted a couple of bucks on gas just to pick up this worthless lottery ticket. When according to the Law of Crissy he doesn't have a snowball's chance in hell of winning the lottery anyway."

Crissy waved her hands in defeat. "Fine. Keep the ticket. But don't blame me when the troubles of the world crawl up your back."

Lynn grabbed her head and moaned. "Oh, please. Don't start quoting your grandmother," she begged, putting the ticket in her wallet.

Crissy gave a wicked laugh, and Lynn knew what was coming. Crissy's grandmother spent most of her day spouting what were intended to be inspirational quotes. Unfortunately, most of them were so garbled that the only thing they inspired was confusion.

"Lynn, you grow what you sow."

"I'm warning you," Lynn tried to sound fierce.

"A penny saved is one less spent. A bird in the nest has salt on its tail."

Lynn lunged at her. Crissy screamed and broke into a run. She continued to yell out her grandmother's jumbled quotes as they ran home.

CHAPTER TEN

Lynn swiped four doughnuts from the courtesy tray that had been set out for the customers and slid them into a folded paper bag she pulled from her pocket. Nevils would give her hell if he caught her, but he was probably in the front office chatting up the new receptionist. Lynn's logic was that if the company could afford to buy doughnuts for customers, they could occasionally spring for a few for their employees.

The Diamond T was a chain of complete car-cleaning shops that specialized in luxury vehicles. When a car arrived it was assigned a personal team. Each team worked in groups of four, sharing the responsibilities. They started on the inside of the car, where they thoroughly cleaned and detailed it from top to bottom, careful not to miss a seam or vent panel. Afterward, the outside of the vehicle was meticulously hand-washed, dried and waxed. For this service the customer parted with a reasonably large chunk of cash, very little of which trickled down to the people who actually did the work.

Lynn worked at the Diamond T during the week. She was hoping to get a shift that included Saturday, since she could earn more in tips on the weekend, but those shifts were saved for Nevils's favorites and she was a long way from being a member of that elite club.

Lynn sauntered into the break room. "I brought breakfast. Who has the coffee?" she called to the table where her three workmates sat.

Deon limped to the coffeepot to pour her a cup. "Man, you gonna get caught snaggin' those things one of these days."

"Yeah, and when you do, Nevils is going to fire your white ass," Jose said.

Sondra, the youngest and newest member of the team, began to fidget with her coffee cup. Lynn noticed the nervous gesture and smiled to herself. Sondra, a small wiry woman whose face betrayed her every thought, had a major crush on her. The guys teased Lynn about it when Sondra wasn't around, but Lynn knew it was harmless and was somewhat flattered.

Deon set the cup of coffee down in front of Lynn. "So how did the LT Hornets do last night?" Deon was an ex-jock who worked two jobs to support his wife and six-month-old son. He lived for anything that dealt with sports. When he was fourteen a drunk driver had ended his dream of playing pro baseball.

Lynn liked her current team. They accepted her for who she was. She had never tried to hide her lifestyle from any of her coworkers and had paid for her honesty a few times. She wondered if that was part of the problem with Nevils but quickly dismissed it. He was an ass to everybody on the line.

"We stole it in the ninth inning. I hit a fly ball out to right field. Luckily their girl was either asleep or else she couldn't catch. Anyway, when she finally nabbed it, she overthrew the ball to second base, and I headed to third." She sipped her coffee.

"That's where I almost got into trouble. Somebody was awake out there and hammered it home. If Crissy hadn't screamed for me to slide into home, I probably wouldn't have made it in. That play turned the game around and we won." She knew she was bragging, so she tore the bag open so they could get to the doughnuts. "And get this. We played the Alamo Ladies."

"Ain't they the ones who hired that ex-college coach?" Jose asked as he bit off half a glazed doughnut.

"Yeah, they're the ones. They have real uniforms and every-thing. Everyone said we didn't have a chance in hell against that team." Lynn sipped her coffee, grateful it was still fresh. As often as not it would be burnt and undrinkable. "It simply shows that money doesn't always win."

"Here comes Nevils," Sondra said quietly.

Jose hissed and crammed the rest of the doughnut into his mouth.

"You ladies waiting for a personal invitation to get to work?" Nevils yelled from across the room.

"Just once I'd like to tell that pompous ass what I really think of him," Jose muttered, spewing the table with crumbs. "Somebody ought to tell him about sexual harassment. He can't be calling me a girl."

"Hey, man," Deon said, "why don't you go do that? I'm sure your old lady will understand how you got fired while defending your manhood."

Jose gave a few incoherent mumbles before he stood.

A quick glance at the enormous clock hanging above the cof-feepot indicated they still had ten minutes before they were scheduled to clock in. Lynn took her time picking up the greasy, torn bag while Jose and Sondra gathered their used cups. Deon took the bag from Lynn and made a perfect shot into the trash can across the room.

"Three points and the crowd goes wild," Lynn said, imitating a radio announcer.

"Unless you ladies won the lottery last night, I suggest you move your butts." Nevils was getting angry. He wanted everyone to jump up and leave the break room whenever he entered.

Lynn suddenly remembered the ticket in her wallet. "Damn. I may have. I forgot to check my numbers this morning." She pulled the ticket from her wallet. "Who's got the newspaper? I need to check my Lotto numbers."

"Here." Deon reached into his shirt pocket and removed a small wad of paper. "I got this to check my numbers this morning." He rummaged through the slips of paper before handing her one. It was the list of the winning numbers that the convenience stores printed out after each Lotto drawing.

Nevils was glaring at them. Even though they still had plenty of time, Lynn knew it was better not to piss him off too much. He could make their lives miserable. As she moved over to get in the time clock line behind her team she began to scan the numbers. "Hey, guys," she yelled. "I've got three numbers."

"Great," Deon replied. "That's almost enough to buy yourself a beer."

"No, wait. I've got four—" She stopped. For several long heartbeats she simply stared at the paper in her hand.

"Come on, Lynn. The line is moving. Get a move on before Nevils starts bitchin' us out again," Jose hissed.

When she didn't respond the three turned back to stare.

"Lynn," Sondra called timidly.

"Yo! Earth to Lynn," Jose said.

When she still didn't respond they came back for her. "Girl, three or four numbers aren't worth getting your ass fired over," Deon said as he tapped her arm.

Lynn looked away from the ticket and then back, afraid her eyes were deceiving her.

"What's the matter with you?" Jose asked.

Lynn looked at Deon. "I—" She looked back at the numbers. They hadn't changed.

"Lynn." Something in Deon's voice made her look up. His gaze held a look that bordered somewhere between hope and fear. "Cut it out. That's not funny."

"I've got them, Deon," she whispered.

"Got what?" Jose demanded.

"Don't mess around," Deon warned again.

Lynn shook her head. "Man, I'm not messing with you." Her voice grew louder. "I've got the damn numbers." She shoved the papers into his hands. "Look at them."

"Fuck," he breathed as he read the numbers. He looked back at Lynn. "You got the fuckin' numbers. That's thirty-two fuckin' million dollars!" He crammed the ticket back into Lynn's hand as a crowd of their other coworkers started pressing in on them.

People demanding to see the ticket quickly surrounded Lynn. Deon stood between her and the crowd and refused to let anyone touch the slip of paper.

"Put it back in your wallet." His hands shook as he took it from her and placed it securely inside her wallet, which he pushed into her front pocket. "Keep it in the front so no one can steal it." His voice sounded hoarse, his breathing so labored he could barely speak.

Nevils shoved through. "What's going on here?" he demanded. "Get to work before I fire the lot of you. It's not like I can't find a hundred more losers to replace you."

Lynn took one look at his beefy red face and finally said the words she had only dreamed of saying for years. "Nevils, you're a jackass. You can take this job and that stupid hairpiece and cram them both where the sun doesn't shine." His face flushed from red to near purple. Before he could find his voice, she made her way through the crowd and walked out.

As soon as she reached her car she quickly locked herself inside and sat clutching the steering wheel, unable to believe what had happened. Her stomach rolled when she realized she had quit her job. In the same instant she burst into hysterical laughter. She had won thirty-two million dollars. She didn't have to work at the car wash ever again. If she wanted to, she could buy the place! For a moment she indulged herself in a fantasy of buying the Diamond T chain and making Nevils wash cars with that disgusting hairpiece.

Suddenly she couldn't wait to tell Crissy. She could have called, but she wanted to see Crissy's face when she told her. Walking away from Nevils had given her such a high she wasn't sure she would ever quit smiling. She dug the keys from her pocket and tried to crank the car, but it refused to kick over. She tried several more times until the battery began to drag. It was no use. It wasn't going to crank. In frustration she slapped the steering wheel and got out to raise the hood. She was almost to the front of the car when she stopped sharply. She didn't have to fix this piece of crap. She could buy any car she wanted. She began to laugh again as she started toward the bus stop.

"Where do you think you're going?"

She turned to find Nevils charging toward her.

"My car won't start so I'm going to take the bus," she said as patiently as possible. She looked at him and realized for the first time just how deeply her dislike for him ran. He acted the way he did because he knew the people working for him all needed those jobs. He knew they'd put up with his bull because they couldn't afford to be fired.

"You're not about to leave that eyesore parked here," he fumed.

She rubbed her chin and tried to control her anger. "Nevils, I told you it won't crank. I really don't think it'll fit on the bus's bicycle rack and I can't carry it, so what would you suggest I do with it?"

"I don't care what you do with it, but you're no longer employed here and if you don't move it immediately I'm going to have it towed away."

Lynn chuckled. "I think that's an excellent idea. Why don't

you take care of that?" she turned and walked away.

"I'm going to have the bill sent to you," he screamed after her.

"You do that." Without waiting for him to respond she headed toward the bus stop, happy in the knowledge that now that she and Crissy were multimillionaires, they would never have to put up with jerks like Nevils again.

When she boarded the bus and found a seat, she felt the corner of her wallet dig into her leg. For a brief heart-stopping moment she started to rip it out of her pocket. What if the ticket wasn't there? What if she had made a mistake in checking the numbers? She started to take the wallet from her pocket but stopped when the man across the aisle from her looked up from his paper. He gave a slight smile before going back to reading.

She longed to check the numbers again but couldn't take a chance in letting anyone see the ticket. Frightening thoughts invaded her mind. What if someone stole it or she lost it before they could claim their winnings? Her heart began to pound. Beads of sweat broke out as she scanned the faces of the people around her. How long had they been sitting there? Had any of them followed her onto the bus? The sweat began to trickle down her sides. Her breathing became so labored she grew dizzy. This was silly, she told herself. She needed to calm down before she passed out or had a stroke. She closed her eyes and forced herself to relax. There was absolutely no reason why anyone would suspect she had a ticket worth thirty-two million dollars in her pocket.

She tried to think of something else, but absolutely nothing but money came to mind. After several minutes she gave up trying to forget it and gave her imagination a little free rein.

What would they do with that much money? Would they put it in the bank or do some sort of investing? She didn't know anything about investing and finances. The one positive thing about being poor was that you never had to worry about what to do with the little amount of money you did have. Day-to-day living took care of it and if by some miracle there was ever anything left over, fate and Uncle Sam took care of that.

She tried to visualize what thirty-two million dollars would look like. When she couldn't she narrowed her focus to the number itself but struggled with the zeros. How many zeros were in a million? She shook her head harshly. Crissy would know the best way to handle the money. She would make sure they were never poor again.

Slowly, she let the dreams emerge. They would help her mom with her new restaurant venture and build her a nice house, send Crissy's folks to Europe. They could pay off all the college loans for the Sunday Brunch crowd. Then she would help Deon, Jose and Sondra. She couldn't stand thinking about them having to stay on with Nevils. Her imagination continued to run wild. She and Crissy would never have to work for someone again if they chose not to. She wondered for a moment if Crissy would drop out of college but quickly vetoed that idea. Crissy had worked too hard for her degree. The money would simply give her the luxury of completing her final semester without having to worry about expenses and without having to work. It was highly likely that Crissy would still want to teach school. Lynn understood that because she certainly still wanted to raise and train horses. She got goose bumps on her arms when she realized how close she was to having the ranch she had always dreamed of. They would buy themselves a small place and a few horses. A hysterical giggle threatened to escape. Small—hell, they could buy a whole county.

CHAPTER ELEVEN

Crissy was making coffee when Lynn walked into the Taco Hut. The midmorning crowd of the non-nine-to-fivers was demanding their coffee and tacos. Lynn could see a small frown of concentration on Crissy's face as she rushed to fill two large Styrofoam cups.

Lynn walked behind the counter and stood beside Crissy. "You have filled your last two cups, baby."

Crissy looked up, startled. Confusion was etched on her face. Lynn was about to burst with happiness. She was eager to share her joy with Crissy, but she couldn't do it here. She would take Crissy somewhere private. She didn't want to share this special moment with any of these demanding people.

"Let's take a walk," Lynn suggested.

Crissy stared at her as if she had lost her mind. "What's wrong? What are you doing here?"

"I came to take you for a walk," Lynn said. Her face was beginning to ache for smiling so much.

"I need those coffees," someone behind them yelled. "Preferably today."

Crissy quickly put the lids on the cups. "Lynn, you have to leave. I don't get a break for another hour. Why aren't you at work?" she asked over her shoulder as she hurried off with the coffee.

A thin, pimply-faced kid came up beside Lynn. "You can't be back here," he informed her. "You'll have to wait on the other side of the counter."

Lynn assumed this was Jason, Crissy's new boss. The guy was all of eighteen.

"We were just leaving," Lynn assured him as she took Crissy by the arm.

"I need a Coke and two potato and egg tacos for here," someone yelled. Crissy turned to pour the drink.

"Oh, no, you don't." Lynn took the glass from Crissy's hand. "Let Junior do it." Crissy gasped as Lynn handed the glass to Jason.

His face flushed a deep red as he thrust the glass back into Crissy's hand. "I'm not joking. Get back to work. And you"—he pointed at Lynn—"need to get out of here now." He spun on his heel and started walking away.

"Lynn, what are you doing?" Crissy looked at her frantically. "You need to leave. You're going to get me fired."

"You're not going to get fired, because you're quitting right now," Lynn said. She took Crissy's hand and led her around the counter. As they rounded the corner, Jason caught them.

"Crissy, either get back to work or you're fired."

Crissy tried to pull away, but Lynn held fast. "You can't fire her, because she has already quit."

"You're fired," he screamed at Crissy.

Lynn led a stunned Crissy outside. She was beginning to

doubt her impulsive decision on how to announce the big news. She pushed away her concerns. In the end it wouldn't matter. As soon as Crissy heard the good news, she'd forget all about that dead-end job. "Where's your car?"

"Around back," Crissy mumbled.

They walked to the back of the building where Lynn spotted the ancient Escort. It looked like the loser in a rust war. *That will be the first thing to go,* Lynn promised herself as she helped a dazed Crissy into the passenger seat and then raced around to the other side. She had to yank on the handle four times before it finally opened. She crawled inside and slammed the door too hard in her excitement and the window dropped down inside the door cavity. She started to curse it but realized they didn't have to worry about it anymore. She laughed instead.

"What the hell is wrong with you?" Crissy's shock was wearing off and anger was quickly replacing it. "You got me fired! And now we'll have to have the window fixed and you're sitting there laughing like a deranged hyena. What are you doing here? Why aren't you at work?" The questions poured out of her faster than Lynn could answer them.

Lynn held up her hands. "Trust me," she said, her excitement almost taking her voice away.

Crissy fell silent and stared at her. "Lynn, this had better be good. I needed that job. It took me a long time to find one that fit into my schedule."

Lynn dug the wallet from her pocket and looked around quickly before opening it. "Lock your door," she whispered.

"What?"

"Your door, lock it." She used her elbow to lock the driver's side door.

"Do you really think that's going to make much of a difference now that the window is missing?"

Lynn glanced back at the gaping hole and giggled. "Oh, yeah. Well, lock yours anyway."

She peered at Lynn closely. "Have you been drinking?"

"No. Humor me. Please lock your door."

Crissy sighed but did as she had been asked.

Lynn handed her the lottery ticket and the printout with the winning numbers. Crissy took it and stared at it for several seconds. Lynn watched the multitude of emotions play across her face as comprehension came. Finally, there was the look that Lynn had been waiting for. The realization. The smile. The scream of excitement.

Crissy continued to scream as she grabbed Lynn and hugged her tightly.

Lynn wasn't sure her eardrums would survive, but what the hell? She could buy new ones!

Crissy was laughing and crying while alternately hugging Lynn and pounding the already battered seat. She tried to speak several times, but no words came.

"We'll never have to work at shit jobs again," Lynn said, wiping tears from her own eyes. "We can buy that ranch we've always wanted." She hugged Crissy to her. "We can help our families. We can do anything we want."

Crissy hugged her tightly. "Is it true, Lynn?" She pulled away. "This isn't a dream or a bad joke, is it?"

"No, baby. It's real. We've won thirty-two million dollars."

Crissy grabbed her chest as she suddenly turned pale and slumped against the car door.

Lynn's heart flew into her throat. She grabbed Crissy's hands. "What's wrong?"

Crissy shook her head and began to cry. "It's not fair." She sobbed.

"You're scaring me. What's wrong?"

"We can't keep the money."

For a moment Lynn thought she had misunderstood.

"We can't keep the money," Crissy said again.

"Why not?" A sick feeling was starting to develop deep in the pit of her stomach.

"It's not our ticket," Crissy reminded her.

"It is so!"

"Lynn, we know who lost it. We saw the man drop it."

"So?" Lynn grew sicker. She had to take several deep breaths to keep from losing the greasy doughnut she had eaten earlier.

"It's not right. We saw his license plate. We have to find him and give it back."

"Like hell I will," Lynn screamed as she snatched the ticket from Crissy's hand. "I found it and I'm keeping it."

"You can't. It's not right."

Lynn shook her head wildly. "Not right! Not right! I'll tell you what's *not right*. It's *not right* that we bust our asses working shit jobs and still can't buy a frigging beer when we want one. Or that almost half of our checks go to taxes that are wasted on crap like studying the breeding habits of frogs. It's *not right* that my mom worked in that god-awful factory until they decided they could make more money elsewhere and she still lives in that crappy trailer court. Or that a quarter of a million people go to bed hungry every night when politicians are sitting—"

Crissy placed a hand on Lynn's arm. "Baby, please."

Lynn watched tears stream down her lover's face. They should be tears of joy. Why was Crissy doing this? They should be celebrating and calling someone to find out how to collect their winnings—or shopping for a new car, finding her mom a new house, sending Crissy's parents on that vacation to Europe that they were always talking about. Now was the time to be happy and Crissy was ruining everything.

"Why do you always have to do this?" Lynn demanded as she turned to face the windshield. "You're so damn moral. Why can't you be like everyone else?"

Crissy began to cry harder.

Lynn felt bad that she hurt her, but there was a deep burning anger at Crissy for spoiling what should have been the best times

84

of their lives. For the briefest instant she wished she had never picked up the ticket, but then she remembered what the money could mean. Why couldn't Crissy understand that this wasn't just about her wanting to be rich? "Why are you doing this?"

"It's wrong to keep the ticket."

"That's bullshit and you know it," Lynn snapped as she turned back to face Crissy. "We have a chance to have a life that most people only dream about. We could help our family and friends. Besides, he doesn't need the money."

"How do you know that?" Crissy whirled to face her.

"You saw that big-ass car he was driving and those personal-ized plates. Did he look like he was hurting for money?"

"What I saw was an old car," Crissy reminded her. "You don't know anything about him."

"I don't believe this. I don't fucking believe it." Lynn flung herself around to face the front of the car again. An uneasy silence fell between them.

Crissy finally put her hand on Lynn's arm. Lynn struggled not to shrug it off.

"I don't want to fight about this. Don't you see we could never be happy taking this money? We would always know it wasn't ours."

"Maybe you wouldn't be happy. I'd sleep just fine, thank you very much."

"Would you?"

"Hell, yes! I'm tired of being broke all the time—of never having enough to do one extra little thing. My car wouldn't crank. I had to take the bus over here." She glanced around. "I'm tired of this piece-of-crap car." She slapped the dashboard and watched in stunned silence as the imitation leather gave way and a long split tore across its length. Suddenly a wave of red fury swam before her eyes. Never in her life had she hated anything as badly as she did that car at that moment. She had to get out of it. She yanked at the door handle. When it failed to work she grabbed it with both hands and tried to rip it off its hinges. She could hear herself howling in frustration but couldn't stop her manic attempt to escape the car. She threw her shoulder against the door repeatedly. Crissy's pleadings for her to calm down only enraged her more. The door latch finally caught and the cheap, lightweight door flew open and sent her sprawling onto the ground. She ignored the stinging scrape on her elbow as she scrambled up and delivered one vicious kick after another into the side of the car.

Crissy leaned across the seat and Lynn could see the fear in her tear-filled eyes. Ashamed of her crazed outburst, she tried to find the words to apologize, but nothing came. Why couldn't Crissy see how much this meant to her?

"Lynn, please. You know finding the owner is the right thing to do."

Her anger was gone. In its place was something colder, darker and infinitely more frightening. "Let me tell you what I know." She leaned down to stare through the open door and watched with a sense of detachment as her lover shrank back from her. "I know that I'm sick and tired of working sixteen hours a day and never having anything to show for it. I've had it up to here"—she slashed her hand beneath her eyes—"with having to work for incompetent assholes like Nevils, and of having to watch every single penny I spend. I'm sick of this damn car." She leaned farther into the car and glared at Crissy. "But above all, I'm sick and tired of your holier-than-thou attitude."

The look of shock and hurt on Crissy's face snapped Lynn out of it. She was filled with a deep sense of shame. How could she have said such a thing to Crissy? She tried to find her voice but it seemed to have abandoned her. They stared at each other for a long horrible moment before Lynn turned and ran.

CHAPTER TWELVE

Lynn heard Crissy calling her, but she couldn't stop. Not even when she heard Crissy's futile attempts to crank the car. The nerve-racking screech of the grinding engine slowly gave way until the only sounds left were the desperate slapping of her running feet and her labored breathing. She ducked into an alley and slowed to a jog. Her lungs burned. A sharp stitch in her side caused her to lean slightly forward. When she could no longer jog, she slowed to a walk but forced herself to keep moving until she came to a small park. Only when she was certain that she was alone did she allow herself to collapse on a bench. As she lay staring up at the sky her breathing gradually returned to normal and the pain in her side eased. How had things gotten so screwed up so quickly? She sat up slowly, propped her elbows on her knees and cradled her head in her hands.

It had started out as an ordinary Thursday morning. They'd

gotten ready for work, had their morning coffee and talked about how they were looking forward to Sunday. Then, two hours later, they were multimillionaires, and now they'd had by far the worst fight of their relationship. Lynn pressed the heels of her hands against her eyes. She and Crissy rarely quarreled in a truly serious way. They might bicker back and forth, but it never got malicious. Neither had ever walked out during an argument.

She opened her eyes and leaned back against the bench. As she did, she heard the rustle of the ticket in her shirt pocket. She removed it and stared at the seemingly benign piece of paper. Without warning her anger began to flare again. This money represented so many things. Her mom could retire and not have to work another day in her life, or if she still wanted to open the restaurant she could do so with a safe financial cushion to fall back on if the venture failed. The Sunday Brunch gang could start life without the burden of the hefty college loans hanging over their heads. She could help Deon, Jose and Sondra. The potential of how much could be accomplished with thirty-two million dollars was almost beyond her range of imagination. She held the ticket closer, as if she was trying to stare into it. With this tiny piece of paper she could help so many. Why couldn't Crissy see that?

Lynn carefully smoothed the wrinkles out of the ticket. "This time I'm not giving in. I'm going to keep it," she whispered.

She tried not to think about what claiming the winnings would do to her relationship with Crissy—if she even still had a relationship.

"This is so stupid." She sighed. Why was she sitting here on this bench by herself? She and Crissy should be together celebrating their good fortune. The psychic had been right. Fate had literally blown this ticket to her. The money was supposed to be hers. A new determination blazed within her. She would use it to help the people she loved and if Crissy had a problem with that, then . . . The thought trailed off. What would she do? She pushed away the stab of fear that shot through her stomach. After a moment, she carefully placed the ticket back into her wallet. She started to slide it into her hip pocket when she remembered Deon's warning and slipped it into the front one instead. Crissy would come around once she saw how much good the money was doing. Right now the important thing was to patch things up between them.

She walked back out to the main street and looked around until she spied a bus stop on the corner. She needed to get home and apologize to Crissy. Together they could work through this. Lynn searched the pockets of her jeans and began to laugh when she realized that she didn't even have enough money for another bus fare. Despite the thirty-two million dollar ticket in her pocket, she was going to have to walk home.

As she walked and her emotions settled she began to see the situation a little clearer and slowly her perspective began to change. To some degree Crissy had been right. They knew who purchased the ticket, so maybe the guy was entitled to it. On the other hand, he had lost it. If she hadn't picked it up, it would probably be lying against some fence rotting away in the weather or down the gutter. That should give her some claim to it. So maybe the standup thing to do was to give him half. Besides, nobody really needed thirty-two million dollars. A mere fraction of that amount would provide them with enough to keep them comfortable for life. She had no desire to spend the rest of her life doing nothing but managing money. The idea of never working certainly didn't appeal to her. She still wanted to raise and train horses. The money merely allowed the opportunity to make their dreams a reality sooner and provided a solid financial safety net. Rather than struggling for years to achieve their dream, it was being handed to them. In the end, nothing was more important than Crissy. Not the money. Not even the ranch and horses. Without her nothing else mattered.

Maybe the money really was a bad thing. Or perhaps it was a

case of too much too quickly. She thought about the horrible argument and how she had run away. She reluctantly admitted that greed had caused her to react that way.

Her next thought lifted a massive burden from her shoulders. There really was a way where everybody won. She would locate the man she now thought of as Mr. Big and split the winnings with him. She didn't know how much would be withheld for taxes, but even after splitting it and paying the taxes, there would still be more than enough left over. She nodded at the idea. It seemed more than fair. Even Crissy couldn't argue with that logic.

Again, she let her imagination run wild with thoughts of how they would spend the money. This time the first thing on her list was securing their financial future. Before a single penny was spent they would seek the advice of a financial planner. Crissy would know who they needed to call. Once that was accomplished then they would be able to help others.

Lynn began to whistle. Crissy would have to agree that the new plan was both fair and responsible.

By the time she turned onto her street she even had a plan to find Mr. Big. Rather than going straight home she would detour over to the convenience store to see if the clerk might know who he was. If he did, then her search would be fairly simple. If not, she'd call Jose. His sister had a friend who worked for the Department of Motor Vehicles and for a few bucks could probably be convinced to look up a license plate number. If that failed, her last-ditch effort would be to approach one of the local television stations. This was the sort of story that they'd all jump at.

Her efforts would show Crissy that she really was sorry for what she had said and done earlier, and hopefully all would be forgiven.

When she stepped into the store, the man behind the counter could have been anywhere between the age of forty and sixty. The large broken veins in his nose and heavy bags under his eyes suggested a problem with alcohol. As she approached the counter she could smell the cigarette smoke that clung to him.

"Hi."

He peered at her through squinted eyes and gave a vague nod.

"I was wondering if you knew a guy I saw here the other night," Lynn began.

"This ain't no datin' service. I don't know nobody." He turned and began stacking the empty candy boxes that were piled on the side counter.

She ignored his comment and pressed on. "He's a big guy. He drives an older Lincoln with personalized plates—Mr. Big."

The guy glanced at her again. "What do you want? You don't look like no cop."

Lynn chuckled. "No. I'm not a cop." She slid her hands into her pocket and rocked back and forth slightly, wondering how she could ask more questions without telling him about the ticket.

"His name is Stoner," the guy volunteered. "He always pays for his gas with a credit card. Edward Stoner is his name." The clerk picked up the empty boxes and walked away toward the back.

It took her a moment to gather herself. "Thanks," she called to the retreating figure.

Lynn knew she had made the right decision when she not only found an almost completely intact phone book at the pay phone outside the store but also a listing for an Edward Stoner who lived less than six blocks away. As she read the address, she experienced a twinge of guilt. Crissy had been right. The guy probably needed the money.

Lynn left the store and rushed home. She was disappointed when she didn't find Crissy's car in the driveway. She cursed her childish behavior in running off the way she had and leaving Crissy with the car. What if the starter had finally gone out? Or any number of other things could have gone wrong with it. Crissy would eventually call her father if she couldn't get the car cranked. But just in case, maybe she should call the restaurant to see if she was still hanging around there.

Lynn went inside to get a couple of bucks for bus fare from their meager emergency stash. The light on the answering machine was blinking. She pushed the button and Crissy's voice filled the room.

"Lynn, why did you run off like that? We need to talk about this. I'm sure we can work something out and maybe split the winnings with this guy. There's more than enough for everyone."

There was a brief pause and Lynn smiled. Crissy was at least thinking about keeping part of the money.

Crissy's voice began again. "I've talked to Jason and I have my job back. I . . ." There was a long sigh. "Even if everything works out with the ticket, I don't know how long it'll take before we see any of the money. Besides, I can't walk out and leave them short-handed. Mr. Salazar has been so good about letting me work around my schedule." Another pause. "Anyway, I guess I'll see you when I get home. I love you." The slight quiver in her voice made Lynn's throat tighten.

As usual Crissy was thinking rationally. Lynn hadn't bothered to think about how they would live until they received the money. Or about the extra work her walking off the job would cause her old team. She didn't care so much about any headaches it would cause Nevils, but she should have thought about her team.

She scanned the list of numbers taped above the phone and dialed the phone number to the Taco Hut. A small sigh of relief escaped her when the voice of an older woman answered. She didn't want to talk to Jason.

"May I speak to Crissy Anderson please?" Lynn asked.

"She's in the back helping to clean up now," the woman

replied.

Lynn shook her head. It was so like Crissy. Despite the fact that she was now a millionaire, she wouldn't change. She thanked the woman and went back outside.

She sat on the front steps for a while and absorbed the sounds of the neighborhood. Mr. Roberts, who lived two houses down, was mowing his backyard. The squeals of the rambunctious four-year-old Jamison twins could be heard from across the street. From the sounds, she guessed they were playing with the border collie, Socks. Sharise Jamison was a single mother with three kids, Jamar and Jamal, the twins, and Althea, her two-year-old daughter. Her husband had been killed in an auto accident shortly after Althea was born. Somewhere nearby a siren began to wail. It was soon lost to the strains of an old blues tune that momentarily reached her as a car drove past the house.

As she sat listening to the comforting sounds of the neighborhood, she began to worry about her childish impulse to run away from Crissy. Nobody was more levelheaded than Crissy and she had been foolish not to listen. If they had talked calmly they could have hit upon the idea of sharing the money, but as usual she had gone off like a cheap firecracker.

She sat up straighter. Maybe there was still another way to make everything better. She wouldn't wait until Crissy came home before going to Edward Stoner's house. She would go now and talk to him. Then Crissy would see that she had worked out the problem by herself and everything would be fine. Half of the ticket would be theirs—free of guilt.

She glanced at her watch. It was almost eleven. Stoner would probably be at work, but maybe he had a wife who would be home. She thought about the arrogant man she had taken an instant dislike to and quickly decided that the idea of talking to his wife was probably a better choice.

"Mrs. Edward Stoner, if you exist, I'm about to make your day," she whispered as she hopped off the steps.

CHAPTER THIRTEEN

Edward Stoner's home brought Lynn's jovial mood up short. The exterior of the house reeked of neglect. The corner support to a postage-stamp sized porch bowed outward at an alarming angle. One of the front windows had been broken out and covered with what appeared to have once been a cardboard box. Old water stains and peeling layers of paper gave proof that cardboard wasn't the best choice of materials for repairing windows.

She cringed when she noticed the older Lincoln Continental parked in the driveway. The concrete beneath it was riddled with cracks that were being further enlarged by a healthy crop of weeds. An overflowing trash can stood at the side of the porch. The garbage scattered across the yard indicated that the can had been full for some time.

Lynn considered leaving. This wasn't merely signs of poverty. This was simply not caring. For a brief moment she resented giving this guy anything but quickly brushed the thought away. It wasn't up to her to judge Stoner. She knew nothing about his life or what had brought him to this point. After taking a deep breath, she went to the door and knocked.

The door flew open so quickly that she took several involuntary steps back and stumbled off the tiny porch.

"Whatever you're selling, I don't want it."

Through the torn screen door, she could see the guy who had dropped the ticket. Up close he looked even heavier than she remembered. She guessed him to be in his late thirties or early forties. The heavy beard concealed most of his face. His eyes looked like raisins that had been pushed into a large ball of dough.

Again, she had an urge to leave without telling him why she was there. She swallowed and summoned her courage. Only the thought of making Crissy happy kept her from leaving. She wasn't there for Stoner. She was there to make Crissy proud of her.

"Mr. Stoner. My name is Lynn Strickland. I'd like to talk to you for a moment."

"Are you one of those Jehovah Witnesses?" He pushed the door open so harshly it banged against the wall.

Lynn couldn't stop herself from taking another step back. "No, sir."

"Well, if you're here to collect on some bill you can forget it. I don't have any money."

Lynn's gaze drifted to the personalized license plate. The senseless waste of money it represented continued to irritate her. If Stoner saw the direction of her gaze he never made a comment. "Actually, I am here about money."

He stepped back and closed the screen.

"Mr. Stoner, please wait."

"I told you I don't have any money." He started to close the entrance door.

Lynn stepped forward quickly. "You don't understand. I'm here to give you money."

He stopped abruptly and gave her a long suspicious look. From somewhere within the house, Lynn heard a baby start to cry, then sounds of footsteps followed by someone softly singing. The baby's cries stopped. The knowledge that she wasn't alone with Stoner gave her a strong sense of comfort.

"It don't look like you've got much to spare," Stoner said.

Lynn suppressed the wave of irritation raised by the smirk on his face. The truth was, she didn't look too prosperous in her faded jeans and a T-shirt that had long since seen its prime. The dress code at the car wash hadn't exactly called for power suits.

"If I could come in for a moment, I'll explain everything." She glanced around her. "I'd rather not talk about it here on the porch."

Stoner moved away from the door. He never invited her in or held the screen door open, but Lynn decided his silence constituted an invitation and followed him inside.

The first thing she noticed was the sound of his loud wheezing. She had on occasion heard the same sound at the nursing home in patients with emphysema. She wondered if that was why he was at home in the middle of a workday. Maybe he was disabled. Another wave of shame at her earlier greediness hit her.

When her eyes finally began to adjust to the room's dim interior it became clear that the inside of the house didn't look much better than the outside. It reeked of cigarette smoke and old grease. Everywhere she looked there were stacks of newspapers and discarded toys.

As she glanced around at the shabby furniture it became obvious that the Stoner family needed the money as badly as, maybe even worse than, she did. In addition to the old sofa, there was a recliner that had an odd tilt to one side and a coffee table with one end being supported by yet another stack of newspapers. Something on the battered sofa moved and she was startled to see that what she had thought were more newspaper stacks were actually three young children. They looked so close in size and appearance that she wondered it they were triplets. Stoner glanced over as if noticing them for the first time also.

"Get in the other room," he yelled. The kids scurried off without a backward glance, leaving Lynn with an almost over-powering urge to flee with them.

Stoner dropped his massive, unkempt body into the recliner with such force that Lynn held her breath, expecting the chair to explode. The chair's frame emitted a frightening screech of protest at the abuse but settled into a more or less upright position. After a cautious moment she slowly exhaled. He didn't offer her a seat, and after another glance at the sofa she decided she preferred to stand anyway.

Unsure of how to explain why she was there Lynn began with the evening she first saw him. "You purchased a lottery ticket last night at the convenience store over by the ball field," she said. "When you were getting into your car, it fell out of your pocket. I tried to tell you, but—" She hesitated when she remembered what an ass he had been. She shook her head to clear the thoughts and repeated her mantra. *I'm not here for Stoner. I'm here for Crissy.* "Anyway, I picked it up."

"So what? You here to give me a lecture on picking up trash?" He snatched a newspaper from the table and flipped it open.

Lynn recalled the overflowing garbage can in the front yard and doubted if Edward Stoner had ever picked up trash. "No. I came by to tell you the ticket was a winner."

He looked at her sharply. As they continued to stare at each other his breathing grew more erratic. "What do you mean, 'it's a winner'?"

"I mean we won the lotto last night—the thirty-two million." To her surprise he chuckled and went back to perusing the paper. "I mean it. The ticket was a winner."

He lowered the paper and peered at her. "Sure it was, and now what? How much is it going to cost me to get it back?" He ran a thick hand over his bushy hair. "Or is this where you tell me that for this reason or that you can't take the ticket in, but you'll gladly give it back to me for a small fee?" He shook the paper at her as if he were trying to shoo off a stray cat. "Get the hell out of here," he snapped.

Again she took an involuntary step back. "Mr. Stoner, I'm not here to try and scam you. I'm telling you the truth. The ticket won. I don't want anything from you. It's like I told you. I saw you drop the ticket and noticed the personalized tag when you drove off. When I realized it was a winning ticket I went back to the convenience store and the clerk remembered your name. He said you always bought gas on a credit card." She could see she was getting his attention. "After he gave me your name I looked in the phone book and"—she shrugged—"here I am."

He stared at her hard. "If you're lying to me, so help me I'll—"

"I'm not lying." She smiled nervously. "Mr. Stoner, we're millionaires."

The paper slipped from his hands as he slowly leaned forward. Sweat crawled down his cheeks to disappear into the dense beard. His breathing grew more shallow as he leaned so far forward that he seemed to be perched on the edge of the chair.

Cold fingers of anxiety tickled Lynn's spine as she watched his face pale and his left eye began to twitch. Suddenly she wanted nothing more than to leave this dark depressing house. "I came by to tell you that I think you're entitled to half the money and that we should make plans to claim the money together."

He heaved himself out of the chair with a speed that shocked her.

She took a quick step back toward the door. It occurred to her that maybe it would have been better if she had called him.

He moved slowly toward her. His chest rose and fell sharply. "You found *my* ticket. *My* ticket worth thirty-two million dollars and *you* decided you would share it with me?" His voice was little more than a harsh whisper, but she found it more frightening than his shouting. His face turned a frightening shade of red.

98

Lynn was too scared to answer. A horrible idea was beginning to slither around the edges of her thoughts. What if he decided to claim the entire amount? Was the ticket legally his? She cursed her impulsiveness.

He moved toward her. "I want my ticket back," he wheezed. By now, his face was nearly purple.

Lynn continued to inch her way toward the door. "Mr. Stoner, I'm here to offer you half. You lost the ticket and I came by it honestly. Now—" Before she could continue, he launched himself at her with such speed she didn't have time to think or run away from him. One massive hand clamped down on her shoulder while the other struck her sharply across the face.

"Give me that ticket," he said between gasps. He gulped in such painfully short breaths that she half-expected him to pass out.

Her concern for him vanished when his hands closed around her throat.

Terrified, she clawed at his fingers. She heard someone scream and caught a brief glimpse of a woman pounding on his back. One hand left Lynn's throat long enough to sweep the woman aside with no more effort than Lynn would use for an annoying fly. When he grabbed her again, some deeply buried need for survival kicked in. She closed her eyes and funneled all of her energy into her right foot, which she slammed down onto Stoner's instep. Instantly, she rechanneled the energy into her arms and shoved them upward between his arms. The heels of her hands struck him beneath the chin with a force that snapped his head back. He stumbled back several steps and flailed his arms wildly as he struggled to maintain his balance, but his weight was working against him. She took advantage of the situation to make her escape, but had only taken a couple of steps when there was a thunderous crash immediately followed by a hush so heavy that it stopped her in her tracks. She spun around expecting to find him standing over her. Instead all she found was a room filled with an eerie, deathly silence.

CHAPTER FOURTEEN

He was so still. In the dimly lit room, it was hard to see him. Was he really hurt or was it a ploy to lure her back into the room. She cautiously eased back toward Stoner. Her stomach churned when she saw the dark pool of blood that was starting to accumulate beneath his head. She didn't remember kneeling down beside him, but that's where she found herself when she heard a noise and glanced up to find the short, painfully thin woman and three small children standing in the doorway staring at her. It was the same woman who had tried to pull him off her earlier.

Lynn's instinct was to run, but she couldn't leave him lying there in a pool of blood. She leaned closer to check the wound on his head. It looked as though he had struck his temple on the coffee table. A nasty-looking knot was already starting to form. Without the steadily growing pool of blood, the wound wouldn't have appeared to be serious, but her extent of medical knowledge was basically limited to splinters and fire ant stings. The silence engulfing the house made her ears ring.

The room gave a sickening spin when she realized that the air seemed so deadly quiet because it was no longer filled with the sound of Stoner's wheezing. She stared at his chest, willing it to move. Nothing. Her hand trembled as she placed it on his wrist to check his pulse. When she couldn't locate it, she cringed and pushed her fingers deep into the mounds of fat of his neck. Could the blow to the temple have been enough to kill him? Sweat trickled down her sides as she grew more desperate in her search for a pulse. There was nothing. The pool of blood was growing steadily larger. "Call nine-one-one," she shouted.

In a panic she checked for a pulse again and once more found nothing. She fought the urge to gag as she began administering CPR. At some point she realized that the woman and kids were still standing in the doorway.

"You need to call nine-one-one," she said. For the sake of the kids she struggled to keep the panic out of her voice. When the woman still didn't move, Lynn lost it and screamed at her, "Now!"

The shout cut through the woman's daze. When she turned and picked up a phone, Lynn went back to work on Stoner. A baby started to cry somewhere in the rear of the house. Then she heard the woman talking on the phone, but the words weren't what she had expected to hear. Instead, she heard her telling the dispatcher that some woman had killed her husband.

Lynn turned to the woman and shook her head. "It was an accident. He fell." The kids were staring at her with round, frightened eyes. She glanced back at Stoner and the growing pool of blood, and suddenly she was on her feet running. Before she reached the street she heard sirens. Terrified, she turned and sprinted toward the alley. After vaulting over the back chain-link fence, she raced down the alley until it connected with a cross street. She cut through another backyard to its alley and kept running until she was several blocks away. Only then did she turn toward home.

Twice she heard sirens on nearby streets. Whether they were in response to her or some other problem, she had no idea. It wasn't as though sirens in this neighborhood were unusual. All she knew now was she wanted to wake up from this nightmare and bury herself in Crissy's arms. She wanted to smell the sweet scent of Crissy's hair and feel the warmth of her skin. She prayed that the day was all a bad dream and that the alarm clock would ring so that she could get up and go to the car wash. Even Nevils didn't seem so bad now.

After making her way across a weed-infested lot that led to the far end of the alley behind her house, she walked as casually as possible until she came to an enormous trumpet vine that draped over the fence in the corner of her neighbor's yard. If anyone walked by in the alley, the plant wouldn't provide much protection, but she was safe enough from the view of anyone who happened to be passing by on the street. She pushed her way beneath the long draping vines. After finding a somewhat comfortable position she sat and rested her head against her knees. Her heart seemed intent on pounding its way out of her chest.

Edward Stoner was dead and it was her fault. She had pushed him. When she closed her eyes she could still see the pool of blood. In one split second her life had imploded and would never again be the same. Memories of Crissy lying in her arms on Sunday mornings and them talking or making love until it was time to go to the field to practice flashed through her mind. She thought of those cold mornings when they would snuggle beneath a heavy layer of blankets. Would she ever have those times again? It didn't seem likely. She had killed a man. She could spend the rest of her life in prison.

The frightened eyes of the three children haunted her.

Because of her, they would have to grow up as she had, without a dad. Suddenly, she saw her mother's face. She would be devastated when she heard the news. This would kill her. Lynn squeezed her eyes shut and shook her head frantically. How had this happened?

A car drove along the street. Its radio filled the air with the pulsing bass of a popular hip-hop song. Lynn pushed herself deeper into the plant's interior. She needed to think. There had to be a way to make things right again. *Nothing would ever be right for Edward Stoner again.* She forced the thought away and tried to concentrate on what she should do.

In hindsight, she realized that running had been a mistake. She had panicked when she heard Stoner's wife telling the dispatcher that her husband had been murdered. Stoner had fallen. His death had been an accident, but with thirty-two million dollars involved, would anyone believe her? She tried to imagine how the media would spin the story. It wasn't hard to picture how the story would be presented. When Stoner had demanded the ticket they had fought and she had pushed him to his death. She began to tremble when she realized that it had really happened like that. She *had* pushed him.

It was self-defense, she told herself. She hadn't shoved him until after he attacked her and tried to choke her. Or was her mind playing tricks on her? Had he been choking her with the intention of killing her? Or had he merely grabbed her by the throat? Even though it hadn't felt like a huge step between the two when it was happening, there was probably a major difference in the eyes of the law. Had she been afraid he was going to kill her? How could she prove it was self-defense?

Stoner's wife had seen it happen. She had even tried to pull him off her. For a moment, Lynn felt a flicker of hope. It was dashed when she remembered the woman's words to the dispatcher. Mrs. Stoner was the only witness and she had called Lynn a murderer.

A new thought sent a chill through her. Prison was the least of her worries. Texas had the death penalty. She slumped over onto the ground. She was going to die. Even if she ran, how far could she get? She had no money and nowhere to go. She couldn't outrun the law. The authorities would flash her face all over *America's Most Wanted*. It would only be a matter of time before someone recognized her. A dog began to bark somewhere down the block.

She pushed herself upright. "Stop it," she whispered harshly. Now was not the time to fall apart. She had to think. How long it took the police to find her would depend on the amount of evidence they had to go on. Had Mrs. Stoner heard her introduce herself to him? A surge of hope rose. She had been in the yard when she gave her name and she hadn't been talking very loud. Maybe Mrs. Stoner hadn't heard. The baby had been crying and she had been singing to it. Had that been before or after she gave her name? Lynn struggled to remember but couldn't be sure. Even if Mrs. Stoner didn't know her name, she could certainly give the police a detailed description of her, and it was only a matter of time before the clerk at the convenience store heard about the incident and reported that she had been in there asking about Stoner. Luckily, he didn't know her name either. She and Crissy seldom shopped there because it was so expensive.

She slapped her forehead. The security camera. She would have been photographed by the store's security camera. The tape would run on the evening news and within a matter of minutes the police would have her name.

Lynn glanced at her watch and was shocked to see it was only ten minutes until twelve. How could so much happen in such a short time? At best, she had five hours before the tape would be shown on television. God, she needed to talk to Crissy.

As she poked her head out of the trumpet vine she noticed the empty house across the alleyway from her. The grass was tall and there were several broken panes in the back windows. She eyed one of them. It looked as if it might be low enough to the ground that she could crawl through it. If so, the vacant house would provide her with a safe place to hide until Crissy came home. She would know what to do.

A door slammed somewhere nearby, reminding her she needed to get out of the alley. The fence that had once enclosed the yard to the vacant house was falling over in the corner. After a quick glance around to see if anyone was out and about, she made her way to the corner and crawled over the fence. She gave another quick check to make sure no one was watching before she ran across the yard to the window. It took her a couple of tries to push the window up, but she was soon inside. Broken glass littered the floor. After closing the window, she tiptoed through the debris and into the interior. Worried that someone might see her moving around inside, she was careful to stay low and near the walls.

The layout of the house wasn't much different from her own. There were four rooms and a tiny bathroom. From one of the back rooms she had a perfect view of her driveway. She sat beneath the dirty window to wait for Crissy. When she pulled her knees up to rest her head her wallet dug harshly into her leg. She twisted the wallet around and tried not to think about how much trouble the ticket had already caused.

She remembered a television special she and Crissy had once watched, about how some people thought the mega-million-dollar lotteries were cursed. The theory had evolved from the fact that several of the major winners had encountered horrible experiences after winning. Despite collecting millions, many of them had ended up destitute. One had died from a drug overdose. Families had been ripped apart and marriages destroyed. All the misfortunes had been blamed on the money. Lynn had scoffed at the idea and insisted it was people's greed and stupidity that caused the problems rather than some dark unworldly curse.

"I still believe that." The sound of her voice sounded hollow in the empty house.

If Stoner hadn't been so greedy they could have started making arrangements to get the money. Instead, his wife would soon be making arrangements to bury him.

Without warning she began to shake. Her teeth clacked together so harshly she expected them to shatter into a million fragments. Sharp pains began to shoot through her stomach and intensified until sweat poured from her as if she were running a marathon. She wrapped her arms around her waist and bent with the pain. It grew so intense she fell onto her side and became nauseous. Terrified that she was having a heart attack, she tried to stand, but it was no use. Her body refused to cooperate. Tears streamed down her face as she twisted in pain. Maybe it wasn't her heart after all. Perhaps this was her punishment for killing Edward Stoner.

She lost track of how long she lay there in agonizing pain. Gradually the pain began to lessen and at some point she dozed. She woke to the sound of someone talking. The searing pain was gone, but her body felt sore and bruised, as though it had been used as a punching bag. It took her a moment to remember where she was and what had brought her there. When she did, she quickly pushed the thoughts away. It was something she would have to deal with later. Right now she needed to find out who was talking and how much of a threat they were to her. With careful deliberation she rolled over and pulled herself to a kneeling position. What she saw nearly doubled her over again. There in her driveway was a police car. The voice she had heard was coming from the police scanner.

They knew who she was. Mrs. Stoner must have heard her after all. It was over. Lynn pulled herself upright. There was no need to drag this out. She would give herself up and tell the truth about what had happened. Surely a jury would believe that she

106

hadn't gone over there intending to kill him. It had been an accident. She stumbled back through the rooms and climbed out the same window she had used to get into the house. Her stomach and sides ached with each step she took. When she reached the back fence she found it was harder to climb over from this angle. She gasped in pain when she hopped off to the other side.

As she slowly made her way across the alley and over to the back gate, she tried to tell herself everything would be okay, but no matter how many times she said the words, she couldn't bring herself to believe them. Nothing would ever be right again.

CHAPTER FIFTEEN

Lynn approached the house cautiously. She didn't want some rookie cop getting scared and shooting her in her own front yard. The police radio had gone silent. In fact, the entire neighborhood seemed extraordinarily quiet. She raised her arms, stepped out into the driveway and froze.

The police car was gone. She ducked back behind the house and pressed herself against the wall.

"What the hell was I thinking?" she whispered. "I can't go to prison. I'd go crazy locked up in a cage."

"*You have to run,*" a devilish voice prodded.

"*No. You need to stay and face up to what you've done,*" a voice of reason replied.

"*You'll spend your life in prison or fry in the electric chair.*"

"*No, you won't. You're innocent.*"

"*You're a dyke from a poor neighborhood. Nobody's going to care if you fry.*"

Lynn shook off the internal debate. It was true. She really only had one choice, but first she needed to get inside the house. Waiting around for Crissy was no longer an option. If she left now, Crissy could honestly say she didn't know where Lynn was. Besides, she already knew how her lover would view her running away.

She pulled her keys from her pocket, strolled as casually as possible to the front and quickly let herself in. From the top of the closet she pulled a small duffel bag down and stuffed a few clothes into it. As she was leaving the bedroom she spied the photograph of her and Crissy. It had been taken at a Christmas party right after they had gotten together. Crissy had gotten a little tipsy and was wearing a pair of those silly fuzzy reindeer antlers. Lynn had always loved the photo. The image blurred through her tears. She quickly brushed them away and tucked the photo into the bag.

In the kitchen she removed an old coffee can from the top of the refrigerator. On the rare occasion they had a few extra dollars they would drop a couple of them into the can to be used for something special. She felt guilty as she pulled off the lid.

Anger replaced the guilt as she counted out the fifteen dollars and twenty-seven cents in the can. How long could she avoid the law without money or a vehicle? She fought the urge to hurl the can through the window. Why had Edward Stoner been such a jerk? They could have all been celebrating now. She slipped the money in her pocket and stood looking around the room. Her anger burned away as quickly as it had flared.

How could she simply walk away and leave Crissy and their life together? There were so many memories in this room— right down to the coffee cups sitting on the drain board. Was it really only a few hours ago that they had sat right here in the room at that crappy Formica table and talked about maybe trying to make a day trip to the coast during the summer? Had they really stood there by the sink kissing until Crissy had slipped away, pleading she had to leave or she'd be late for class?

"That's my Crissy, always doing the right thing," she said.

Without warning she slapped the can off the table and sent it careening across the floor. If Crissy hadn't been such a goody-two-shoes, none of this would have happened. It was all her fault. If she hadn't pulled her holier-than-thou crap, Lynn would never have gone to find Edward Stoner and he would still be alive. She stormed out of the house without bothering to lock the door behind her.

She cut through alleys and parks until she was several blocks away from her neighborhood. Only then did she use some of her precious cash to catch the bus. She didn't know exactly when the idea came to her, but an hour later she was standing at a phone booth down the street from the Morning Sunrise nursing home.

She fed more money into the phone and dialed the number to the phone in Beulah Mae's room. When it rang for the fifth time, she started to worry that maybe the older woman had fooled her and already taken off. If so, all her plans were useless. She would have to give herself up. The pitiful amount in her pocket wouldn't get her far. At last, the phone was answered.

"Do you remember what we were talking about earlier?" Lynn asked.

"I may be old, but I'm not senile yet," Beulah Mae replied.

She ignored the sarcasm. "If you're still interested, it has to be now."

"You mean tonight?"

"No. I mean now. This minute."

"But, I'm not ready. Besides, I haven't told you about my latest strategy. I think it's starting to work."

Lynn had no idea what Beulah Mae was rambling about. "What new strategy?"

"I've started spending a lot more time up front. You know, where people can see me more."

"Look, there's no time for this. We need to leave now."

"But I told you. I'm not ready."

Lynn struggled to keep her temper in check. The woman had a three-foot-wide closet and a dresser. How much time would she need? "How fast can you be ready?"

When the older woman didn't reply right away, Lynn pushed on.

"I'm telling you it has to be now or you're on your own."

"Okay. Can you give me fifteen minutes?"

Lynn wanted to say no but knew she was being unreasonable. "I'll be waiting at the bus stop on the corner." She hesitated. "Do you really have money?" She felt like a jerk for asking, but without Beulah Mae's money they wouldn't be going anywhere.

"You held it in your hands. I'll be there as quickly as I can."

"Fifteen minutes." She started to hang up.

"If I get a little delayed, you won't leave without me, will you?"

Ashamed that she had bullied the old woman, Lynn dropped her head against the phone. "No. I won't leave without you. Just get here as soon as you can." She hung up and looked at her watch. It was a little after four. Would this day never end? She slowly made her way back toward the bus stop.

She didn't feel good about using Beulah Mae, but she justified her decision with the knowledge that she would also be helping her with her desire to return home. Ultimately it would benefit them both. Beulah Mae had offered the money when she'd originally asked for help, so it wasn't as if it had never been mentioned.

When Lynn reached the bus stop she was too restless to sit. She kept walking. Not wanting to get too far away in case Beulah Mae was early, she turned after about half of a block and made her way back to the bench. Her nerves practically hummed with excessive energy. Unable to sit still, she placed her bag on the bench and strolled in circles around it, grateful that no one else was there waiting for the bus.

She was beginning to get dizzy from her numerous circuits when she finally spotted Beulah Mae scurrying toward her. The poor woman was gasping for air by the time she reached Lynn.

"We need a car," Lynn announced without preamble.

Beulah Mae patted the bag she was toting. "Let's go rent one."

Lynn noticed the bag and frowned. "How did you get that out without anyone seeing you with it?"

Beulah Mae gave her a disgusted look. "I threw the bag out my window. There's a row of box hedges there that hid it until I could get around and retrieve it. I waited until the nurse at the desk was busy. Then I walked out the front door, made my way around back, picked the bag out of the bushes and hightailed it down here."

Lynn only half listened as she gazed around them. She had no idea where the nearest car rental agency was. She gave herself a swift mental kick for not checking the phone book before she left the house. Reluctantly she passed on her lack of knowledge to Beulah Mae.

"There's an Alamo Rental three blocks over on Howard," Beulah Mae replied quickly.

"How do you know that?" Lynn asked, surprised.

"I looked it up in the phone book, nimrod."

Sufficiently chastised, she reached for Beulah Mae's bag only to have it pulled out of her hand.

"I can carry it," Beulah Mae replied. She turned and headed down the street, leaving Lynn no choice but to follow her.

As they made their way toward Howard Street Lynn began to worry about people noticing them. Their bags must surely stand out like flashing neon signs. She didn't calm down until she saw the large yellow and blue sign. Soon they would be on their way and she would be able to relax.

"May I help you?" a cheerful young woman called out as soon as they stepped into the rental agency.

"We'd like to rent a car," Beulah Mae informed her.

"Well, you're in the right place. Do you have a reservation?"

"No. I never was much of one for reservations. I've always preferred spontaneity."

The woman giggled when Beulah Mae winked at her.

Lynn had hoped they could get in and out without much fuss. She didn't want anyone remembering them. Although she had the sickening feeling that Beulah Mae never left anyplace without being remembered. She had seen her in action before when they went out to eat or if one of the female nurses happened to come into her room when Lynn was there. The woman was a hopeless flirt and for some reason all the women lapped up her flirtation. Maybe it was because she looked so harmless.

"Well, don't you worry," the woman said. "It's been a slow day. I think I can find you something you'll like. What size car were you interested in?" She turned to the computer.

"Whatever's the cheapest," Lynn said.

Beulah Mae gave her a stern look before turning back to the woman. "Ignore her. I'd prefer something in the line of a Buick or a Caddy."

The woman perked up. "Oh, you're interested in a luxury vehicle."

"I like to ride in style," Beulah Mae said as she leaned toward the woman slightly.

Lynn bit her tongue when the clerk began to giggle and actually blushed.

"If I could see your driver's license and a credit card, I think I can find you something special and it'll only take a moment."

Beulah Mae turned to Lynn. "She'll be doing all the driving, so I guess it'll be her information you'll need."

Lynn opened her wallet and the lottery ticket fluttered to the floor. She stared at it. There was a moment when she considered leaving it there, but she couldn't. She picked it up and tucked it back into her wallet. As she started to remove the license from the see-through pocket of her wallet, she realized that renting a car was a mistake. When she wasn't found right away and her car was discovered still sitting at the car wash, the police would start checking the airport and other transportation options. It wouldn't take them long to get around to checking the rental agencies. On the other hand, if Nevils had followed through with his threat and had her car towed it might work in her favor. The authorities would be looking for her in her car, thus allowing her a little breathing room.

How long would it take them to connect her to Beulah Mae's disappearance? Crissy would put it together immediately. Would she tell the authorities? Lynn wanted to believe she wouldn't, but Crissy's need to always do the right thing worried her.

As she pretended to struggle with her wallet, she considered telling the clerk that they had changed their minds, but she couldn't think of a better way for them to get out of town.

"Where will you be taking the vehicle?" the clerk asked.

Before Lynn could respond, Beulah Mae calmly chimed in. "Colorado. We're going back to my hometown."

Lynn almost passed out. Where in the hell was Beulah Mae's classic *play your cards close to your chest, don't tell anybody your business and hide your money from the government* persona now? She realized they were both staring at her.

"Your license," the clerk reminded her.

"Oh, yeah." This time her fumbling with the tight pocket was real. She could feel their gaze on her and started to perspire worse. Finally in desperation, she yanked the stubborn card from her wallet so hard that it slipped from her sweating fingers and went flying over the counter.

For an agonizing eternity the thin plastic rectangle sailed through space. Lynn's gaze locked on her photo as it smiled back at her. As she watched, the image slowly morphed into a mug shot. The world returned to real time as the card slapped the clerk square on the forehead. Lynn had a sinking feeling that Beulah

114

Mae's lapse in judgment in revealing their destination would no longer be the first thing the clerk remembered about them.

Lynn sputtered an apology and glanced over in time to see Beulah Mae look toward the ceiling and shake her head.

After another flurry of apologies, the clerk assured them she was fine and tried to move the process along. "I'll need a credit card also," she prompted as she gave Lynn a slight small. "You can just hand it to me."

Mortified, Lynn looked down at the wallet in her hand. "Um . . . I don't have a credit card." She and Crissy had gotten a card for emergencies, but it was tucked away in a drawer back at the house. It had never occurred to her to take it.

"You don't have a credit card?" The woman frowned and looked as though Lynn had suddenly sprouted two heads.

She straightened her back and met the woman's gaze. "No. I don't have a credit card."

The clerk turned to Beulah Mae, who was beginning to fidget.

"I don't have a card either," Beulah Mae admitted.

"Oh, dear, then I'm afraid I can't rent you a car." She pushed Lynn's license back across the counter.

Lynn grabbed it and quickly put it away. She was almost certain the woman hadn't even glanced at it.

"I'll pay in advance." Beulah Mae started to reach into her bag.

"That still won't do. I have to have a credit card number on file in case there's an accident."

"Can't I sign something accepting personal responsibility for any damage to the car?" Beulah Mae asked.

"Well, that would have been part of the rental agreement, but I'm afraid there's nothing I can do for you without a card."

The bell over the door dinged as a young couple with two kids walked in. The woman quickly excused herself and rushed to greet them.

Lynn and Beulah Mae remained silent until they were outside.

"What in the hell were you thinking of?" Lynn demanded as soon as they stepped out the door. "What possessed you to tell her where we're going?"

Beulah Mae's confident smirk and calm demeanor only infuriated her more. "I know what I'm doing." She glanced at Lynn. "Although I am a little curious about that unusual performance you gave."

Lynn backed down quickly. "It was an accident."

"Ah, that's too bad. Regardless, it was a stroke of brilliance."

Lynn's head snapped up. "Are you crazy? That woman will still remember us five years from now."

"She sure will."

Lynn could only stare. The judge who had committed Beulah Mae had been absolutely right. The woman was completely off her rocker. It was a miracle someone hadn't already arrested them. Lynn grabbed her head in frustration. What had she been thinking? There was no way they could pull this off. The smartest thing she could do was give up now. Edward Stoner's death had been an accident. She should throw herself on the mercy of the court and pray for the best. Her agitation evaporated. She couldn't turn herself in. She was too scared. The thought of spending the rest of her life in prison or being sentenced to death was more than she could handle. "What do we do now?" she asked, defeated.

"We could buy a car."

"Buy a car!" Lynn glanced at Beulah Mae's bag and wondered how much money it held.

"Sure. I used to buy used cars all the time."

Lynn counted to ten before speaking. "We don't have time to buy a car. We need to leave now."

"No, we don't. I'll give you the money to buy the car and I'll go back to the nursing home. I'll bet no one has even missed me.

You shop around and buy a decent car. When everything is settled we'll leave."

Lynn shook her head harshly. "Damn it. I told you. I have to leave now!"

Beulah Mae looked at her suspiciously. "What's going on here? Are you in some sort of trouble?"

Lynn considered telling her everything that had happened, but she couldn't bring herself to do so. Again, she justified her decision with the logic that the less Beulah Mae knew, the better off she would be. "Nothing's wrong." She quickly improvised. "It's just that I took off work to do this. I only have a couple of days. So if we don't leave today, I can't help you." She felt horrible about lying but reminded herself that in the long run it would be better for Beulah Mae. If they didn't leave today and the authorities caught her, there wouldn't be anyone to help Beulah Mae get home. She didn't allow her conscience to analyze the excuse too closely.

"Shouldn't this have been planned for a weekend? Then you wouldn't have missed any work. You could easily drive up and back in a weekend. Once I'm there I'll be fine. I don't expect you to wait around—"

"No. My weekends are full."

The older woman glanced away. "Oh. I see."

Ashamed of her outburst, Lynn tried to think of something to say. She didn't know how Beulah Mae expected her to drive all the way to Colorado and back over a weekend and still manage to make it to work on Monday morning. "What part of Colorado are we going to anyway?"

Beulah Mae ignored her and nodded toward a small restaurant across the road. "Let's get inside where we won't be so obvious. I always think better with a cup of coffee anyway."

Lynn took a deep breath to keep from yelling. Since she didn't have a better idea, she finally gave in and fell into step alongside Beulah Mae.

CHAPTER SIXTEEN

They sat staring into their coffee several minutes before Beulah Mae finally nodded. "Okay," she began. "I think I know where I can get us a car." She dug into her pocket and pulled out some change. "You wait here. I have to make a phone call." She started to get up.

"Wait a minute. Where are you going?"

"Are you deaf? I told you I'm going to make a call." She pushed her cup toward Lynn. "If by some miracle that waitress comes back by, get me some more coffee." She shook her finger at Lynn. "And try smiling at her. We'll get better service. I swear I've never seen anyone with such a surly scowl. I don't know how you ever got a woman to look at you, much less that cute Crissy. If I was ten years younger, I'd be making my move on her."

"If you were ten years younger?" Lynn asked, incredulous. "You'd still be seventy-five. Crissy is barely twenty-five."

Beulah Mae brushed her comment aside. "That's okay. As long as they aren't jailbait, I like them young." She gave a loud chuckle as she rushed off and left Lynn with her mouth hanging open.

Lynn watched her leave. This obviously wasn't going to work. She had no idea who Beulah Mae was going to call. She couldn't remember her ever talking about having friends here in town, and there didn't seem to be anyone coming to the home to visit her.

Maybe it wasn't such a good idea to take Beulah Mae from the home anyway. What if there really was something wrong with the old woman's mind? What would happen once they got to Colorado? Was she supposed to simply drive away and leave Beulah Mae standing on the street somewhere? Apparently it had been seventy years since she had been home. What were the odds of any of her family still being around there? This whole thing was a bad idea. She should have never made the call and gotten Beulah Mae involved.

Lynn rubbed her chin. At this point it wasn't too late. If she left, Beulah Mae could simply walk back to the nursing home and no one would ever know what she had been planning to do. Besides, it wasn't fair to entangle anyone else in her problems.

She made a quick decision that would be better for both of them in the end. At least that's what she told herself as she slid out of the booth and pulled some money from her pocket. For all she knew, Beulah Mae might not have a penny in that bag. She didn't want to leave her with the bill. She glanced at the few dollars left in her hand and shrugged. What difference did money make in the end? She had a ticket worth thirty-two million dollars in her wallet and it certainly wasn't doing her any good.

Lynn was almost to the door when she spied two police officers walking up the sidewalk. She froze. Unable to move, she watched them come steadily closer. They were pulling the door open when Beulah Mae slipped an arm beneath Lynn's and led her back to the table. To the casual viewer it no doubt looked like the younger woman was helping the older one back to her seat.

Lynn couldn't take her eyes off the police officers who were seated two booths down from them. The coffee she'd drunk earlier was burning a hole in her stomach, or maybe it was simply guilt for the horrible thing she had done. She was vaguely aware of the waitress refilling their cups and Beulah Mae laughing with her as she did so.

"Stop staring at them and drink your coffee," Beulah Mae hissed after the waitress left.

Lynn tore her gaze away from the two men and tried to pick up her cup, but her hand shook so that the coffee sloshed over the side.

"I've got us a car," Beulah Mae said barely loud enough for Lynn to hear.

The statement was enough to snap her back to reality. "What? How?"

Beulah Mae sipped her coffee before giving Lynn a smug look. "I have my ways. It'll be here in about an hour."

"I don't understand. How did you get a car?"

"I still have a few favors to call in." She picked up a menu and in a bizarrely normal tone announced, "I think I'll have some peach cobbler. I truly love a good peach cobbler." She stopped the waitress as she passed by. After giving her order she looked at Lynn. "What about you? Do you want something to eat?"

"No. I'm not hungry." The mere thought of food made her already unstable stomach churn.

Beulah Mae looked at the waitress and shook her head. "Since when do you have to be hungry to eat dessert?"

"Now, ain't that the truth," the waitress replied before rushing away.

Beulah Mae stared into her coffee for a moment. "I'll bet your blood sugar is low. That's probably why you're so grumpy." She sipped her coffee again. "Did I ever tell you about the girl I dated who had a problem with her blood sugar?" She went on without waiting for Lynn to respond. "She would faint whenever she got overly excited, which was a real problem every time we—"

"Stop." Lynn held up her hand. "I don't want to hear about you . . . you . . . making girls faint."

Beulah Mae shrugged. "Fine." She paused for a moment. "She's the only one who ever fainted." She twisted her coffee cup slowly in the saucer. "Don't you love the way a woman's eyes roll back and flutter when she comes?"

"Damn it, Beulah Mae, I told you I don't want to talk about your lovemaking excursions."

"Why do you curse so much?"

Confused, Lynn stared at her. "What?"

"You're always cursing. It's not very becoming." She tilted her head slightly. "I'll bet Crissy doesn't like it."

Lynn grabbed her head. This was not going to work. It irked her that Beulah Mae was always right. The cursing was a habit that she had picked up from working with so many men. Crissy and her mom were always getting after her about it.

The waitress arrived with Beulah Mae's peach cobbler and a fresh pot of coffee. She made a great production of serving the cobbler and waiting for Beulah Mae to taste it.

"This is excellent," Beulah Mae said. "Was it made here?"

The waitress nodded. "The night cook does all our baking."

"Please, pass on my compliments."

"Oh, I will. I know he'll be happy to hear you enjoyed it so." After topping off Beulah Mae's coffee she glanced at Lynn's nearly full cup and grudgingly topped it off.

Lynn shook her head in amazement. "How do you do that?" she asked after the waitress left. "I'm positive that woman is straight, but she was practically drooling on you."

Beulah Mae took a bite of the cobbler before she put her fork down and chewed with agonizing slowness. Only after she swallowed and took another drink of her coffee did she answer. "The first secret I learned about women is to make them feel as special as they truly are." She tapped her table with her finger. "I may be an outdated old dinosaur, but I truly believe that principle is still true."

"I don't want to always be on the make," Lynn said. "That's what men do."

"You're not getting what I mean. You're on the make if you're only doing it to get in their pants. That's the wrong reason. What I'm talking about is . . ." She seemed to be trying to find the perfect word. "Let's see if I can explain it another way. I've never met an ugly woman."

Lynn rolled her eyes. "Now I know you're lying."

"No, I'm not. I truly believe from the bottom of my heart that there is something beautiful in every woman. For example, tell me what you see when you look at the woman at the booth in front of the register."

Lynn looked across the room. "I see a woman who's about fifty pounds overweight and in serious need of a haircut."

"What about the woman in the red sweater over by the window? The one who's reading."

Again, Lynn looked where she had been directed. "She's a little frumpy for my taste."

"And the two women behind her?"

"The younger one is sort of cute, but neither one of them really does anything for me. Why don't we stop the quiz and you tell me what you see?"

"Okay, I will. Look at the first woman really close. She has beautiful soulful eyes. Those are the sort of eyes that will look up at you after you've made love and make you feel like you're the most important thing on earth." She turned to the woman in the red sweater. "She's reading poetry. Look at the graceful movements of her hands when she turns a page and the way she holds the book. It's almost as if she were caressing it." She smiled softly. "Those are hands to cool a fevered brow, comfort a

122

broken heart and hold a lover. You could get lost forever in those hands."

"I think you need a cold shower," Lynn mumbled.

Beulah Mae pushed her coffee cup away. "I swear you're as dense as a tree stump." She drummed her fingers on the table-top. "You know what the trouble with you young people is?"

Lynn leaned back in the booth. "No, but I'm sure you're about to tell me."

"You're dang right I am. You're rude, crude and . . . and . . . you've got no manners. That's why you're moving in with a woman two weeks after you meet her."

"That doesn't make sense. It's a complete contradiction of what you just said. If I'm so rude and crude, how did I even find a woman to move in with?"

"Well, now, that is the sixty-four-million-dollar question, isn't it?" She shook her finger. "I'll tell you how. You all are like bumper cars, out there scurrying all over the place until, *wham*, you actually run into each other, and for six months you're stuck together like superglue. Then you start to notice how she bites her fork when she eats, or leaves the cap off the toothpaste, and before you know it you're back out there bumping around on the floor again."

"That is the most asinine explanation I've ever heard. Besides, who are you to talk about a long-term relationship? I thought you were the honor graduate of the wham-bam-thank-you-ma'am school of lovers."

Beulah Mae stood suddenly. "The car should be here soon. I'm going to wait outside." She tossed some bills on the table.

"I've got the check."

"Keep your money. I told you I'd cover the expenses for the trip and I meant it." Without waiting for Lynn to respond, she grabbed her bag and headed to the door.

Lynn watched until Beulah Mae was out of sight. Only then did she turn to look at the woman she had moments before called fat. The woman saw her and quickly bent her head before Lynn had a chance to see her eyes. The unruly hair hid her face. As Lynn stared at her, she realized that the hair was a defense shield the woman hid behind. Embarrassed, she turned to the woman she had described as frumpy. Again, she saw that Beulah Mae had been right. The woman's hands were very pretty. As she studied the graceful movements and the long, slim fingers she was surprised by the unexpected tingling in her groin. Taken aback by her body's reaction, she scooped the bills from the table, grabbed her bag from beneath the table and rushed to the register to pay their bill.

The cashier was a middle-aged woman with salt-and-pepper hair that a few minutes ago Lynn wouldn't have looked twice at, but now she suddenly noticed the woman's delicate mouth and full lips. *She's probably a great kisser.* The thought shocked her so that she took a step back. The abrupt movement caused the woman to look up from the register. Caught off-guard, Lynn smiled and the woman smiled back, drawing Lynn's gaze back to her full luscious lips.

CHAPTER SEVENTEEN

After leaving the cashier, Lynn went to the restroom to splash water on her face. Afterward she stood staring into the mirror. It seemed odd that she was staring at the same face she did every morning. Surely, after all that had happened today, there should be some mark, some indication of what she had done. How could you watch someone die and simply walk away with no consequences? Her stomach twisted sharply to remind her that there would always be some scars.

Her thoughts turned to the two police officers sitting in the restaurant calmly eating their meal. When she walked past them, they had been talking and hadn't even noticed her. What would they have done if she had stopped and informed them that she had killed a man?

She leaned closer to the mirror and tried to look herself in the eye. After adjusting her gaze a few times, she realized that it was impossible to look oneself in the eye. She could look at her eye, but it wasn't the same as when she was looking at another person. She wondered if the eyes really were the windows to the soul. If so, she couldn't see into hers. Maybe she had lost the ability when she killed Edward Stoner.

At the sound of the outer door opening, she tossed the paper towel in the trash, picked up her bag and started out. When the woman saw her, she did a double take at Lynn's short hair and scruffy clothes before moving to the side and giving her a wide berth. Lynn tried to ignore her. It wasn't as if this was the first time it had happened, but for some reason this time it bothered her. She ducked her head and rushed out.

When she left the restaurant she glanced at her watch. It was a few minutes after six. It took her a moment to spot Beulah Mae. She was standing beside a black convertible talking to an older white man. Lynn went over to join them. They were looking down into the interior of the car with their backs to her.

" . . . wished you had let us know you were staying there," the guy said. "We tried to find you, but nobody knew where you'd gone."

"I didn't want you to see me in that place."

"Didi and I have plenty of room. You know you can stay with us for as long as you'd like."

Lynn must have made a noise because the guy suddenly turned to face her.

"Jay, this is Lynn Strickland," Beulah Mae said. "Lynn, Jay Mason."

"Good to meet you, Lynn." He stuck out his hand.

Lynn shook his hand. Jay had the gravelly voice of a long-time smoker. The pack of Camels in his shirt pocket verified her suspicions. He had a full mane of silvery gray hair that was combed back sharply from his forehead and a deep tan that would have horrified a dermatologist. He wore expensively tailored tan slacks with a chocolate brown silk shirt. A diamond-encrusted pinky ring caught the sunlight and sent a dancing rainbow skittering across the hood of the car.

"Jay is going to lend us a car." Beulah Mae nodded toward the small, sporty-looking convertible.

"That's nice of him," Lynn replied.

Jay gave a sudden harsh laugh. Beulah Mae exhaled loudly and started to say something, but Jay stopped her. "It's okay. I'm used to it."

Beulah Mae rolled her eyes and looked skyward. "I'm sorry about that. I swear, the kids nowadays."

"What's wrong?" Lynn asked, puzzled. She was getting sick and tired of Beulah Mae's attitude.

"It's nothing," Jay assured her. "Can you drive a standard?"

Before Lynn could answer, Beulah Mae cut in. "I'm a little nervous about taking this car. I know how special it is to you."

Jay waved off her protests. "Don't worry about it. Like I told you on the phone, I'm right in the middle of overhauling my truck and . . ." He shrugged. "Well, you know Didi. She still can't drive a standard."

Beulah Mae looked at Lynn. "Are you sure you can handle this car?"

Something in her attitude made Lynn bristle. "Hell, yeah, I can drive it."

"Here you go then." Jay tossed Lynn the keys. She almost handed them back and admitted that she had never driven anything other than an automatic, but they were both watching her, almost as if they were expecting her to do so.

She tried to appear confident as she slipped the keys into her pocket and gave the car another visual once-over. She had never been much of a car buff. Automobiles were simply a means of transportation to her. Although she had to admit that this one looked nice. "What's so special about this car?" From the reactions of the other two, she knew she had stuck her foot into it again. Jay actually paled.

He cleared his throat before saying. "This is a fully-restored nineteen fifty-seven Corvette."

They seemed to be waiting for her to say something, but she had no clue what. She finally nodded and said the only thing that came to mind. "Oh." It was apparently not what they were expecting to hear, because they continued to stare at her. "I like the red interior," she added lamely.

Jay abruptly burst out laughing. Soon Beulah Mae was laughing too.

Lynn's face burned as they continued to laugh. She failed to see the humor. As soon as Jay left she fully intended to expand Beulah Mae's knowledge on the meaning of rude.

Finally, Jay wiped his eyes and slapped Beulah Mae on the back. "Beu, you've got your hands full. I wish you the best."

Beulah Mae shrugged and smiled. "It's rough getting old."

"That's the truth, for sure," They stood staring at each other for a long moment before he cleared his throat roughly and said, "I've got to get going."

"It was good to see you again, Jay. You won't forget to make the call."

"No. I'll do it exactly as you asked."

Beulah Mae nodded. "Thanks for letting me use the car."

"Hey, it's the least I can do after what you did for me."

Beulah Mae looked down and shrugged. "That was a long time ago. Those old debts have long since been paid."

Jay shook his head. "It'll never be paid as far as I'm concerned. I'll always owe you."

As Beulah Mae looked away, Lynn caught the glimmer of tears in her eyes. "I'll call you as soon as we get there."

He nodded. "You take care of yourself."

"Yeah, you too." Before he could leave Beulah Mae gave him a long hug.

When they broke away, Jay swiped a hand across his eyes before throwing a quick wave toward Lynn. "Take good care of my girl." Without waiting for her to respond he turned and left.

Lynn wasn't sure if he meant the car or Beulah Mae.

They stood in silence as he climbed into a Mercedes that had been parked a few slots over. In the instant before he closed the door, Lynn caught a glimpse of a beautiful blond woman sitting in the passenger seat. A moment later the car glided past them. Beulah Mae waved good-bye before turning back to the Corvette.

"It's getting late," she said gruffly. "Let's get out of here."

A knot began to form in Lynn's stomach as she went around to the driver's side and stared down into the small two-seater. There would be hell to pay when Beulah Mae discovered she didn't know how to drive a stick shift. She wondered if she could fake it. When she was littler her mom had driven an older model car with a standard transmission, but the gear stick had been on the steering column, where this one was on the floor. She got a boost of confidence when she looked closer. Compared to today's cars with their multitude of buttons, levers and gauges, the Corvette's instrument panel was uncluttered. Her confidence began to grow. Nothing about the setup looked complicated. She remembered sitting beside her mom and imitating her as she pressed the clutch when she shifted. Besides, she had seen actors on television do it hundreds of times. From listening to her own car change gears she had a vague idea of when to shift. The tightness in her stomach eased. This wasn't going to be such a big deal. She noticed Beulah Mae standing at the back of the vehicle watching her and realized there was no backseat to store their bags. She tried to act as if she knew what she was doing as she unlocked the trunk and tossed her duffel in.

Beulah Mae gave a small grunt as she closed the trunk. "Before we get started there's something I want to get clarified."

"What's up?"

"When I do business with someone, I always like to put everything right out front so that there are no misunderstandings later."

Lynn's heart rate accelerated. Did Beulah Mae suspect something?

"I intend to pay you for helping me get back to Williamstown."

Lynn started to protest, but Beulah Mae stopped her.

"I'm guessing that it will take about nine or ten hours of straight driving to get there. My initial thought was that you could drive the rental car back, but since that fell through, I'm thinking the best thing to do is for me to put you on a plane as soon as we get to . . . there. Then you can be back here in plenty of time to go to work on Monday morning. I'll cover all expenses for the trip and pay you a hundred dollars in cash." She removed a money clip from her pocket, peeled off a crisp fifty-dollar bill and held it out to Lynn. "I'll give you half now and half when we get to the airport."

"I don't want you to pay me."

"I didn't ask you if you wanted me to or not. I'm paying you, period." She shoved the bill into Lynn's hands.

"What about Jay's car? How are you going to get it back to him?"

"Don't worry about that. It's taken care of already." Beulah Mae started back around to the passenger side. "And by the way, Jay is a woman."

"What?"

"I said Jay is a woman."

Lynn cringed when she thought about how she had used the male pronoun in reference to Jay. No wonder they had laughed at her. "I'm such an idiot. I'm sorry. I didn't realize."

"Don't worry about it." Beulah Mae eased her way into the car. "It's not like it's the first time someone's been confused about her gender."

When Lynn opened the door and slid into the low-slung seat she had to admit it was pretty cool. She'd never been in a sports car before. It actually seemed to radiate a sense of power. A wave of confidence settled over her as slipped the key into the ignition and turned it. Nothing happened. She swallowed the sense of dread that began creeping up her spine. What had she missed? She stepped on the brake harder and turned the key again.

"I thought you had driven a standard before," Beulah Mae said.

Lynn heard the suspicion in her voice. "Hey, I didn't say it was yesterday. Give me a minute, okay."

"You have to push the clutch in before it'll start."

"Oh, yeah. I forgot." Lynn stepped on the clutch and brake. As soon as the key turned the engine sprang to life. She smiled and a deep sigh of relief escaped her. Now all she had to do was fake her way through changing gears. She tried to act nonchalant as she glanced around them as if checking for oncoming traffic. All she had to do was figure out where first gear was located. The rational assumption would be to move in a clockwise motion. She kept heavy pressure on the clutch as her hand closed around the knob on the gearstick. It felt cool and smooth in her hand. She pushed it up and over. As if by magic the well-maintained mechanisms responded and slipped effortlessly into a notch. Elated by the smooth movement Lynn almost laughed aloud. This was going to be a snap. She took her foot off the clutch. The car jerked sharply and died. She could almost feel Beulah Mae glaring at her. "Sorry. I'll get it this time." She reached for the key.

"It's still in gear."

Lynn began to sweat. This wasn't going to be quite as easy as it had seemed a moment ago. She tried to remember where the gearshift had been before she moved it.

"You don't have the first clue on how to drive a standard, do you?" Beulah Mae asked quietly.

Lynn attempted to swallow, but her throat suddenly seemed extremely dry. "No," she admitted. She kept very still as Beulah Mae took a deep breath and slowly released it.

"Did I or did I not ask you if you could drive this car?"

"Yes, you asked."

"And remind me again what it was you said."

Lynn's throat was starting to ache. "I said I could handle it."

Without warning, Beulah Mae threw the car door open and got out surprisingly fast for a woman of her age. When she started around the car, Lynn scrambled out. "Give me the keys," she demanded as she approached with her hand out.

Lynn handed it over and quickly stepped out of her reach.

Beulah Mae opened the trunk. A moment later, she closed it and slipped on a pair of glasses. "Get in the car."

Lynn turned and started to slide back into the driver's seat.

"The other side, nimrod."

She hopped out and rushed around to sit in the passenger's seat. She fastened her seat belt and fought the urge to ask if Beulah Mae could see well enough to drive. She was fairly certain she didn't have a driver's license. She decided not to worry about it. If they were stopped, driving without a valid license would probably be pretty far down on their list of transgressions.

Beulah Mae put the car in neutral, cranked it, deftly shifted it into gear and drove out of the parking lot. Within minutes, they were gliding up the ramp to the interstate. She merged into the heavy traffic and expertly maneuvered the Corvette into the fast lane. Neither of them spoke as the little car picked up speed and the city traffic began to fall away behind them.

Lynn closed her eyes and let the warm air wash over her. She wished it had the power to blow away this entire day. Twinges of guilt, about not leaving a note for Crissy, were beginning to pluck at her conscience, but she quickly reminded herself that the less Crissy knew, the better. She tried not to think about Crissy arriving home to find her gone. Or how hurt her mom and Crissy would be when they found out about Edward Stoner. Crissy would have friends to turn to for comfort. Suddenly, Lynn hoped that her mom's friend Jaime Treviño was more than just a friend. Her mom would need someone now.

CHAPTER EIGHTEEN

When Lynn opened her eyes again it was dark and the wind was no longer whistling through her hair. "What time is it?" she asked as she stretched.

"A little after eight, I guess." Beulah Mae was hunched slightly forward over the steering wheel.

"Gosh, I can't believe I slept for so long. I'm sorry."

"That's okay. I've always loved driving," Beulah Mae said.

Lynn noticed the top was up. "You stopped?"

"Yes. It was starting to get a little cool so I stopped and put the top up and filled up the tank while I was at it. I tried to wake you, but you were out like a log." She glanced toward Lynn. "I guess you've had a pretty tough day."

Lynn leaned back in the seat as all the events of the day came back to her. "Is it really still Thursday?"

"I'm afraid so."

"Did you ever have a day that simply wouldn't end?"

Beulah Mae nodded. "I've had a lot of those days in the last couple of years."

Lynn closed her eyes. By now Crissy and her mom would know what she had done. They would be sick with worry. The nursing home would have reported Beulah Mae missing. It wouldn't be long before dozens of volunteers would be out scouring the street for the elderly woman. Her eyes flew open at the sound of the tires hitting the warning grooves on the edge of the highway. "Are you okay?"

"Sure." When Lynn continued to stare at her, Beulah Mae added, "The fool behind me has his high beams on. I was only trying to get the glare out of my eyes."

Lynn glanced behind them. The car didn't have its high beams on, or maybe it was a different car. "I'll bet a lot of people are looking for us by now," she ventured.

"I thought about that when I started planning all this. I didn't want anyone to worry. That's why I asked Jay to make a call for me."

"What sort of call?" Blood rushed to her head so quickly her ears buzzed. Was Beulah Mae inadvertently going to lead the police right to her?

"I asked her to call the nursing home and let them know I had left on my own and that I was going home to Colorado."

Lynn stared at her in amazement. "You what?" She closed her eyes and rubbed her forehead. "Why didn't you tell me about this before?"

"Because I knew you would get all huffy and start yelling before I had a chance to explain."

"God, I hope I wake up soon from this nightmare of a day."

Beulah Mae ignored her. "Are you hungry?"

"No. Not really."

"Well, we're approaching a truck stop. I need some coffee." Again she glanced at Lynn. "I thought we could stop for a while and have a little talk."

"Where are we anyway?" Lynn would have preferred to keep moving. The farther they got from San Antonio the better, especially now that their destination was known.

Beulah Mae hesitated. "We're a ways north of Austin."

"Austin? Why are we headed in that direction? Shouldn't we be headed toward Amarillo?"

"That's one of things we need to talk about, but let's wait until we get the coffee."

Lynn wondered if they were already lost. She had assumed Beulah Mae would know the route or else they would stop somewhere along the way for a map. The one thing she was sure of was that they shouldn't have gone through Austin to get to Colorado.

As soon as she spied the truck stop Lynn felt calmer. It was one of those big, busy places where hundreds of cars stopped every hour. If they didn't do anything to draw attention to themselves, it wasn't likely anyone would ever remember them.

Once they were inside Beulah Mae excused herself and headed toward the restroom while Lynn went to find them a seat in the dining room. She worried about how brightly lit the place was until she realized it was packed with hungry and exhausted travelers. No one would pay them much attention. The Fates gave Lynn a second break when a sullen waiter showed up to take their order. There was nothing about him to attract Beulah Mae's attention. She ordered two coffees and settled in with her back to the main dining area. She wondered if she should try to eat something. She hadn't eaten anything since the doughnut she'd swiped from the customer waiting area at the car wash that morning, but she still didn't feel hungry. All she really wanted to do was crawl into bed beside Crissy and sleep for a week. Tears stung her eyes when she realized that she might never again do that.

Doubt plagued her decision to involve Beulah Mae. Maybe

she should have headed for Mexico and hid out there for a while. It wouldn't have been easy for many reasons, mainly because she didn't have a passport and her command of the language was almost nonexistent. When she thought about the difficulties in trying to sneak across the border, she felt a little better about her decision. She wouldn't stand out so much if she lost herself in some small Midwestern town. If she could avoid the law long enough, eventually they would stop actively searching for her. When it was safe, she would contact Crissy and maybe they could find a way to be together again. Would Crissy want to live with a fugitive? She tried not to think about her mom.

Beulah Mae slipped into the chair across from Lynn. "Why are you crying?"

Lynn quickly wiped a hand across her face. "It's the smoke in here," she answered quickly.

Beulah Mae frowned. "Are you sure it doesn't have anything to do with those bruises on your neck?"

Lynn's hands went to her throat. She couldn't tell Beulah Mae about Edward Stoner choking her. If she did, she'd have to tell the entire story. "I'd rather not talk about it right now."

Beulah Mae started to respond, but the waiter arrived with the coffee, bringing an effective end to her questions.

Lynn quickly took advantage of the pause. "What did you want to talk about?" When Beulah Mae ran a hand over her face, Lynn noticed how tired she looked.

"I need to tell you something. It's not a big deal, really, but we're not going to Colorado."

"Where are we going?"

"Arkansas. That's where I grew up."

Lynn frowned. "Why did you tell me Colorado?"

"Everything I told you about Williamstown was true, except for the state. When I told you about it, I had already made up my mind to go, with or without you."

"I see. You lied about the state because you were worried I'd

136

tell someone."

Beulah Mae glanced away and nodded guiltily. After a long second, she looked back at Lynn and shrugged slightly. "I guess I might have some trust issues."

"You're probably right." Lynn was puzzled by the sense of hurt she'd felt at her friend's lack of trust in her. It took her a moment to realize that in Beulah Mae's situation she would have done the same. In essence, she'd done the same thing to Crissy by leaving without giving her a chance or even leaving a note. She had been certain that Crissy would insist she do the right thing, even to the point of calling the police herself. "I'm such an ass."

"I know you wouldn't have turned me in unless you were worried about me." Beulah Mae slowly stirred her coffee and cleared her throat nervously. "This isn't easy for me. Since the day I left Williamstown, I've pretty much been on my own. Now it seems as though there is always someone around poking into my business." She set the spoon aside. "I . . . I thought that if I could get out of there, then maybe I could make it on my own again."

An awkward silence descended over their table. At least the direction they were traveling now made sense, as did the fact that Beulah Mae had estimated that the trip could easily be accomplished in a weekend. After a long moment Lynn finally asked, "Did you really tell Jay we were going to Colorado?"

"That's what I asked her to tell everyone, but Jay knows all about me."

"You two go way back, don't you?" Lynn wondered if there had ever been more than friendship between them.

"I've known Jay for more than sixty years."

"How did you meet?" Lynn regretted her question when she saw the look of sadness cross her friend's face.

"That's water under the bridge." Beulah Mae tasted her coffee and grinned. "We've been flapping our lips and let the coffee get cold." She pushed the cup away. "I guess we should get back on the road anyway. I'm sorry I lied to you. I felt bad about it, but I didn't feel like I had a choice."

Lynn cringed. Beulah Mae's little lie was nothing compared to the information she was withholding. She stared into her cold coffee. What would Beulah Mae do if she knew about her killing Edward Stoner? Her worries must have shown on her face.

"You look as though you have a few problems yourself."

Lynn licked her lips. How well did she really know this woman? Could she trust her?

"We're in this together," Beulah Mae said. "If there's something I need to know, now might be a good time to fess up."

Lynn looked across the table into those dark eyes and had the sinking sensation that her secret was already known. She shook the thought off. There was no way Beulah Mae could know. She leaned forward. "The police are looking for me. I—"

"More coffee?"

Stunned by the waiter's unexpected appearance, Lynn flinched.

"No. We're leaving." Beulah Mae handed him some bills and motioned for Lynn. "Come on."

Lynn stared at her, unable to believe that after psyching herself up to tell all, she wasn't going to be able to do so. "I need to tell you," Lynn started.

"In the car," Beulah Mae hissed.

As soon as they were inside the car, Beulah Mae started it.

"I think you should listen to what I have to say," Lynn said.

"Give me a minute."

When Beulah Mae backed the car out of the parking slot, Lynn noticed that she was squinting. She felt guilty for lying about being able to drive a standard. Beulah Mae had hired her to drive her to Williamstown, not to simply ride along. As Beulah Mae drove around to the back of the parking lot and pulled into a well-lit area between two idling eighteen-wheelers,

Lynn reached into her pocket and removed the fifty she had been given as advance payment.

"We shouldn't attract too much attention sitting out here." Beulah Mae killed the engine and turned to Lynn. "Now, spill your guts, and this time don't leave out the part about those bruises on your neck."

Over the next several minutes, Lynn related the surreal events that had started the previous evening when she and Crissy had first seen Edward Stoner, right on through until the time she had placed the call to the nursing home. Her traveling companion remained silent throughout the story.

When she finished, Lynn sat quietly, waiting as Beulah Mae drummed her fingers on her knee. She had started to fidget by the time Beulah Mae finally stopped and exhaled sharply.

"God sure has a wicked sense of humor," she said tiredly.

"We can still go on to Arkansas," Lynn insisted. "You telling everyone that we were headed to Colorado will actually help. I even told Crissy about Colorado. She'll think that's where we are."

"And that's okay by you? It doesn't bother you that Crissy and your mom don't know where you are?"

"Of course it bothers me. Don't you think I'd rather be home right now?"

Beulah Mae held up a hand. "Let's not start this. I'm sorry. I didn't mean to sound so judgmental." She eased back around in the seat. "When did cars become so uncomfortable? I remember when you used to have room to move around."

Lynn didn't bother to remind her that the car was fifty years old.

Again Beulah Mae's fingers began to drum, this time on the steering wheel. Lynn forced her attention away from the sound, determined not to interrupt.

"I'm going to tell you how I met Jay. In a strange way, I think it might help you. Before I do I want you to swear to me that you'll never tell a soul."

Lynn shrugged. "Sure."

Beulah Mae looked at her sharply. "I mean it. Jason Mason is one of my dearest friends. If she knew I ever told anyone about . . . that night, she would . . ." She left the sentence hanging. "Swear to me you'll never tell anyone, not even Crissy."

Exasperated, Lynn held up her hand. "I swear I won't tell anyone. Do you want me to prick my finger and sign an oath in blood?"

"What I want is for you to put that attitude away somewhere, before I put it away for you."

Surprised by Beulah Mae's sharp tone, Lynn backed down. "Sorry. I didn't mean to upset you."

Beulah Mae shook her head. "No. It's . . . I'm . . ." She stopped and took a deep breath. "It's just that it's been a long time since I've talked about this and it's not easy." She turned to look at Lynn. "You see, you aren't the only person to have killed someone."

CHAPTER NINETEEN

"It was the spring of 'forty-six. I was living in—" Beulah Mae stopped. "I'm not going to tell you where this happened." She glanced at Lynn. "No so much because I don't trust you, but because I've made promises that I'm breaking and there are other people besides me who could be hurt if this was ever brought into the open."

"I told you I wouldn't tell." Lynn was hurt by Beulah Mae's lack of trust in her.

"I made the same promise over sixty years ago."

"If you're so worried about it, why are you telling me?"

"Stop pouting. I'm telling you because I think it might help you to not make the same mistake that I did."

Lynn wanted to tell her she wasn't pouting, but knowing Beulah Mae as she did, her comment would simply make things worse. "I'm listening," she said. "But just so you'll know if I really wanted to know where this happened it wouldn't be too hard to find out where you were in nineteen forty-six." Lynn had seen the amazing things that could be accomplished with a computer. Even with the antiquated recordkeeping practices of the past, there was still plenty of information out there, if you knew where to look.

Beulah Mae nodded. "Yes, I suppose that's true." She looked hard at Lynn. "I'll trust you not to do so." Without pause she launched into what had happened on that long ago night. "It was around two thirty in the morning I had just left the home of a young woman I had been seeing for a while." She settled back into the seat.

Lynn turned to face her.

"I had parked my car several blocks over, because this particular woman was married to a rather prosperous businessman. He was often out of town, but it was best not to have my car seen outside their place, especially at that time of morning. I had only gone a few blocks when I heard a scuffle going on down the alley. My first instinct was to go on and mind my own business, but then I heard a woman cry out." She glanced at Lynn "I had spent the previous two years working on a fishing boat in Alaska. Hauling those nets in was hard work and I was pretty strong, plus I never went anywhere without a little extra protection."

Lynn wondered if she was talking about the gun she had mentioned she once carried.

"Anyway, I eased into the alleyway. There was a full moon that night, or maybe it was just a streetlight. I just remember how patches of the alleyway were lit up. As I was walking I remember thinking how pretty the shadows played along the wall and ground. When I came upon them, they were by a huge pile of crates. I could see them struggling on the ground. Even though they were little more than silhouettes, I didn't need a light to figure out what was happening. I yelled at the guy to stop." She shook her head. "I didn't realize it then, but I must have been standing in the shadows myself, and when he heard my voice he recognized it as a woman's voice. When I yelled at him, he simply looked over his shoulder at me and told me to either get the hell out of there or get in line and he'd be with me in a moment."

Lynn recoiled at the vision Beulah Mae's words brought to life. She had a sickening feeling she knew where the story was headed. She braced herself as Beulah Mae continued on with the details of that horrible night.

"It was then that I noticed a second woman lying near the crates. I started toward her and guess my size got his attention because he jumped up. After that everything is a jumble. I remember he pulled up his pants and that something shiny on his shirt pocket caught the moonlight. I was so scared I couldn't move. Then he started toward me and there was another flash of moonlight, but this time it was from something in his hand. That knife got my attention pretty dang quick. I told him to leave and no one would get hurt." She ran a hand over her mouth. "It was such a stupid thing to say. There were two women on the ground and I told him to leave and no one would get hurt."

Lynn lay a hand on Beulah Mae's arm. "You were in shock. The point is, you went into that alley to help when you heard the woman scream."

Beulah Mae seemed to give Lynn's last comment some consideration. "I've wondered about that a lot over the years. I'm ashamed to say that I may have taken my part-time male role too much to heart. At that time, I didn't see other women as equals to me. I thought I was special because I had lived in a man's world and passed. I had been 'one of the boys.' Women were a source of entertainment, objects to be conquered for my own pleasure." A tear ran down her cheek. "So you see, in some ways I wasn't any better than that bastard standing in the alleyway."

"You were nothing like him. I've seen how you treat women."

"That's now. Back then, I was a different person." For a moment she seemed to be lost in her memories.

Lynn kept quiet to give her a moment to regroup. As she sat there she realized she was still holding the fifty-dollar bill in her hand. She started to hand it to Beulah Mae but decided to wait. She needed to hear the rest of the story.

After a while, Beulah Mae started talking again. "He laughed and lunged at me." Her hand went to her side. "The blade caught me here. Luckily it wasn't deep enough to do any real damage. When the knife sliced me, I struck out at him and he stumbled. I hadn't hurt him, but it gave me all the time I needed. When he turned back toward me I had the gun out and pointed at him. It didn't faze him in the least. He said something about me not having the balls to pull the trigger." She wiped her face. "He was wrong."

A thousand questions tumbled through Lynn's mind, but Beulah Mae didn't give her time to ask any of them.

"Jay was the woman he was on when I got there. He had followed her and her girlfriend, Joanie, after they left a bar. He had held the knife to Joanie's throat and forced Jay to handcuff herself to one of those crates. Then he . . . he . . . raped Joanie right there in front of her." Beulah Mae's voice grew hoarse with emotion. "Afterward he stabbed Joanie and tossed her aside before he grabbed Jay and started trying to rape her. That was the struggle I heard. He had managed to rip most of her clothing away by the time I came along."

Lynn's stomach lurched. She threw open the car door and suffered a bout of dry heaves. When she regained control of her stomach, she closed the door and rested her head on the back of the seat. "I'm glad you shot the son-of-a-bitch." She wiped sweat from her face. "Did Joanie die?"

"Not physically, but she was never the same after that. None of us were. She and Jay split up a short time later."

"At least the court understood you did it in self-defense.

Unless his wife decides to tell the truth, there's no way I can prove I was defending myself against Stoner."

"That's why I decided to tell you about this." She glanced at Lynn. "You see, we never reported it. When I finally got the nerve to check to see how badly I had hurt him, I discovered what had been shining on his shirt pocket. He was a cop—a dead cop who had been killed by a black woman who was dressed completely in men's clothing. That was more than enough to have gotten me hanged, and killing him over another dyke and her girlfriend would have only added fuel to the fire."

"Christ," Lynn breathed. "What did you do?"

"After I got Jay loose, I got my car and put him into the trunk. Then, I took Jay and Joanie to a doctor Jay knew who for a few extra bucks wouldn't bother asking questions. He stitched us up, handed over some antibiotics and kicked us out."

"What did you do with the body?"

"After we left the doctor's office, I drove them to the home of a friend of theirs where we left Joanie. Jay insisted on helping me. She borrowed some clothes from her friend, and then we drove out to the city dump and left him with the rest of the trash."

"They never found the body?"

Beulah Mae shook her head. "Not to my knowledge they haven't."

Lynn tried to imagine the two women dumping a body in the middle of the night.

"That's why you have to go back and turn yourself in," Beulah Mae said softly.

Lynn's head whipped around. "Are you crazy? I can't go back. I'd go to prison."

"Things are different today." In a rare display of affection, she took Lynn's hand. "Don't you see? I've spent my whole life looking over my shoulder and worrying about when that dead cop was going to rise from the grave and pull me in with him. That's one of the reasons I never went back home. I'm telling you this because I don't want the same thing to happen to you."

Lynn continued to shake her head.

"It's the only way," Beulah Mae said. "No one in their right mind would assume you went there to kill that man. You had the ticket already and no one except you and Crissy knew about him losing it."

"You don't understand. His wife told the emergency operator that I had killed her husband."

"She was scared and you said she tried to help pull him off you." She squeezed her hand. "Trust me. You don't want to spend the rest of your life running. What about Crissy and your mom?"

"What about them?" Lynn could almost feel her determination slipping away.

"Do you want them to go through life not knowing what really happened? Always worried about where you are. If you have enough to eat or a place to sleep, or if you're even alive."

"After everything calms down I can call or write them and let them know what happened."

"Do you love them so little?"

Lynn yanked her hand away. "What the hell does that mean?"

"You care so little that you're willing to give up your life with them. Has it ever occurred to you that maybe the law will believe you? Do you think so little of yourself?"

The truth hit hard. That was it. She had doubted her own innocence. She hadn't gone there with the intention of harming Stoner, but she had convinced herself that she had fought him over that stupid lottery ticket when in truth she had been protecting herself. She looked at the wadded-up bill in her hand. "I promised to help you get home." She smoothed the bill and held it out to Beulah Mae.

"You hang onto that. We made a bargain and I intend to hold you to it."

146

"But I don't know what's going to happen. What if I go to prison?"

"I don't believe you will. I think I'm going to put my trust in the system this time."

"Yeah, now that it's not your ass on the line."

Beulah Mae chuckled. "Well, yes, that does make it a little easier. But now I have to go back and convince a judge that I'm sane and healthy enough to be sent back out here into the real world." She shook her head. "I'm afraid my little disappearing act may not reflect too well in my favor."

Lynn grinned. "I think he'll see that you're more than capable. And as an old friend once told me, 'I'm going to put my trust in the system.'"

"You keep calling me old and I'm going to introduce my boot to your rear end."

"I'll bet you can't even kick that high," Lynn teased back.

"I can if I stand on a chair," Beulah Mae muttered as she turned the car around and headed south.

CHAPTER TWENTY

Beulah Mae was clearly struggling with the traffic long before they made it back to San Antonio. Lynn lost track of the number of times they had hit the warning grooves and been honked at by irritated drivers whipping past them. She had volunteered to try driving again, but Beulah Mae quickly declined the offer.

"How do you want to handle this?" Beulah Mae asked as they entered the San Antonio city limits.

Lynn glanced at her watch. It was almost a quarter after eleven. "I've been thinking about it. We should go to my mom's place first. She doesn't live far from the nursing home and she can follow us over there." Beulah Mae started to object, but Lynn stopped her. "No. I have to know that you're back at the home safe. After we get you back, Mom can go with me to get Crissy and they can go with me to turn myself in." She stopped. "No." Something about hearing the idea aloud made her change

148

her mind. "No. Wait. I don't want them with me when I turn myself in. I should go alone." Her head was beginning to hurt again. "But if I do, they won't know where I am or what has happened."

"You'll get one phone call." Beulah Mae's reply seemed too blasé for Lynn's frazzled nerves.

"How can you be so calm?"

"At this point, worrying won't fix anything."

"I'm glad to see that you'll be able to sleep tonight."

"I'm almost eighty-five. I don't even remember what sleep is." When Lynn didn't respond she went on. "Here's my suggestion, for what it's worth. I drive you directly to the police station. That way it's obvious that you're turning yourself in. I'm sure the police have someone watching your house and maybe your mom's as well. If you go to either place and they arrest you, then there's room for speculation as to whether you really intended to turn yourself in."

"That makes sense," Lynn agreed.

"After you turn yourself in, I'll call Crissy and she can call your mom. Then they can make arrangements to get you a lawyer."

Lynn's shoulders slumped. "They can't afford a lawyer."

"The court will appoint you one and if you don't like him then I have money to help you."

"I can't take your money."

"Call it a loan."

"No, I can't pay you back. I don't have a job. I may be going to prison and—"

"You have lottery ticket worth thirty-two million dollars. I think you'll be able to afford to repay my measly two-thousand-dollar loan."

Lynn gave a short chuckle that slowly escalated to hysterical laughter. Poor Beulah Mae's life's savings was two thousand dollars and they were both trying to escape on it and in a borrowed car, no less. She was so tired she could barely think.

"I really do believe your blood sugar is messed up. You should see a doctor about that."

Lynn slowly regained control of herself. "We'll go with your idea." She didn't add that at this moment facing the cops didn't worry her as much as facing her mom and Crissy.

By following Lynn's directions, Beulah Mae soon had them at a precinct near Lynn's neighborhood.

"This is probably the best choice of places," Beulah Mae said as she parked the car in a visitor's slot. "Since the . . . ah . . . accident happened near here, they should be better acquainted with the facts." Her rambling betrayed how nervous she was.

As Lynn watched a police officer leave the building her knees began to knock. "I don't know if I can do this," she admitted.

Beulah Mae placed a hand on her arm. "I'll be right there with you."

"Maybe that's not such a good idea for you. If your name gets caught up in all this it might make things harder for you."

"Pooh. Either they'll let me go or I'll eventually go on my own. I'm not worried about it."

"Don't you dare leave for Arkansas without me."

Beulah Mae lightly slapped her leg. "Well, I guess I can hang on another ten or fifteen years," she said, laughing.

Lynn glared at her. "That's not funny."

Beulah Mae suddenly turned serious. "I know this isn't much help right now, but in my heart I know you're going to be fine."

Lynn was amazed that the words actually made her feel better. "Let's go do this before I change my mind."

Together they got out of the car and started toward the building.

"You'll call Crissy, right?" Lynn asked nervously.

"Of course I will."

"Make sure she calls my mom."

"I will."

Lynn pulled the door open. It was eerily quiet inside. She began to tremble as if she was freezing. "I thought it would be busier," she whispered. "Where is everyone?"

"Police stations are always such madhouses on television," Beulah Mae whispered back.

"Can I help you?"

They both jumped and turned to the sound of the voice behind them. The speaker was an older man of medium height and weight who looked more like someone's grandfather than Lynn's mental image of a cop.

"I . . . uh . . . um . . ." Lynn began. "I . . . I . . ." The words refused to come. She glanced to Beulah Mae and found her staring straight ahead. She wondered if she was remembering her own brush with the law.

He looked from Lynn to Beulah Mae and smiled. "Why don't you come with me?"

They nodded and silently followed.

He led them to a small conference room and got them seated at the table. "Can I get you some coffee or something?"

The both declined.

He sat across from them. "Now, what can I do for you ladies tonight?"

Lynn took a deep breath and blurted as quickly as she could, "I killed a man this afternoon and I'm turning myself in. I didn't mean to. It was an accident, but I got scared and ran. Then I broke Beulah Mae out of the nursing home and—"

The man's eyebrows shot halfway to his hairline as he held up his hand. "Whoa. Let's slow down and take this one step at a time. By the way, I'm Sergeant Davidson." He pulled a notepad and pen from his pocket. "Let's start at the beginning with your names."

Lynn gave him the information for the both of them.

"Now," he said, "who did you kill?"

"Edward Stoner. I didn't mean too, you see—"

Again he held up his hand. "I'm sorry, you said Stoner?"

She nodded.

"I remember something about that." He looked at her a moment. "Wait here a minute. I need to check this out." He started to leave but stopped and turned to Beulah Mae. "Which nursing home did you . . . uh . . . escape from?"

"Morning Sunrise."

"Okay, I'll be back with you in a couple of minutes." He closed the door softly behind him.

After he left they sat in silence, Lynn lost in her own world and Beulah Mae seemingly lost in hers. Lynn kept wondering how her mom and Crissy were doing. She was beginning to regret her decision to come to the station first.

When Sergeant Davidson opened the door a few minutes later they both flinched. "Sorry to keep you waiting, but things have picked up a little since you came in. That's what I get for anticipating a slow night."

Lynn realized for the first time that the noise level from outside the room had risen considerably.

Sergeant Davidson sat down across from them and placed a file folder in front of him. "Now, Ms. Strickland, let's begin with you. Start at the beginning and fill me in on your version of this lottery ticket business."

Lynn hesitated slightly. She didn't remember mentioning the ticket to him. Then she realized the information was probably in the file folder lying on the table. She cleared her throat and told him the story.

He interrupted her occasionally to ask her to clarify some point of information or to jot something down on his notepad. When she finished, he nodded and glanced back at his notes. "This other young woman, Ms. Anderson, she was with you when you found the ticket?"

"That's right."

"Did anyone else see you pick it up?"

"No. I don't think so."

"How did you get the bruises on your neck?"

"They're from when Stoner was choking me."

He jotted some more. "Where is the lottery ticket now?" he asked.

"It's in my wallet." She started to reach for it.

"Let's leave it there for the time being," he said, leaning back in the chair. "You know, you could have saved yourself a whole lot of trouble if you hadn't of run away."

Lynn looked down at her hands. "I know. I got scared."

"I have the proverbial good news/bad news scenario for you."

Lynn looked up. Maybe he was going to believe her story.

"The good news is that Edward Stoner isn't dead."

Unable to believe her ears, Lynn leaned forward. "What? He didn't have a pulse. I'm sure of it. I checked it twice."

He shrugged. "Maybe you missed it because you were so frightened."

"What's the bad news?" Beulah Mae asked.

Davidson flipped the file folder open. "Mr. Stoner has filed a charge against Ms. Strickland. He claims she stole the ticket from him when she was at his house."

"That's ridiculous," Lynn protested. "Before I went to his house to offer him half the winnings, I had no idea who he was."

"We'll get into all that in a few minutes. Would you still be willing to split the ticket fifty-fifty?"

"Sure. If it means I can put this all behind me, he can have the ticket."

"No, he can't," Beulah Mae cut in. "You found the ticket and you did the right thing by trying to return it. I'm not going to stand by and let Stoner walk away with the entire thing."

Sergeant Davidson closed the folder. "I'm sorry, but I'm going to have to ask you to stay here a while longer. Stoner is on his way in. As soon as he gets here we'll try to get this ironed out." He pointed to her throat. "You can press charges against him for assault."

Lynn shook her head. "I want to put this all behind me and go home."

"Hopefully, it won't take long to straighten this mess out." He turned to Beulah Mae, "Now, for you, Ms. Williams. I've called the Morning Sunrise nursing home and there seems to be some confusion. According to the nurse at the desk, they received a call this afternoon informing them you had left to go to Colorado. They reported your disappearance to the authorities." He looked at her. "You obviously didn't go to Colorado."

"I stayed because I wanted to help my friend." Beulah Mae placed a hand on Lynn's arm.

He nodded and smiled. "That was very nice, but I'm afraid that you're going to have to go back to the nursing home. They're sending someone over to pick you up."

"Can't I stay here until I find out what's going to happen to Lynn?"

"No, ma'am, I'm afraid not. As I said, someone is already on their way over."

There was a loud banging from the hallway. It sounded to Lynn as if someone had thrown a metal trash can.

Sergeant Davidson sighed and stood. "I need to get out there. It would help if you both waited here. I'll get back to check on you as soon as I can." Without waiting for them to reply he rushed out the door. There was another flurry of noise and then silence.

"It looks like we'll both be sleeping in our own beds tonight," Beulah Mae said.

"I guess so. I don't see how Stoner can make anyone believe I stole that ticket from him. I'm sure that once he's here and they question him again, they'll see through his lies. They'll have to let me go then." Lynn suddenly remembered that the gang at the car wash could testify that she'd had the ticket before she went to Stoner's house. She didn't want to pull them into her mess, so she decided to keep the information to herself until she absolutely needed it. Davidson would call Crissy to verify that she had been with her when she found the ticket. When Davidson faced Stoner with the new facts, Stoner would probably fold.

"Don't you go crazy on me and hand that ticket over to Stoner. It's not right," Beulah Mae said.

Lynn nodded. "When I first found out that I'd won, it was as if all my prayers had been answered. I thought the money was going to be the end of all my troubles. But it has been nothing but trouble. I'm beginning to think those people were right about there being a curse on the lottery."

Beulah Mae stretched her legs out slowly. "Horsefeathers. The only curse there is on any money is people's greed. You take your half of the money and you use it to do good things."

Lynn nodded again. "I never thanked you for coming back with me."

"It's nothing. You just hurry up and get this mess straightened out. I still want to go home."

"You know they'll be watching you."

"I know. That's why I'm going to tell them that I want to leave Morning Sunrise. At least then I'll find out what I need to do to get out of there."

"What are you going to do if they let you go?"

Beulah Mae chuckled before leaning closer to Lynn. "Well, when I thought you were headed to prison I was going to keep your pretty girlfriend company, now I guess I'll just wait around until you're rich enough to buy a car that you can handle. Then I'll let you drive me home in style."

"You are so full of yourself," Lynn said. She tried to sound gruff, but she couldn't keep the smile off her face. What mattered now was that Edward Stoner was still alive, which meant she would soon be home cuddled next to Crissy.

CHAPTER TWENTY-ONE

Sergeant Davidson returned about twenty minutes later to tell Beulah Mae that a nurse had arrived to take her back to the nursing home.

Lynn struggled to keep from smiling when she looked up and saw Janelle, the nurse Beulah Mae had hinted at having a fling with. She couldn't resist a final whisper as she gave her friend a good-bye hug. "Do you think she's going to spank you for being a bad girl?"

Beulah Mae chuckled and whispered back. "If there's any spanking to be done, it'll be me doing it."

"You are unbelievable."

"That's what they all tell me," Beulah Mae replied as she waved good-bye and left on Nurse Janelle's arm.

Just as Lynn was about to sit back down, Sergeant Davidson motioned for her. "Edward Stoner is here. Why don't you come with me?"

Suddenly the thought of seeing Stoner again made her nervous. Her lack of enthusiasm apparently showed.

"It's okay," Davidson assured her. "We won't leave you alone with him."

She reluctantly followed him out of the room. As they walked down the hallway, she happened to glance through a partially opened doorway and saw Crissy sitting at a table. Their gazes met at the same moment. Lynn started toward her, but the look of anger on Crissy's face stopped her cold. When Crissy turned her back to the doorway, Lynn slowly followed Davidson into the next room.

Stoner looked even larger in the enclosed space. The gauze pad didn't completely hide the ugly knot on the side of his head. His labored breathing filled the room.

In a strange way, Lynn now found the sound comforting, but she still chose a chair as far away from him as the small table allowed. As she sat down she noticed another police officer sitting behind the door.

"All right," Sergeant Davidson began. "I'm sure this has all been a big misunderstanding and no one intentionally filed a false police report." He nailed Stoner with a hard stare. "Because we all know how serious that is."

Lynn was glad to see that Stoner at least had the decency to drop his gaze.

"Mr. Stoner," the sergeant continued, "Ms. Strickland has assured me that she is still willing to split the ticket with you fifty-fifty."

"It's my ticket," Stoner replied gruffly. "She's got no right to any of it."

Davidson leaned across the table toward him. "Let me explain something to you. If you two can't reach an agreement, this matter will eventually end up in court. When that happens, there's good chance the decision will go against you. It won't really matter either way because once it gets in the court system the lawyers are going to drag it out until they siphon off every penny they can. Then you two will be left to either split the little that's left or winner takes all. Either way, after the government gets it share and the lawyers get their portion, there won't be enough left for you two to fight over. So what's it going to be?" The glare he gave Stoner made Lynn grateful it wasn't directed at her.

"It's my ticket," Stoner said again.

Davidson pushed away from the table. "Fine, Mr. Stoner." He turned to Lynn. "Ms. Strickland, my advice to you is to get to Austin and file your claim with the lottery commission as quickly as possible."

"Wait a minute," Stoner shouted as he jumped up.

Lynn pressed herself as far back as the chair would allow.

The policeman behind the door came swiftly to his feet. Davidson had turned to face Stoner.

"Sit down," Davidson ordered.

"You can't let her walk out of here with my ticket," Stoner protested as he sat down.

"I have a witness who will swear that Ms. Strickland tried to tell you that you had dropped the ticket. Do you remember what your response was?"

Stoner glowered at Lynn. "It's my ticket and she knows it."

"That's a decision for the court to make," Davidson replied. "Unless, of course, you're willing to compromise, in which case you'll both be enjoying the comforts of approximately . . ." He did some quick mental math and whistled. "After taxes you're still looking at something around ten million each."

The number seemed to finally penetrate Stoner's anger.

"Ten million today is a heck of a lot better than what you'll see after the lawyers tie it up for three or four years," Davidson said.

Finally Stoner gave in and nodded.

"That's what I like to see," the sergeant said cheerfully, "reasonable people who know how to compromise." He leaned forward. "We're going to do something a little different, to ensure that there aren't any further problems." He nodded toward the policeman who had returned to the chair behind the door. "Patrolman Ramos is going to escort you both to Austin and stay with you while you each claim an equal share in the ticket." He looked at Lynn and Stoner. "Any problems with that idea?"

They both agreed that there weren't.

"Good. He glanced at his watch. "It's already a little after three, so I suggest you find yourself a nice quiet room with a comfortable chair and try to catch a few winks of sleep."

"Are you saying we can't leave?" Stoner asked.

Davidson seemed to give the question some consideration before answering it. "I would rather you didn't," he began. "The reason being is that sometimes greed makes us forget that small part of ourselves that is normally rational. If I let you leave and something was to happen to either one of you, I'd have to tell myself every single day that I could have prevented it if only you had stayed here. So I prefer to think of it as me allowing you to remain here as our guests for a few hours." He shrugged. "Besides, with the morning traffic being what it is between San Antonio and Austin, you'll have to leave here around five anyway, so you'll be waiting on the steps when they open, and in no time you'll both be millionaires."

Lynn waited for the surge of happiness to hit her, but it was gone. All she could think about was how Crissy had turned away from her.

"Can we agree?" Davidson asked.

"It's fine with me," Lynn said, wanting nothing more than to get out of there and talk to Crissy.

Stoner finally mumbled his agreement.

"Good. Mr. Stoner, if you'll go with Patrolman Ramos he'll help you find a quiet room."

"Where's she going to be?" Stoner asked as he nodded toward Lynn.

"I'll see to it that she'll have a comfortable place to wait as well," Davidson assured him.

Stoner finally gave in and followed the patrolman into the hallway.

"There's a cot in back that you can use," Davidson said as soon as Stoner was out the door.

"I'm really not sleepy," Lynn admitted. "Is it okay if I go talk to Crissy?"

He nodded. "Why don't you stay here and I'll send her in."

"Thanks."

Davidson left and pulled the door closed behind him. It seemed like only seconds passed when the door opened again.

Expecting to see Crissy, Lynn hopped up. Her excitement faded when Davidson stuck his head in.

"I'm sorry," he said. "Ms. Anderson said she was tired and has gone home."

Lynn swallowed her pain and fear as she nodded and sat down.

"Can I get you anything?" he asked.

She shook her head. As she sat there alone all she could think about was the curse of the lottery. She lost track of time as she sat staring into space. She needed to get home and talk to Crissy. Had Davidson told Crissy they would be going to Austin in a few hours, or was she sitting at home waiting for her? Lynn sat up suddenly and slapped herself on the forehead. If she couldn't go home at least she could call. A phone sat on a table against the wall. She practically ran and snatched it up. It took her a moment to get an outside line. By the time her home phone was ringing, she was already beginning to doubt the advisability of her decision. She knew her doubt was justified when Crissy slammed the phone down the moment she heard Lynn's voice. After a silent prayer that the disconnection had been caused by a glitch in the phone system, Lynn dialed her home number again. This time there was no answer. Not knowing what to say that wouldn't make matters worse, she finally hung up when the answering machine kicked in.

CHAPTER TWENTY-TWO

The next ten hours were a blurred nightmare. From the minute she and Stoner walked through the doors at the lottery commission someone was beside her pushing papers at her to sign or posing her alongside the obnoxious Stoner for a photo.

His disposition hadn't improved when he discovered that because he'd purchased the ticket with the cash value option, which provided the winner with an instant lump sum, rather than disbursing the amount over several years of annual payments, the ticket's value had been drastically reduced. Then there was the huge chunk for taxes. In the end, they were to receive a little over seven million each. Stoner went ballistic when he heard the amount. He started threatening lawsuits and demanded an audit of the entire lottery system.

Lynn no longer cared. All she wanted was to get home to Crissy and get their life back on track. If she could have reversed time, she would have gladly given all the money to Stoner. The only thing that kept her there was Beulah Mae's counsel that she should take the money and do something good with it. She didn't know what she would do yet. Simply thinking about all the people who needed help made her dizzy. Compared to the overwhelming needs of the world, seven million wasn't even a good Band-Aid.

After what felt like an eternity, she was finally in the car headed back to San Antonio with Patrolman Ramos and Stoner, who thankfully had finally shut up. She tried to grasp the fact that at that very moment a deposit for a little less that seven million five hundred thousand dollars was in the process of being wire-transferred to her checking account. A twinge of panic threatened when she thought about all that money. What would she do with it? She pushed the thoughts away. Crissy would know the best way to handle the money.

As they rode in silence, Lynn began to worry. She didn't know what she would do if Crissy kept refusing to talk to her. Maybe she should leave her alone for a couple of days to let her cool off, but on the other hand, if she waited, Crissy might get the idea that she didn't care. She still hadn't made a decision about the best way to approach Crissy, when they arrived back at the police station.

She was careful to make sure Stoner was gone before she went to the nearest bus stop and caught a bus home. Stoner had settled down after they had gotten in the car and he had lost his audience, but his anger had frightened her and she intended to be extra vigilant for a while.

The trip from the bus stop by the police station to the one near her house was much too short. When she stepped off the bus and watched it pull away, she still had no idea what to say to Crissy. She slowly made her way home, praying that Crissy had cooled down. When she turned on their street she was surprised to see her old car sitting in the driveway. She wondered if Nevils had arranged to have it towed to her or if Crissy had been forced to take care of it. Crissy's car was nowhere in sight. It took her a minute before she realized that it was still Friday and that Crissy was in class.

When she walked past her car and saw her stuff inside it was obvious that Crissy wasn't over being mad. She stood staring into the car for several minutes. No one had even bothered stealing it. Finally she dug her car keys from her pocket and climbed inside. She breathed a sigh of relief when the engine finally caught on the third try. At least she wouldn't have to bear the humiliation of having to ask her mom to come get her. She patted the dashboard of the old car. Now that she was only hours away from having all that money available to her, material items no longer seemed so important.

Her mom wasn't at home when Lynn arrived. She had her old key, but she didn't feel like being inside. Instead, she went to the backyard and stretched out on top of the picnic table.

It was almost dark when her mother shook her awake. "Why didn't you go into the house?" she asked.

"Crissy kicked me out." Lynn looked at her mom and shrugged slightly. "I didn't know where else to go."

"I can't say as I blame her."

Shocked, Lynn could only stare at her.

"Don't look at me that way. How could you simply run off like that and not let us know? We were worried sick about you."

"I wasn't gone that long," Lynn snapped.

Suddenly her mom was standing over her with that look she had used when Lynn was much younger and in trouble. She truly expected to hear her mother announce that she was grounded for two weeks.

Instead, she took a deep breath and stepped away. "Come on in. There's no need to give the neighbors a free show."

Lynn obediently followed her inside. As soon as the door closed behind them, she tried to apologize. "Mom, I'm sorry.

Everything got crazy and I didn't know what to do."

"Why didn't you come to me?"

Lynn really felt like a heel when she realized her mom was on the verge of crying. "I was afraid it would cause you trouble. I didn't want that."

Her mom dropped into her chair. "Sit down and tell me everything. Crissy called last night to let me know they weren't going to lock you up." She pointed a finger at Lynn. "By the way, that was a call that should have come from you."

Lynn tried to weasel out from under her condemning eyes. "I wasn't even sure if you knew what had happened. I didn't want to upset you if you hadn't heard, plus I knew Crissy would call you once she knew something."

"So there are no charges against you? Not even something for dragging that poor old woman out of the nursing home?"

"Mom! I didn't drag anyone out of the nursing home. Beulah Mae wanted to go home and I needed to get out of town." When her mom didn't relent, she added lamely, "It seemed like the right thing to do at the time."

For a moment they sat in silence.

"Are you hungry?" her mom asked.

Lynn shook her head.

"When was the last time you ate?" Her mom asked. "I'll bet your blood sugar is low."

The familiarity of the words stopped Lynn. "You've been talking to Beulah Mae," she said accusingly. "She kept saying that."

Her mom smiled slightly. "Crissy gave her my number and she called to check on you this morning." She fluffed her hair. "She's actually a very charming woman. She invited me to the nursing home to have dinner with her next week." She looked at Lynn and frowned. "She can't leave the home until all this mess with you is straightened out."

Lynn's jaw nearly dropped. Even her mom hadn't been

immune to Beulah Mae's charm. She stood up and hugged her mom suddenly and was rewarded with a solid smack on her fanny.

"I swear I don't know what I'm going to do with you."

Lynn's stomach rumbled loudly.

"See," her mother said. "You are hungry. Come on and let me fix you some dinner."

"I've got a better idea," Lynn said. She still had the fifty that Beulah Mae had given her. "Why don't I take you to dinner? Let's go to that little steak place where you used to work."

"Oh, no. That's too expensive. I can fix us something here."

Lynn started laughing.

"What's so funny?"

"Mom, by tomorrow morning I'll have over seven million dollars. I think I can afford to buy us a couple of steaks from Billy Bob's." She stopped. "There's only one hitch."

"What?" her mom asked, eyeing her suspiciously.

"I'm not sure my car will get us there and back. You'll have to drive."

Her mom pushed her toward the hallway. "Go get yourself cleaned up. I'm not going out with you looking like a refugee."

Lynn suddenly remembered that all of her stuff was in the car. She swallowed the lump that tightened her throat. "Is it okay if I stay here for a while?"

Her mom hugged her again. "You know you can stay as long as you want."

"I don't have a job anymore." After missing the past two nights at LaCasita she assumed she wouldn't be welcomed back there either.

"Well, it so happens that I know this great new restaurant that's going to be opening soon and they'll have plenty of work to keep you busy."

Lynn smiled. "I don't know. What are they paying?"

"We're offering room and board and my undying gratitude."

Lynn kissed her mom's cheek. "That sounds perfect."

"Lynn, give Crissy time. She's really hurt."

"I never meant to hurt her. I really thought I was doing everyone a favor by not getting you all involved."

"Sweetie, we love you. We want to be involved in your life all the time, not just during the good times. Crissy loves you."

Lynn nodded. "I'd better shower." She rushed off before her mom could see the tears in her eyes.

CHAPTER TWENTY-THREE

When they arrived at the restaurant, Lynn was surprised by the number of people who approached their table to speak to her mom. Coworkers came by to say how much they missed Violet's humor, and customers dropped by to say how sorry they were that she had left. Lynn wondered if anyone other than her own team missed her at the car wash.

Lynn's biggest surprise came when a man and a woman stepped up to the table.

"Hey," he began, "aren't you the woman who found that winning lottery ticket?"

The last thing Lynn wanted was the attention that acknowledgment would bring. She laughed lightly. "Me?"

The woman grabbed his arm. "See, I told you. Come on and stop bothering these people." She started pulling him away. "I'm sorry," she called over her shoulder. "He watches the news and swears he knows everyone they show."

Lynn smiled and quickly turned her attention to her steak.

"Wow," her mom whispered. "You're famous."

"Stop it," Lynn hissed. "Why do they air those clips? Don't they know it gets the attention of every crackpot in the city?"

"I doubt if they care. They're probably more interested in the publicity it brings. Think about those times when you saw the beaming face of a winner. Didn't it make you want to run out and buy a bunch of tickets?"

"Yeah, you're right."

"Remind me to set the VCR when we get home. I'm sure they'll show it again at ten." Her mom stopped and looked in the direction of the couple. "I wish I had thought to ask him which channel."

"Mom, please. Let's not encourage this."

"You're right." They ate in silence for a while before Violet asked, "How does it feel to be a millionaire?"

"You're not going to believe this. I had the money electronically sent to mine and Crissy's joint checking account, but with everything that's going on I've not really had time to think about it." She shrugged. "I guess I should go by the bank tomorrow and open another account and move some of the money into it."

Her mom stared at her. "Are you telling me you dropped all that money into a checking account?"

"What was I supposed to do? It wouldn't fit in my pockets."

"Don't get smart with me."

"I wanted to talk to Crissy about what we should do with it, but then I got home and found my things in my car."

"What are you going to do about that?"

"Are you taking about the car or the money?"

"I'm talking about your problems with Crissy."

"Mom, I can't do anything until she's ready to talk." She set her fork down. "Look, it's not like I woke up yesterday morning and decided that it was a good day to screw up everyone's life. I went to see Edward Stoner because Crissy insisted we give the ticket back to him. I didn't agree, but after thinking it over I was willing to split it with him." She leaned forward. "I still don't agree that he was entitled to it. Hell, I don't think he should have gotten any share of the ticket. It has nothing to do with the money. That guy was a butt head. I tried to tell him he'd dropped the ticket and he flipped me off."

"I'm sorry I brought it up. I didn't mean to upset you." She patted Lynn's arm. "Let's enjoy our dinner."

After an awkward moment, Lynn tried to return the conversation to a more agreeable subject. "How are the renovations on the new restaurant going?"

Violet's dark eyes sparkled. "Good. The inside is really messed up. We've gotten all the junk hauled out. There are some walls that need new sheetrock hung. We want to replace the floors. The previous tenant put in a cheap ceramic tile and it's slippery. We can't afford to have someone fall." Her voice took on a soft lilt. "Jaime's uncle tears down old buildings for the lumber which he refurbishes. He's going to give us a good deal on some really nice old pine boards that we're going to use for the floor. It'll be beautiful with all the bright colors we've chosen for the décor."

As her mom continued talking about the restaurant, Lynn saw an animation in her mother that had been missing for too long. She was happy for her and realized she was actually looking forward to seeing Jaime again. He had been a nice guy. She had been around twelve or thirteen when he left. "So you've already met the family, have you?"

Her mom started to respond until she noticed the look of devilment on Lynn's face. She blushed.

"When do I get to see him again?"

"Whenever you're ready. We had been talking about having you and Crissy over to the house for dinner before . . ." Her mom began to fidget with her napkin. "I meant to tell you sooner, but so much has been going on. I hope you like him and that—"

Lynn covered her mom's hand with her own. "Mom, I want you to be happy. If you like him, I'm sure I will, too. Heck, I liked him before so why wouldn't I now?" She leaned back. "Don't worry about me and Crissy. We'll work this out somehow." She sipped her iced tea and wished she felt as confident as she sounded.

They topped off their meal by sharing a slice of pecan pie.

"I'm stuffed," her mom said as they made their way to the car.

"I enjoyed talking with you tonight," Lynn said as she unlocked the car doors.

Her mom stopped and stared up at her. "You seemed different tonight, more mature. How did that happen?"

Rather than her usual flip response Lynn stopped to think about the question. "I think it might have been last night somewhere just outside of Austin." She couldn't have explained it had she been asked to, but there had been something in Beulah Mae's story about Jay and Joanie that haunted her and made her look at things differently.

After they arrived home, Lynn programmed the VCR for her mom. They sat down together to watch the news. Sure enough, shortly into the segment a photo of her and Stoner accepting the oversized cardboard check popped onto the screen.

"Why didn't you comb your hair?" her mom scolded. "And look at how you're dressed. You look like a ragamuffin."

"I'm more concerned about how many crazies are watching this," Lynn said after the short spotlight was over. "Maybe everyone went to bed early."

"Well, you know that's a pipe dream. You're lucky they settled for the press photos and didn't come looking for you." With that her mom pleaded exhaustion and went off to bed.

Lynn wasn't sleepy and she had eaten too much at the restaurant. To work off some of the food, she carried the rest of her meager belongings in from the car and put them in her old room. She tried to relax and read, but she had forgotten how small the room was. When the walls threatened to start closing in she went back to the living room and dialed Crissy's number. When it went to the answering machine she left a simple message. "Hi. It's me. Look, I'm sorry I hurt you. I never meant to. I thought I was doing the right thing by not getting anyone else involved." She hesitated a second to arrange her thoughts. "You won't have to worry about money. I made a *small* deposit into the checking account today." She bit her tongue. It was probably not a good idea to sound too cheerful. "I guess we should talk about the best way to handle the money. I'm staying with Mom. Please call me. I love you." The tape shut off. Lynn stared at the phone for a moment before hanging up.

CHAPTER TWENTY-FOUR

The following morning Lynn was dragging. She hadn't slept much the night before. Every little noise had brought her fully awake, listening for the telephone, but Crissy hadn't bothered to return her call. She had finally given up on trying to sleep and crept out of bed around four. She had sat on the tiny steps at the front of the trailer and tried to find a solution to her problems. Crissy had never been one to remain angry for long, and her decision not to return Lynn's calls spoke volumes. Lynn felt certain that when Crissy finally did call it would be to tell her it was over between them. The irony wasn't lost on her. All this time she had thought their problems stemmed from the lack of money and now that there was plenty, it looked as if it were too late. She loved Crissy, but she had to admit that she was tired of the arguing. It might be best if they both stepped back and reevaluated their commitment to the relationship.

The sun was beginning to peek over the horizon when she made her decision. If Crissy needed time to think things through, she would give it to her, but she intended to move on with her dreams. Maybe her mom was right. She needed to start doing things to secure her future.

By the time her mom woke, Lynn had breakfast almost ready.

"What are you still doing here?" her mom asked. She was dressed in a pair of old jeans and a faded work shirt. Her hair was tied back in a red bandana.

"You said I could stay," Lynn said defensively.

Violet sighed. "I meant, why aren't you at the nursing home? It's Saturday morning."

"I didn't think I'd be welcomed back after the thing with Beulah Mae."

Her mom poured herself a cup of coffee. "There are a lot of people there depending on you."

"Yeah, but what will I do if they kick me out?"

"I don't think anyone is going to kick you out." She smiled slightly. "I wouldn't recommend you try taking any of the patients to lunch though."

"Mom, it's not funny."

"Oh, come on. Don't you think it's a little funny?" She sipped her coffee. "I for one would have loved to have seen your face when you put the car in reverse and tried to drive off."

"I don't believe Beulah Mae told you about that. She's nothing but a big blabbermouth." Lynn removed the bacon from the skillet and began to fry the eggs.

"What possessed you to think you could drive a stick?"

"I don't know. It always looked so easy when you did it."

"Lord, I guess I should be grateful I'm not a brain surgeon."

"Ha ha. You're a real barrel of laughs." She turned back to the stove. "The eggs are ready if you want one."

Her mom took a plate and served herself. "Don't be a grumpy Gus." She pulled out a chair and sat down. "Sit down and let's

174

have breakfast together. Then you need to get on over to the nursing home and I need to get to the restaurant. We're going to start pulling down sheetrock today.

Lynn made herself a plate, refilled her coffee and sat down at the table. They ate in silence for a few minutes.

"Have you decided what you're going to do with the money?" her mom asked.

"I've been giving it some thought. The woman at the commission who talked to me suggested financial planners, and I'll certainly look into that, but I don't need all that money. I know what I want to do with some of it, but I have to be careful. Apparently there are some serious tax issues if I give it away."

"I thought they took out the taxes before they gave it to you."

"Believe me, the government got their share and then some. But there's something about gift taxes if I give it away to someone. So I have to think of some way to get around that. I don't intend to pay a penny more than I have to in taxes."

Her mom chuckled. "You're already starting to sound like a millionaire." She began to clear the table. "Have you talked to Crissy yet?"

"Not really. I called last night, but I guess she was still working. I left a message. I may try to call her again tonight."

"Good." Her mom patted her arm. "Now, get on over to the nursing home."

"Mom, I really don't think that's a good idea."

"How is Mr. Greenberg going to e-mail his son if you don't go? Not to mention all those other poor souls who have been sitting there all week waiting for you to come back. You're all that some of them have."

Lynn nodded. "Okay. Let me get my keys." She went back to her room to grab her keys. When she came out her mom was waiting for her by the door.

"Why don't you come and play bingo with me tonight?"

"Mom, please. I hate bingo."

175

"Okay, then we'll stay home and watch a movie or something."

Lynn wrapped an arm around her mom's shoulders and hugged her. "You don't have to stay home with me. I'll be fine."

"I know you will, but you shouldn't mope around here by yourself."

"I'm not moping," Lynn protested. "Besides, don't you have a date with Jaime or something?" She noticed the warm blush that rose to her mom's cheeks.

"Maybe, but that would be after bingo."

"Oh, so nothing comes between you and bingo, huh?"

"Hurry up. I'm going to be late."

"I'm sure the boss will give you a little leeway," Lynn teased.

"For your information, Ms. Know-It-All, this is an equal partnership."

"All right. You go, Mom." Lynn kissed her mom's cheek and climbed into her battered old car. When she turned the key she got a resounding click. She tried again with the same result.

Her mom tapped on the window. "Come on. I'll give you a lift to the nursing home."

"No. That's okay. I'll take the bus."

"Are you sure? It's not that far out of my way."

Lynn reassured her mom and watched her drive away before going back into the house. The truth was that after paying for dinner last night she only had thirty-eight cents left. She went into the house and called the automated service at her bank. Even though she knew roughly what the balance should be, she was still so stunned when she heard seven million that she missed the rest of the balance. Satisfied that the money was in place, she went to her mom's room and ripped a blank check out of her book. She smiled when she saw that her name was still on the joint account. Her mom had added Lynn's name to the account when she turned sixteen. Lynn had never used the account and was a little surprised that her name was still on it. After folding the check and slipping it into her wallet, she took two five-dollar bills from her mom's "secret" stash.

In the kitchen she found a phone book and called the Taco Hut. When a woman answered she asked to speak to Crissy. The woman was soon back on the line telling her Crissy was busy.

Lynn thanked her and hung up. She immediately dialed their home phone. When the answering machine kicked on she didn't hesitate with her message. "This is important, so please listen. I'm leaving half of the lottery money in the joint account. No matter what you decide, that money is yours to do with as you please. I'm going to open a separate account today. Please don't think that I'm doing this because I want to end anything between us. I love you with my entire heart and soul, but I've finally realized that I need to do some things for myself. I'm going to start looking for land. I would like for you to be with me when I do, but if you can't, I understand. All that I'm asking is that you recognize that I have to do this. Take all the time you need." Her voice broke slightly, but she quickly recovered. "I want things to work between us, Crissy. I still want us to grow old together. I want that whole rocking-chairs-on-the-front-porch dream." She swallowed. "I won't bother you again. Call when you're ready to talk."

CHAPTER TWENTY-FIVE

After placing the call to Crissy, Lynn changed into her nicest jeans and shirt. She swapped out the tennis shoes for boots. Then she took a bus to the bank. When she arrived she explained that she wanted to open an account, and after a short wait she was ushered back to an office. The man who greeted her was young and seemed to be genuinely eager to help her. She rather enjoyed the look of shock on his face when she told him she wanted to transfer over three million dollars from her current account into the new one. Then she handed him the blank check she had taken from her mom's checkbook and instructed him to transfer five-hundred thousand to that account. When he finally found his voice and made discreet inquires as to why she was keeping so much money in a checking account, she explained her situation.

He immediately set out to find the best products for her.

When she explained her intention to buy land, he suggested she keep some of the money in a liquid savings account that paid a decent rate of return. The rest would be placed in a short-term certificate of deposit. This would give her time to review her investment options. He helped her apply for a bank credit card. Then he convinced her to sign up for a series of free financial seminars the bank provided for its customers during the last week of each month. She left the bank with a sense of accomplishment and a stack of temporary checks.

From the bank she hopped on a bus and had to change three times before she reached the location where several automobile dealerships were located. It took her a while to find what she wanted, and then the salesman balked when she informed him she intended to pay the full balance off with a temporary check. She finally convinced him to call the bank to have the check verified. He returned with a wide smile and a tray of coffee and pastries. She was treated like royalty during the rest of the transaction.

It was a few minutes before two when she pulled her new Dodge Ram out of the parking lot. Compared to the old Honda she had been driving for so long the truck was gigantic. It was more vehicle than she needed for running around in the city, but she rationalized the purchase as eventually needing it for the ranch.

She stopped at a bakery, a candy store, a flower shop and, after a few false starts, finally found the tobacco store she was searching for.

When she arrived at the nursing home she gathered her packages and rushed inside. She found Mrs. Harmon asleep on the couch in the entryway. As quietly as possible she placed a large bouquet of daisies beside her before she rushed back to see Mr. Greenberg.

"Hey, Mr. G.," she called out as she entered. To her consternation his grumpy roommate, Ray Cook, was in. "Mr. Cook," she said with a much cooler nod.

"I thought you had forgotten about us," Mr. Greenberg said as he shuffled over to her.

"She was probably too busy kidnapping old people," Cook answered.

Lynn wasn't surprised that everyone would know about Beulah Mae. This place was one big gossip mill. She ignored him and handed the tobacco to her friend. "I have a present for you," she whispered.

Mr. Greenberg smiled when he pulled the bag out and saw the label. "It's my favorite."

"I remembered the name from that first time I visited you."

"This is too much," he protested.

Before she could respond, Cook piped up again. "She wins thirty-two million dollars and all she brought you was a measly bag of tobacco. What did you bring me?"

She removed one of the bags of soft peppermint sticks and offered it to him. "I thought this might sweeten your disposition." She knew she shouldn't let him get to her, but she had never met anyone so bitter.

He turned up his nose and left the room.

"If I had known that was all it would take to get rid of him, I would have bought him candy years ago," Mr. Greenberg said after Cook had left.

"I shouldn't have done that," Lynn said. "I let him get to me."

He made his usual rude sputtering sound. "Please, that man could make Mother Theresa spit."

Lynn noticed that the laptop was sitting on his bed. "So, did you e-mail David?"

He shook his head. "No, but I think I have that solitaire game whipped."

"Good for you."

"Maybe I should start thinking about this e-mail business a little more. It might not be so bad." He looked at the laptop.

"But not right now."

Lynn nodded. "That sounds like a good idea. We'll take it slow." She picked up the laptop and settled into her usual chair. "Okay, let's see what David is up to this week." As she had promised him the week before she stayed longer than usual with him.

Still, he seemed reluctant to see her go. "Will you keep coming back to see us?"

She looked at him and frowned. "Of course I will. Why would I stop?"

He shrugged. "You're rich now."

She put her hands on her hips. "Did you think I only came to see you because I was poor and didn't have anything better to do?"

He looked taken aback. "No. Of course not."

"Well, then why would I stop coming now?"

He nodded and patted her arm. "You'd better hurry on over and see Beulah Mae. She's been by here a dozen times already today looking for you."

"I'll see you next week. You keep working with the laptop."

"Okay." He hovered nearby as she gathered the remaining bags and started for the door.

"By the way, how is everything going with Mr. Garza's iPod? Has he gotten it to work?"

He sputtered again. "I told him what you said about those earbugs and now he walks around with them stuck in his ears all the time. He can't hear a thing. I tried to warn him that they would make him as deaf as a post, but he couldn't hear me."

Lynn laughed. "Well, I'll see you next Saturday." With a final wave good-bye she headed toward Beulah Mae's room. The trip took much longer than she had anticipated because people kept stopping her to congratulate her on winning the lottery. More than one person wanted to talk to her about a great investment idea they had. She carefully avoided those minefields and slowly made her way to Beulah Mae's room.

"Whew," she replied when she finally slipped into the room. "I figured it was you out there causing all that ruckus."

"Money sure has a way of getting people's attention," she said as she hand the bakery box to Beulah Mae. "Here are the cinnamon rolls I promised you last week. I'm sorry I'm so late today, but"—she leaned forward—"I bought myself a brand new truck."

"I hope it's an automatic."

"You're not going to let that go, are you?"

Beulah Mae pulled one of the cinnamon rolls from the box and bit into it, chewing slowly. "Why should I? You have to admit it was a pretty boneheaded thing to do. If you had damaged Jay's baby she would have ripped your head off."

Lynn thought back to the woman she had mistaken for a man and decided that despite her advanced years Jay still looked feisty enough to inflict some serious damage. "How did you get her car back to her?"

"She and Didi drove back in and picked it up from the police station."

Lynn had been so exhausted and worried on Friday morning when she left the police station she hadn't even noticed whether the car was there or not. "How have things been around here?" she asked.

Beulah Mae shrugged. "I had a meeting with the administrator and told her I wanted to leave. She's sending me to be physically and mentally evaluated. I have an appointment to see a psychiatrist in two weeks. I'm not worried about the physical portion. I had a physical a few months back and I passed it with flying colors, but you know how those psychiatrists are. They can make a sane person crazy, so I'm not holding my breath."

"Let me know if there's anything I can do to help."

Beulah Mae smiled. "You make sure you keep that new truck gassed up in case I decide they're taking too long." She was silent while she finished her cinnamon roll. As soon as she was done she turned to Lynn. "So, how is my girlfriend? Are you treating her right?"

Lynn sat down in the chair across from her. She considered lying but didn't see the point. "Actually, I haven't seen Crissy. I've been staying at my mom's."

"Why?"

Lynn shifted in the chair and stared out the window for a moment. "When I got home from Austin the other night she had put all my stuff in my car." She picked a hangnail on her thumb. "Now she won't return my calls or anything."

Beulah Mae released a long-suffering sigh. "You silly kids. If you had any idea how short life was, you wouldn't waste a minute of it."

"I thought you didn't believe in long-term relationships."

"Since when do you listen to me?" She set the box of pastries aside. "I give you all this great advice and all you latch onto is the garbage."

Lynn let her vent.

"What are you going to do about it?" Beulah Mae asked finally.

"What can I do? I'm going to buy my ranch and start raising horses. That's my dream. If she wants to join me then I'll be happy. If she chooses not to, then I'll have to learn to live with it." She tried to sound more sure of herself than she felt.

"That's it?" the older woman asked, obviously vexed.

"I can't barge in and carry her off. She has to decide what she wants."

Beulah Mae waved both her arms in exasperation. "Nimrod, she doesn't know what she wants any more than you do."

"Well, I guess that leaves us both in a world of hurt." Lynn's anger was building. She hadn't come in here to be yelled at. "You're so smart. What would you do?"

"I'd woo her."

"Woo? Nobody *woos* a woman now."

Beulah Mae shook her finger at her. "That's exactly why the divorce rate keeps rising and why you're living with your mama." She scooted forward on her seat. "Just once I want you to really listen to me."

Lynn fought the urge to roll her eyes. "It's not going to make any difference. Crissy is pissed, and she's going to stay that way."

"So, that's it? Just like that you let her go."

"Hey, it wasn't my idea."

Beulah Mae sat up straighter. "Am I to understand that as far as you're concerned Crissy is free to see other women?"

Lynn pushed aside the pain the image of Crissy with someone else caused. "If that's what she wants. I can't stop her."

"Okay, then. I'm glad I have your permission." Beulah Mae stood. "I hate to cut our time short, but I have to make a phone call."

Dumbfounded, Lynn stared at her. "Are you telling me to leave so you can call my girlfriend?"

Beulah Mae gave her an innocent look. "What girlfriend? You said you didn't care. Crissy was free to do as she pleased."

Lynn jumped up. "Fine. Knock yourself out." She stormed from the room. Let the old fart make a fool of herself, she thought. There was no way Crissy would go out with her. She tried not to dwell on the effect Beulah Mae had on women. No way, she told herself. Crissy wouldn't fall for that act.

She was almost to the main door when she heard her name. She turned to find Mrs. Harmon sitting on the couch holding the daisies she had left her.

"Come and look at the beautiful daisies my Allen brought me."

Lynn pushed her anger aside and went back to sit by the woman. "They're very pretty. Would you like for me to find a vase for you, so you can put them in water?"

"One of the nurses is looking for one," she replied.

Lynn sat down beside her. She wondered if it was a mistake to feed the poor woman's delusions, but when she saw the sparkle in the age-dimmed eyes she couldn't bring herself to tell the truth.

Mrs. Harmon picked at the tissue paper wrapped around the daisies. "He has never wrapped them in paper before." She seemed to be talking to herself. "He would pull them from the field until his little hands were full." She looked at Lynn and smiled. "Sometimes when the dirt was soft enough he'd pull so hard he'd pull them up roots and all."

Lynn smiled. "I'm sure he picked these special."

A nurse came up with a vase of water. "Here you go, Mrs. Harmon." She gave Lynn a sharp look.

Lynn assumed it was her show of disapproval over the antics with Beulah Mae. Lynn stood. "I have to go." She touched Mrs. Harmon's shoulder. "I'll see you next week."

The old woman looked up at her with confused, frightened eyes.

Lynn could see that in those brief moments, the spirit of Agnes Harmon had once more surrendered to the empty void.

CHAPTER TWENTY-SIX

Lynn drove back to her mom's. Her argument with Beulah Mae and then the episode with Mrs. Harmon had left her with a deep sense of depression. She told herself to stay busy and started by finding a company that would tow the Honda away. When she began cleaning out the trunk she was amazed by the strong emotional response she had to getting rid of it. To lessen the pain she focused on recalling all the times it had left her sitting on the side of the road, or how it seemed to always break down when she could least afford the repairs. Still, when the wrecker arrived and towed it away, she felt a strong sense of loss.

She was at the table flipping through a magazine about quarter horses when her mom came home.

"Is that behemoth in front of the house yours?"

"It sure is. What do you think of it?"

"I think you're going to have one heck of a gas bill."

"I know it's too big for the city, but I'm going to need it on the ranch."

Violet slid into the chair across the table from her. "So, you're still thinking about raising horses?"

Lynn nodded and braced herself for her mom's disapproval.

"Then I suppose you'll need a big truck."

Lynn looked up. "You're not going to try and talk me out of it?"

"Is that what you want me to do?"

"No."

"Then I won't." She stood and started toward her room. "I need to get cleaned up. Lea will be here to pick me up soon for our weekly bingo date."

"Hey, wait a minute."

Her mom turned back.

"Do you really think I can do it?"

"I think you can do anything you set your mind to."

Lynn thought about Crissy. "I don't know about that, but I want to give it a try."

"Then do it. You have the money and you're young enough to handle the risk." Her mom started to walk away.

"Oh, by the way, I borrowed ten bucks from your secret stash this morning. I didn't have any cash."

Her mom waved it off.

"I'll pay you back with interest," Lynn said.

"I charge twenty-one percent," her mom called back.

Lynn smiled when she thought about the money she had transferred to her mom's account. She wondered how long it would take before her mom discovered the deposit. She went back to reading her magazine.

"Are you sure you don't want to go to bingo with us tonight?" her mom asked when she reappeared freshly showered and wearing a cheerful pale lavender outfit that Lynn couldn't recall seeing before.

187

"I'm positive."

"If you get hungry there's lunch meat in the fridge."

"I'm fine, Mom."

There was a knock on the door.

"Oh, that's Lea. I'll see you later." She gave a small wave and rushed out.

Lynn listened to them chatter like schoolgirls as they hurried to Lea's car. Nothing got in the way of bingo. She went back to reading the magazine. Engrossed in the articles, she lost track of time. When the light coming through the kitchen window grew too dim to read by, she moved to the living room and flipped the lamp on. She was about to lie down on the couch when the phone rang.

Still reading the article she went back into the kitchen to answer it. She froze when she heard Crissy's voice.

"I don't want the money," Crissy said.

"Then give it away."

"Why do you always have to be so difficult?"

Lynn tossed the magazine onto the table. "I'm not being difficult. I mean it. If you don't want the money, give it away. I don't care what you do with it."

There was a moment of awkward silence.

"I heard you bought a truck," Crissy said.

"How did you hear that?" Lynn asked, amazed at how quickly news traveled.

"Beulah Mae mentioned it when she called."

Lynn felt an inkling of jealousy. "I see. What was she calling about?"

"She was inviting me over to the home to have dinner."

"Oh." She wrapped the phone cord around her finger. "Are you going?"

"I thought I would. She sounded lonely."

Horny was more like it, Lynn thought. She glanced at the clock on the stove. "Aren't you late for work?"

There was a slight hesitation before she replied. "I decided to quit working and concentrate on school."

Lynn bit her tongue. Apparently Crissy didn't find it as disagreeable as she had tried to make it sound. "That's good."

"Mr. Salazar's niece started working and they didn't really need me anymore."

"I see," Lynn answered evenly.

"Are you going to come to practice tomorrow?"

"I had planned on it, but if you'd rather I didn't, I guess I could make an excuse to miss it."

"No. I think you should be there. The team is depending on you and the season is almost over with anyway."

"All right. I'll be there."

Another awkward pause occurred.

"Are you coming to the house for the barbecue after practice?"

Lynn gripped the phone. "Will I be welcomed to stay afterward?"

"If you're asking if you can spend the night, the answer is no."

"Then it's probably best if I don't stop by."

"Oh."

She could hear the surprise in Crissy's voice.

Crissy quickly recovered and blurted, "So when are you going to start looking for your ranch?"

Lynn hadn't missed the fact that the ranch was now being referred to as hers. "I was thinking about driving up into the Hill Country on Monday and looking around. Maybe pick up a few flyers from the local Realtors."

"I thought you were leaning more toward land south of San Antonio."

"Actually, you talked about that area. I always liked the Hill Country more. It seems better suited for horses."

"You never told me that."

"Yes, I did. You never listened."

"Why are you trying to pick a fight?" Crissy demanded.

"I don't want to fight. I'm merely trying to be truthful. That's what you wanted, isn't it?"

"I have to go. I'm going to be late for dinner with Beulah Mae."

"Have fun."

Lynn hung up the phone and picked up her magazine, but the article no longer held her interest. She couldn't get the thought of Crissy alone with Beulah Mae out of her head. She had seen how women responded to her magic too many times. Under normal circumstances she wouldn't be worried, but Crissy was vulnerable now. Would she fall for Beulah Mae's charm?

She wandered aimlessly around the trailer. In desperation, she picked up the phone a couple of times to call Deb or Karen, but she really wasn't in the mood to talk to any of that old gang. There would be too much explaining to do.

She had actually reached the point of regretting her decision not to go to the bingo hall with her mom. When she grew tired of pacing, she stretched out on the couch and flipped on the television. This was silly. Why was she worrying about Crissy and Beulah Mae? For all her chatter, she didn't for one minute believe that Beulah Mae would try putting the moves on Crissy.

At some point she fell asleep. Her mom woke her when she came home from bingo. Lynn didn't feel like talking, so she pleaded exhaustion and hurried off to her room. It wasn't until she had turned off her bedroom light that she realized it was raining. She prayed it would rain hard enough that practice would be cancelled. She wasn't sure she'd be able to be so near Crissy without touching her.

CHAPTER TWENTY-SEVEN

Lynn woke to a loud clap of thunder. Rain pounded the metal roof of the trailer. She closed her eyes and turned over. Practice would be cancelled, so she could sleep late. Her peaceful mood was ruined when she realized that Crissy would be left to explain why she wasn't there for the Sunday get-together. Lynn was secretly glad she wouldn't have to be there to tell their friends that they had separated, but part of her felt bad for Crissy having to do it alone.

She got up and slipped on a pair of shorts and an old sweatshirt. She found her mom at the kitchen table with the Sunday paper.

"There's coffee in the carafe and a box of doughnuts on the stove."

For as long as Lynn could remember her mom had spent Sunday mornings with the paper and a seemingly never-ending cup of coffee. She poured her coffee and plucked a chocolate-covered doughnut from the box. She sat at the end of the kitchen table and idly began to thumb through the television guide.

"Why did you put all that money into my account?" her mom asked without looking up from the paper.

The suddenness of the question caught Lynn off guard. "Because I wanted you to have it," she replied finally. "How'd you find it so fast?"

"I started to balance my checkbook this morning and noticed I was missing a check. Imagine my surprise when I called the automated system and discovered that I had over five hundred thousand dollars in my checking account."

Lynn realized that her mom was actually upset. "I'm sorry. I took the check because I needed your account number. I wanted to surprise you."

"It's too much."

"Use it to help with the restaurant or buy yourself a new house or whatever you want."

The paper in her mom's hand began to tremble and then her mother was crying.

Lynn jumped up. "Mom, I'm sorry. My God, I never dreamed it would upset you." She knelt beside her and slipped an arm over her shoulders. "Don't cry. If it bothers you that much I'll take it back." She continued to hold her until the tears stopped. "What's this all about?"

Her mom sniffed "Everything is going so well for me. The restaurant is moving along. Things with Jaime are finally beginning to . . ." She waggled her head from side to side. "Well, you know."

"No, I don't and, respectfully, I don't want to know," Lynn replied.

Her mom gave a quick laugh. "Why is the thought of our parents having sex so unpleasant?"

Lynn jumped up. This was not an avenue she wanted to

explore. "I don't know and I'd really rather not dig into the subject too deeply."

"Sit back down. I'll be good." Her mom pulled a tissue from her pocket and dabbed her eyes.

"I'm sorry about the money," Lynn said. "I should have asked first."

"I know your heart was in the right place. I guess I get nervous when things go too well."

"Why? You're a good person. You deserve to have good things happen to you."

"I know all that. It's just that there seems to be some law of averages that if things are too good for too long then it all blows up in your face."

In a flash of insight, Lynn suddenly realized her mother wasn't talking about the money at all. "You're really in love with this guy, aren't you?" she asked.

Her mom blushed. "Yeah, I am." She glanced at Lynn. "He asked me to marry him."

"Wow. That was sort of quick, wasn't it?"

"Yes and no. We've known each other almost fifteen years. I never stopped loving him, even after he moved to Laredo." She rubbed the back of her hand. "Maybe I've been waiting all this time for him to come back."

Lynn looked at her mother and for the first time saw her as someone other than a parent. She saw her as a woman who had been more concerned about the happiness of her child than she had her own.

"Do you think we're moving too fast?" her mom asked. "I mean, how do you feel about me getting married?"

Lynn grinned and came back around to hug her. "For once stop thinking about me and concentrate on your happiness."

Her mom blushed again. "I think I will."

"Congratulations. When is the wedding?" When her mom didn't respond, she stepped back. "Wait a minute. I was assuming you had already said yes."

"I told him I'd have to think about it."

"Why? You said you love him."

Her mom sprang up and began to pace. "I loved your dad. You loved Crissy." She turned back to Lynn. "Look at us now." She shook her head. "I don't want to go through that again."

Lynn leaned against the counter. "Mom, it isn't fair to compare Jaime to anyone else. I always liked him. I remember how he used to take us to the Mission's baseball games and the museums. He was always talking about art," she recalled. "The most important thing I remember is how he made you laugh."

"He still does." She sat down. "It was hard when he left to go back to Laredo to help his mom."

"Why didn't you go with him?"

"It was complicated. At the time, I had never officially filed for a divorce from your father. Please, I didn't want to throw you into an upheaval by making you move or change schools. You had just turned thirteen and seemed to be so miserable."

Lynn remembered that horrible time. She'd turned thirteen and developed a major crush on her English teacher, Ms. Ponder, all around the same time. To this day, she still thought about Veronica Ponder's sky-blue eyes every time she smelled Chanel Number Five. Her mom's voice pulled her back.

"When he left it was only supposed to be for a couple of months. He thought he'd be able to help his mom put her affairs in order and then come back here. Once he was there, though, he couldn't convince her to sell the restaurant, and since his dad had taken care of the management side, she couldn't handle it by herself. Somehow, the months dragged into a year. We both were caught up in day-to-day living and sort of drifted apart."

"But you kept in contact with him."

"We continued to write letters and he'd call occasionally. But it wasn't the same. Not until he came back and we started seeing each other again. It was like he had never left."

Lynn looked across the table at the woman who had given up so much to raise her. "Mom, all I can say is that a truck could run over us tomorrow."

Her mom looked up, horrified. "Is that supposed to make me feel better?"

"I mean, there are no guarantees in life. Maybe things between Crissy and me are over. I don't know. But if I had it all to do over again, I wouldn't change a thing." She stopped and frowned. "That's not true. I wouldn't make the mistake of going to Edward Stoner's house alone."

Her mom laughed. "You always were a strange child."

Lynn looked offended. "I'm not strange."

"Sweetie, you have millions of dollars in the bank and you had to sneak ten bucks out of my dresser. That's pretty strange."

"No. That's poor money management."

Her mom wiped her eyes again.

"So, are you going to invite me to your wedding?" Lynn asked.

"I'm going to do better than that. I'm going to let you be in it."

"Whoa. Wait a minute. I'm more of a spectator."

"Would you prefer to give me away or be my maid of honor?"

Lynn struggled not to grimace. "Mom, do you know what I think would be a great idea? I think you guys should elope to Vegas."

"No way. When I married your father, we went to a justice of the peace. This time I want a big wedding." She smiled brightly. "And thanks to my generous daughter I can afford a really big one."

Lynn grabbed her head and pretended to moan. "Will I never learn?"

"What are you doing today?"

"I don't know. Softball practice has been rained out. I'll probably hang around here and read. I need to do some laundry."

"That can wait. I want you to go shopping with me."

"Shopping."

"I need to start looking for a wedding gown."

"Isn't it too soon to buy a dress?"

"I'm not buying. I'm looking."

Lynn frowned. "Why? Can't you wait and look when you're ready to buy?"

"No. That's why it's called shopping."

Lynn would have rather washed the neighbor's dog than go shopping, but if it made her mom happy, then she could handle a couple of hours of leaning against dress racks. "All right, but don't you think you should inform your future husband that there's going to be a wedding? I've noticed lately that news seems to travel extra fast around here. I'd hate for him to hear from someone else that he's getting married."

Her mom hopped up. "You're absolutely right. You can get dressed while I call him." She went off toward her room.

"Would it be okay if I finished my coffee first?" Lynn called after her.

"There's a travel mug in the cupboard. You can use it."

Lynn smiled. It was good to see her mom happy again. When thoughts of Crissy tried to seep in, she pushed them away. She wasn't going to allow her own problems to dampen her mom's happiness.

CHAPTER TWENTY-EIGHT

The following morning Lynn woke up eager to start her excursion into the Hill Country. She hobbled slightly as she got out of bed. Her feet were sore from all the walking she and her mom had done the previous day. She had lost track of the number of stores they went to looking at dresses, shoes and a host of other things. Under normal circumstances this would have driven her to tears. Thankfully the rain had stopped by mid-afternoon. At the end of the day the only thing they had to show for their efforts was a pocketful of business cards and sore feet. But her mom was literally glowing, and for that Lynn could easily endure a little discomfort.

As she showered and dressed she tried not to think about Crissy or how many times they had talked about this day. She wondered how Crissy's date with Beulah Mae had gone. It was dinner, she reminded herself. They didn't have a date.

She was making toast when the phone rang. She grabbed it before it woke her mom.

"Good. I didn't miss you," Beulah Mae said.

"What's up?" Lynn asked, surprised by the early call.

"I heard you were going to look for land today."

"Damn, is there some new communication system that I don't know about? Everybody seems to know my business ten minutes before I do."

"That's because none of us have anything better to do than sit around talking about you. Are you going to pick me up or not?"

"Beulah Mae, I'd gladly take you with me, but are you sure it's okay with the nursing home?"

"Yeah, it's fine. I have a day pass. I'm pretty sure they're going to let me go." She chuckled. "I really think that new strategy I was telling you about before we left is working."

"What are you talking about?"

"I tried to tell you about it the other day."

Lynn shook her head. "I'm sorry. Refresh my memory."

Beulah Mae gave her trademark long-suffering sigh. "I've started spending a lot more time up front. You know. Where I'll be a lot more visible to everyone coming in. I make sure I'm there during peak visiting hours or when families are here to check the place out."

"What are you up to?"

"Nothing. But you'd be amazed at how many families seem to be a little nervous about leaving dear old mom here after they get a look at me, especially when I wear my gray suit with the nice striped red and blue tie. They turn three shades of pale when I start winking and giving them my best come-hither look."

Lynn rolled her eyes. What the heck was a come-hither look? She wasn't about to ask for fear that Beulah Mae would launch into one of her long-winded explanations. "Are you sure it's okay for you to leave? I don't want any more trouble."

198

"I'm sure. Is it okay if I bring a friend along?"

"Oh." Lynn started to refuse, but she was too slow.

"Great. We'll meet you out front in twenty minutes." She hung up before Lynn could argue.

Lynn stood staring down at the toast she had been intending to sit down and enjoy. She quickly slathered some butter and jelly on it before slapping the two pieces together to make a sandwich. She could gobble it on the way. She jotted her mom a quick note and ran out the door.

When she arrived at the nursing home and saw Crissy waiting with Beulah Mae, she didn't know whether to laugh or cry. She made herself take a deep breath and count to ten. She would not let them ruin her day. As soon as she stopped the truck, she got out and went around to the other side. She had parked by the curb and the truck had running boards, but she was still concerned about Beulah Mae climbing in.

"I like your truck," Crissy said as Lynn approached.

"I read somewhere that trucks are phallic symbols," Beulah Mae said. Rather than backing down when she saw Lynn glaring at her, she added. "This is one big . . . truck."

"Come on, I'll give you a boost up," she offered.

"Don't worry about me." Beulah Mae shooed her away before she turned to Crissy and offered her hand. "Come on, sweetie, in you go."

Lynn fumed as Crissy took the offered hand and stepped up into the truck. She waited until Beulah Mae had struggled into the vehicle before she slammed the door and headed back to the driver's side. Since when did Crissy need help getting into a vehicle, and why wasn't she at her biology class? She started to ask but decided it was probably no longer any of her business.

She climbed into the truck and threw it into gear.

"Where are we headed?" Beulah Mae asked cheerfully as she slipped an arm across Crissy's shoulders.

Lynn threw them a deadly look, but neither seemed to notice.

"I thought I'd start looking around Boerne or maybe Comfort," she replied between clenched teeth.

"I've always like Boerne," Crissy said.

"I've always been more partial to Comfort," Beulah Mae replied as she winked at Crissy.

Lynn ignored them. As she drove away from the curb she changed her mind and decided to go to Bandera instead.

The other two chatted all the way up. When they tried to pull Lynn into the conversation, she pointedly ignored them. When they reached Bandera, they insisted on tagging along with her. She would have preferred to not have watched them, but they seemed determined to make her miserable. Crissy had turned into a giggling teenager. Everything that Beulah Mae uttered sent her into nearly hysterical laughter.

Lynn picked up a local newspaper and redoubled her efforts to ignore them. She was amazed to discover that there were several real estate offices in town. After a quick glance through the few land listings shown in the paper, she chose an agent who seemed to specialize in larger parcels of property. The office was several blocks away.

"Why don't I meet you two back here later," she suggested. "I'm going to be doing a lot of walking and I wouldn't want to tire you out." She looked pointedly at Beulah Mae.

"Hey, don't you worry about me. If I start to lag behind I'm sure Crissy will let me lean on her." She took Crissy by the arm and stared at Lynn. The smirk on her face seemed to dare Lynn to say something.

"Fine." Lynn turned and stalked off. She deliberately increased her normal pace, hoping they would fall behind, but no matter how fast she walked, the traffic lights were against her. They were able to catch up as she stood trapped by the lights. She got so desperate that she finally almost broke into a run.

By the time she reached the real estate office she was only about twenty feet ahead of them, but she was paying for her childish behavior. She was breathing so hard she could barely talk to the receptionist. When she finally managed to explain that she wanted to talk to a Realtor about some property, she was told that he was currently with another customer but should be out soon.

Lynn took a seat and tried not to notice that Crissy and Beulah Mae had plopped down on a bench directly outside the office window. She had a front-row seat to their laughter and cavorting. It seemed like forever before a young couple came out from the back. A burly man trailed behind them. He sported a lush steel-gray handlebar mustache and ponytail. Except for the ponytail he looked like he would've been more at home in a John Wayne western than a real estate office. Lynn suspected he was in his mid-sixties, but he moved like a man half that age.

After assuring the couple that he would contact them in a few days, he saw them out the door before turning his full attention to Lynn. "I'm Nathan Bainbridge. What can I do for you today?" he asked as he shook her hand.

Lynn introduced herself and told him she was looking for a small ranch.

He waved her back to his office. "How small of a place are you looking for?" he asked.

"Well, I saw this ad." She opened the paper. "It was for a place with seventy-five acres, two barns and a mobile home."

"That was the Simpson place. I'm afraid I sold it last week. A deal that good doesn't stay on the market long." He pulled a pad of paper from a wire basket on the corner of his enormous oak desk. "Why don't you tell me what you're looking for and then we can get down to brass tacks."

"I want to raise quarter horses."

He glanced up at her but didn't comment. "What's your price range?"

"I don't know. I guess a million or less."

He stared at her hard for a long second before he nodded.

"What's more important to you—acreage or buildings?"

Lynn gave it some thought. "I suppose acreage would be. I can always add buildings."

He nodded his approval. "Now you're thinking." He continued to scribble. "If you're running stock you'll need water." He stopped writing. "Mary," he called out.

The receptionist came to the door.

"Where is that flyer I gave you this morning?"

"You mean the one on the old Burton place?"

"Yeah, that's the one."

"I'll get it."

"I may have something that might interest you. This place only went on the market a couple of days ago."

Mary returned with a folder and handed it to him.

He quickly flipped it open. "It says here that it has good grass, mature oaks, two wells and a spring-fed stock tank with water year-round. I'll vouch for that tank. I've lived here all my life, and I've never known that tank to go dry." He flipped the page over. "They're selling off a hundred acres of the original homestead. There's a house and a couple of old outbuildings. The barn burnt when I was a kid and was never rebuilt. I'll warn you the old house needs a lot of work. This is the original homestead of the old Samuel Burton place. The original deed was for eight hundred acres, but the family has been selling off bits and pieces for years. Now, there's only the one boy left and he's got no interest in living out there. He has moved off to California and wants to sell off the last of the land."

"How much do they want?" Lynn asked.

"The asking price is six hundred and fifty thousand." He leaned back in his chair. "This isn't one of my listings, but if you're interested I can give the agent a call and see if we can run out there."

"I'd like to see it."

As soon as he picked the phone up to call the other agent she began to sweat. What the heck was she doing? Was she seriously considering spending six hundred and fifty thousand dollars on land when she didn't know squat about ranching? By the time he stood up and picked up his Stetson her knees were starting to knock.

He looked at her and chuckled. "Wait until you actually have to sign your name to the check," he said. "I was so nervous when I bought my first house, I completely forgot how to spell my name. I just sat there like a babbling idiot. I finally had to take my driver's license out and copy it."

Lynn laughed. "You're just trying to make me feel better."

He motioned for her to precede him to the front. "Let me tell you when you're really going to feel better. That's going to be the first time you wake up, look out your window and see your horses grazing in the field." He nodded. "Now, that's when you know you made the right decision."

Lynn's imagination produced the image of her and Crissy waking up to the view he described. She practically floated out of his office on the dream.

CHAPTER TWENTY-NINE

Some of Lynn's elation evaporated when she remembered that Crissy might not be a part of that dream anymore. Her euphoric mood was further dampened when she found Crissy and Beulah Mae still sitting on the bench when she walked out with Nathan Bainbridge.

"I'm here with friends," Lynn explained as she made a quick round of introductions. "I can follow you if you'd like."

"No, I have a Jeep. We can all ride out together."

Lynn tried not to notice that Beulah Mae and Crissy climbed into the backseat while she was left to sit up front with Nathan.

As he drove, he gave them a nonstop monologue on the history of the county. Once they left the city limits he began to point out individual ranches and rattled off the names of the owners as smoothly as a mother could her children.

They hadn't traveled far when he pulled over and pointed to

a fencerow. "The property starts here. It doesn't look like much at this point, but I think you'll soon notice a difference." He drove on another mile or so before turning off onto a graveled road. "From here on we're on your property."

Lynn liked the sound of that, even though she knew it was a selling ploy intended to get her to start identifying with the land. She couldn't keep from glancing over her shoulder at Crissy. Her heart missed a beat when she found Crissy staring at her.

Beulah Mae spoiled the moment by starting to ask questions about water-level tables and mineral rights.

Lynn faced forward and grudgingly found herself glad that Beulah Mae had asked. She hadn't known that the rights weren't automatically transferred with the land. "You mean I can own the property, but someone else can own the mineral rights?"

He nodded. "It's pretty common, actually. You'd be surprised how many people don't know that."

"Is that something I should be concerned about?"

"I always tell people to get them if they can, but unless you're planning to drill for oil, which would be a waste of time around here, don't give up a piece of property you really want because of the mineral rights."

"What about endangered species?" Beulah Mae asked. "Are there any golden-cheeked warblers or blind salamanders being protected around here?"

He smiled. "No. As far as I know there are no endangered species that would affect his property." They traveled in silence for a few minutes. They were starting up a good-sized hill when he spoke again. "You might want to turn your attention to the front here. As soon as we top this hill I think you'll be impressed."

Lynn heard a seat belt being released and a moment later Crissy was peering over the seat. Lynn had to sit on her hands to stop herself from reaching back and taking Crissy's hand. This could be the moment they had waited on for so long.

The Jeep topped the hill and stopped. Lynn's heart practically stopped with it. After stepping out of the vehicle, she did a slow one-hundred-and-eighty-degree sweep of the beautiful valley below. The gentle slopes gave way to natural plateaus and panoramic views that took her breath away.

"It's beautiful," Crissy whispered beside her.

For once Beulah Mae was being useful and had pulled Bainbridge off to the side and was peppering him with questions.

"It's everything we ever wanted," Lynn said as she turned to Crissy.

"But it's all happening so fast. I'm scared. What if we can't do it? What if we spend all this money and then fail?"

"We could always sell and move back to the city."

Crissy looked out over the view again. "How could we leave this?"

Encouraged that Crissy was still including herself when talking about the property, Lynn took a chance. "I know I'd have a much better chance of making it if you were beside me."

"What about all the arguing? Aren't you worried that we might not make it?"

"I think things will be a lot different now. I'm not saying there won't be hard times, but I really believe our roughest times are behind us."

"I want to believe that. I really do." Crissy's eyes clearly reflected her doubt. "Maybe we need some more time apart."

Lynn motioned to the valley below them. "There's a hundred acres. That should give us both plenty of room."

Before Crissy could respond Nathan called them. "If you ladies are ready, we can go on down and look at the house."

Crissy raced off to the Jeep, leaving Lynn to follow.

"The house was built in the late eighteen fifties," Nathan said as they pulled into the driveway and stopped. "Of course, there have been several renovations to add electricity, plumbing and such, but the integrity of the original design has pretty much been kept intact."

The house was a two-story, clapboard farmhouse. The large front porch made Lynn smile. All it needed to fit into her dream was a couple of rocking chairs. Along with a few planks to set them on, she thought as she looked closer and noticed that one side of the porch had collapsed.

"As I said, it needs a lot of work," Nathan said as they sat staring at the house. "It's on pier and beam, which I personally like a lot better than a concrete slab for this area. It makes it a lot easier and cheaper to fix. I doubt you'll have many problems with the foundation. When this house was built, it was made to last. Let's go in and have a look."

As they piled out of the Jeep, Crissy spied an old rose garden. She asked about it. Apparently, it was the only incentive Nathan needed to launch into a long lecture on antique roses.

Lynn tuned them out and went to examine the porch closer. A moment later, Beulah Mae slapped her on the shoulder. "It has been my observation that as long as you've got a solid foundation everything else is fixable."

Lynn looked back at the older woman grinning at her. "Why do I get the feeling you've been pulling my leg?"

"Lynn, I'm quite certain that some people would find playing with your skinny leg pleasurable. Luckily, I'm not one of them." She grasped Lynn's shoulder and held her gaze. "I want you to know something. I consider you a friend. I would never make a move on your girl. We were trying to make you jealous."

"You mean Crissy knew what you were doing?"

"Yes, nimrod, she knew. When are you two going to figure out that you love each other?"

Lynn looked away.

Beulah Mae sighed. "Okay, I'm going to break one of my longstanding golden rules and put my two cents in."

"You mean you don't normally?"

Beulah Mae gave her a scorching glare. "One of these days

me and that sassy mouth of yours are going to tango. Now listen up, nimrod."

"Will you please stop calling me that?"

"Not until you stop acting like one."

Lynn started to ask what the heck a nimrod was, but Beulah Mae's tight grasp on her shoulder stopped her.

"You two don't respect each other."

Again Lynn started to interrupt but was stopped.

"You think Crissy is a goody-two-shoes who is hell-bent on holding you back."

Lynn blushed to the roots of her hair. It was true. How many times had she thought of Crissy as an overactive do-gooder?

"And she thinks you have no ambition and that you only want to take the easy way out."

"I work my ass off. All I've ever done is dream about the day I'd have a ranch."

Beulah Mae tapped Lynn's forehead. "That's her point. All you do is dream." She shook her head. "Let me ask you something. If you hadn't won this lottery, do you think you would have ever been able to afford a ranch?"

Lynn folded her arms across her chest. "Once Crissy went to work teaching we could have saved everything I made."

"How long would it have taken you to save enough? Sure, maybe you could have scraped enough together for a down payment in ten years, but you're fighting an uphill battle, because while you're saving the cost of living is still climbing." She stopped short. "Look, I'm not going to say you couldn't have eventually done it. I mean, after all, that's the whole point of the big American dream, right?" She patted Lynn's shoulder. "I'm simply trying to tell you that you two need to sit down and have a real heart-to-heart talk." She looked Lynn square in the eye. "If you don't, you aren't going to make it." She turned and slowly started making her way to where the other two were still talking about roses.

Lynn stood staring after her and feeling more confused and scared than ever.

"Come on, let's look inside," Nathan called out to her.

Lynn glanced over and saw Crissy following Nathan. *I'm not going to lose her*, she told herself as she fell into step with them. She filed the conversation with Beulah Mae away. She would analyze it word by word later when she was alone. Right now she needed to concentrate on looking this place over.

Once they were inside, Lynn had serious doubts about the condition of the house, but Crissy and Beulah Mae scoffed at her doubts. Within ten minutes, Crissy already knew what colors the walls should be painted and what type of furniture should be in each room. Lynn tried to convince herself that Crissy was picturing herself in this house. That she saw them living here together.

"What do you think?" Nathan asked when the other two had wandered off.

"You're right. The house needs a lot of work. I really like it, but this is the first place I've looked at. Maybe I should look at a few more before I decide."

He nodded. "I understand that and I don't mean to pressure you, but you might not want to put it off too much. I don't think this place will stay on the market long."

"Can you give me a minute?"

"Sure. I'm not suggesting you decide right now."

She nodded and walked outside onto the large back porch. A slight southerly breeze ruffled her hair. She wondered how many people had stood here in this very spot and looked out over the land as she was doing. Had some woman stood here to survey the area for Union soldiers or marauding Indians before making her way out to tend the livestock or her vegetable garden?

She noticed the two sheds. Both needed work. She carefully made her way down the rickety steps and over to the nearest shed. It was the smaller of the two and appeared to be a toolshed.

She peeked inside. It was empty except for a couple of rusty paint cans. The second shed was larger and might have been a workshop at one time. She tried to open the door, but it was jammed.

Between the outbuildings was a large overgrown garden. Her heart gave a small leap. Crissy would love it. She continued on around the larger shed. As she stepped around behind it she stopped and stared in awe at the large patch of wild daisies. She smiled and turned back to the house. There was no longer any doubt in her mind that she had found her home.

Lynn found Crissy and Nathan in the kitchen. He was telling her how to restore the old hardwood floors. When he saw Lynn he nodded toward the large side windows.

"I was telling your"—he hesitated slightly—"friend that the morning sun will pour through these windows."

Lynn studied the room. The appliances were old but could easily be replaced. The counters and lower cabinets were in bad shape, but the glass-paneled doors on the top cabinets would definitely remain.

"Mr. Bainbridge, I'd like to talk to Crissy a moment."

"Hey, call me Nathan. I'll run along and find Beulah Mae." He smiled and winked. "I'll bet by now she'll have a couple of more questions for me."

"Come on," Lynn said to Crissy. "I want to show you something." She led the way back out to the garden area. "Look at this garden."

Crissy gasped. "It's huge."

"It's overgrown, but together we could work it back into shape."

"Lynn, this place is everything you ever wanted."

"It's everything *we* wanted," Lynn said.

Crissy took a step away from her.

Lynn thought of the conversation she'd had with Beulah Mae. If she could take this place and turn it into the ranch she had dreamed of for so long, then Crissy would see that she wasn't just a dreamer. She'd get this place back in order, and once the barns were built, she'd buy a few horses. "You're right. I need to do this."

Crissy looked at her, clearly taken aback.

Lynn quickly validated her point. "The ranch was always more my dream than it was yours. Your dream was to teach at a small school. I simply took it and incorporated it into my fantasy life."

"But—" Crissy began.

"No, you're right." Lynn glanced at her watch. "Come on. It's getting late." She rushed back to the house and found Nathan sitting on the back porch step talking to Beulah Mae. "I've changed my mind," she told him. "This place has everything I was looking for. I want it."

He smiled brightly. "Then let's get on back to the office and put in a bid."

The trip back to the real estate office was much quieter, but Lynn didn't mind. She was busy wondering how long it would take to get the ranch operational.

When they reached the real estate office Crissy announced that she and Beulah Mae were going to a nearby café for coffee. Lynn agreed to meet them there as soon as possible.

"Have you given any thought to how much you want to offer?" he asked as he settled behind his desk.

Lynn had no experience with buying property, but she didn't want to appear completely naïve. "I'm not familiar with land prices here. To be honest with you, I wasn't really expecting to find anything so quickly. Do you think their asking price is fair?"

He leaned back in his chair. "The house is going to need a lot of work, but if you're ready to do it you'll have a beautiful home. You can't get a house of that quality built today. I believe the strongest selling points are those panoramic views and the water." He seemed to give it some thought. "I never recommend a bid price to a client, but I will tell you this. If you're planning on living out here and you're able and willing to put some sweat equity into the old place, you'd have yourself a beautiful place at a fair price. However, if you're just looking for some land to run some stock on you might think about offering a little less or even looking at other property."

"That's good enough for me. I'll offer full asking price." She didn't want to chance offering less and have someone outbid her. She had the money, so why take the risk?

Nathan prepared the paperwork to submit the bid on the property. When he tactfully probed about financing, she floored him when she announced she wouldn't be requiring outside financing.

After they had completed the paperwork for the bid proposal, he accompanied her back into the outer office.

"Mary, this is Lynn Strickland. She put a bid in for the old Burton place."

Mary smiled. "Oh, that's a wonderful old spot. I remember my grandpa telling me about the dances they used to have there. He called Old Man Burton a fiddle-playing fool."

"Both of his boys were too," Nathan said. "I remember listening to them play."

"How long will it be before I know if they've accepted my bid?"

"I normally tell my clients that it'll be five to seven days before they hear back from a bid," he said. "Sometimes it's less and on rare occasions more."

Lynn thanked him for all his help and walked out. As she strolled down the sidewalk she couldn't stop smiling. She wouldn't allow herself to think about her bid not being accepted. In her heart she truly believed that property was meant for her. She couldn't wait to bring her mom up to see it.

CHAPTER THIRTY

The ride back from Bandera had been quiet. Once more Crissy sat in the middle but it seemed to Lynn that she sat closer to her. She warned herself not to let her imagination run wild. When she dropped them off at the nursing home, she was pleasantly surprised when Crissy hung back.

"Did I tell you I got the starter fixed on my car?"

Lynn stared at her in amazement. It was so like Crissy to have three million dollars in the bank and still drive that broken-down heap. "Why don't you start thinking about buying a new car? You need something dependable."

"I'll think about it." Crissy hesitated. "Maybe we could go to dinner either Friday night or Saturday and talk about it."

"That would be a nice change, us in a restaurant being waited on rather than the other way around." Lynn chuckled. "Friday would be better for me." Friday was better because it allowed her to be with Crissy sooner. "I could pick you up around seven. We could go to Kim's." Kim's was a burger joint that they loved to eat at whenever they could spare the money.

"I'd like that." Crissy started to lean forward.

For a moment Lynn thought she was going to kiss her, but she stopped sharply, turned and hopped out of the truck.

"Call me if you hear anything about the land," Crissy said from the safety of the ground.

"I will."

After the door closed behind Crissy, Lynn waved to Beulah Mae then drove away. She had intended to go straight to her mom's but changed her mind and stopped to get a cell phone. She wanted to make certain Nathan Bainbridge would be able to locate her.

It was almost five when Lynn arrived back at her mom's and found a strange car parked in front of the trailer. When she went in, her mom and Jaime were sitting at the table.

"Hey, it's the happy couple," she said.

He stood to shake her hand. "I'm not sure half of the happy couple is very happy right now," he warned, nodding to her mom.

"What's wrong?" she asked as she placed a hand on her mom's shoulder.

"I want a June wedding," Violet announced.

"Okay. So what's the problem?"

"She wants it to be this June," he said.

Lynn frowned. "Mom, I don't know much about weddings, but don't they take a long time to plan?"

"Yes, but there has to be some way around that." She pushed a calendar around so that Lynn could see it. "Look, we could have it on the thirtieth of June. That's a Saturday and it gives us almost ten full weeks. If God built the world in seven days I don't see why we can't put a simple wedding together in ten weeks."

Lynn shrugged. "Strangely enough, when you put it that way

I can see your point. I guess finding a church would be the hardest part. I can get my friends to help me with the food."

Jaime moved back to the table. "Maybe you had better sit down and hear her plans before you start volunteering too much," he said.

Lynn held up a hand. "Can you give me a couple of minutes?" She quickly explained about getting the cell phone as she plugged it in to charge the battery. She wasn't taking any chances on Nathan not being able to locate her. She found his card in her pocket and used the landline in the kitchen to call. When Mary answered, Lynn gave her the new number as a backup contact. Then she went to the table and sat down. "Okay, I'm ready. What's going on?"

"I've already told you I want a big wedding," her mom said.

"Yes, you did." Lynn noticed the expression on Jaime's face and asked, "How big?"

"The guest list is teetering at three hundred right now," he said.

Lynn blinked in amazement. "Do you even know three hundred people?" she asked without thinking. Her thoughtlessness earned her a scorching glare from her mom. "Sorry," she mumbled. After a moment she added, "Mom, how are you going to find a hall big enough for that many people on such short notice? You know I'll do anything I can to help, but I can't handle cooking for three hundred people. I was thinking more like a couple of dozen. We'll have to hire a caterer and I'm not sure there's enough time. Since June is such a busy month for weddings. Won't everything already be booked?"

Violet folded her arms on the table. She looked down to hide the tears but not before Jaime saw them.

"Ah, chica," he murmured. "If you want to be married in June, then June it is and you can invite as many people as you want. We'll find some way to feed them."

"You mean it?" she asked, wiping the tears from her eyes.

"Yes." He patted her hand. "But don't yell at me if we have to hold the reception at Alamo Stadium and serve bread and water." He looked at Lynn and winked. "If we can't get a caterer, I have a cousin who drives a delivery truck for Mrs. Baird's Bread, so I'm fairly certain I can get enough loaves of bread to feed everyone."

Her mom pushed him away gently. "We can do this if we all pull together," she insisted as she leaned over and kissed his cheek. "I know June is a busy month, but I can't believe that every caterer in this city is booked. We'll just have to dig a little deeper until we find one."

Lynn saw her point but wondered how many calls would have to be made before they found someone.

"Violet said you were looking for land," Jaime said.

Lynn suspected he was more interested in changing the subject than he was in her land search. "I actually ended up putting a bid in for a place in Bandera." She gave them a rundown on the property. As soon as she finished she started to the refrigerator. "I'm starving." Beulah Mae and Crissy had eaten while she was filling out the paperwork on the bid. They had offered to sit with her while she ate, but she was too eager to get home.

"Why don't I take everyone to dinner?" Jaime offered.

"No. Let's order pizza and finish going over the invitation list," Violet said.

Lynn hid her smile as she reached for the phone. She had a feeling the next ten weeks were going to be a little hectic for Jaime. After placing the pizza order, she asked how the restaurant renovations were coming along.

"Slow," Jaime said. "I thought we could tear out the sheetrock in one day, but we only got about half of the work I expected done today."

"I'm not doing anything tomorrow," Lynn said as she poured herself a glass of milk. "If you like, I can come over and help out."

"We could use the help," he said before turning his attention back to his fiancée. "Now, chica, let's see if we can look at that list a little bit more."

By nine o'clock her mom had settled down and become a little more rational about the wedding. The invitation list had been reduced to two hundred and twenty-seven people. Jaime had been placed in charge of locating a hall for the reception and finding a church. Lynn volunteered to find a caterer and a band. Violet took on making arrangements for the cake, the invitations and flowers.

With a rough plan in place, Lynn bid them good night and went to her room. She heard Jaime leave a short time later. Despite being tired, she couldn't sleep. She was too busy thinking about the place that she was already beginning to think of as home. The house needed a lot of work that was way beyond her limited hammering-a-nail-in-a-board skill level. Once her bid was accepted, and she refused to believe it wouldn't be, she'd speak to Nathan Bainbridge. Maybe he could recommend a company to handle the renovations.

Her thoughts turned to Crissy. She had looked tired today. Was it possible that she wasn't sleeping either? Lynn considered calling her but quickly changed her mind. Crissy needed time. Once the house was repaired, she would have the barn and corrals built. Then she would purchase a few horses. Crissy would see that there was more to her than talk.

She closed her eyes and envisioned the house repaired and boasting a new coat of paint—white with green trim. On the front porch were two sturdy wooden rocking chairs. In the chairs sat two older women. She strained her eyes to see who they were. She almost had them identified before she drifted off to sleep.

CHAPTER THIRTY-ONE

The following morning Lynn rode with her mom to the restaurant. As soon as she saw the building she remembered it. Crissy had been right when she'd said it was huge.

"Mom, this place is enormous. Do you think you'll ever be able to fill all this space?"

"We've talked about turning the back portion into a party room."

"It's certainly big enough, and you've got a decent-sized parking area."

"Oh, parking isn't a problem. All of those businesses in that strip mall next door close around eight and we can use that lot then," her mom said as they made their way toward the building.

Once inside Lynn gave a slow whistle. "This place is a disaster." She looked around. It presented a seemingly endless task. She could see where they had ripped out some of the sheetrock.

"I think you guys had better start thinking about hiring someone to renovate this place for you."

"Oh, no. We know it's going to be a lot of hard work, but we want to do it ourselves."

Lynn knew when not to push. "What happened to that wall?" About twelve feet of the wall was riddled with holes that ranged from fist-sized to a couple of feet in diameter. It looked as though a gigantic shotgun had blasted it.

"The owner let his brother use the place as a warehouse. He tried to open up the space by removing the wall, but the police found him before he finished it."

"What did they get him for?"

"He liked to collect things that didn't belong to him." She shrugged. "The condition of the building is the reason the rent is so cheap. We agreed to handle all the repairs if the owner would split the cost of the materials."

"When are you planning on opening?"

"We were hoping to open in May."

Lynn looked around the room and smiled as a thought came to her.

"Why are you smiling?"

"I think you can kill two birds with one stone."

"What are you talking—oh, no, ma'am. I'm not getting married in this dump."

"It won't be a dump by June. Look at this place. It would be perfect. If you moved the wedding up to the first of June and moved the opening date of the restaurant back a little it would be perfect."

Her mom glanced around. "I don't know."

"We'll decorate it. Crissy is good with stuff like that and her mom . . . Well, you've seen all that foofaraw in her house."

Violet nodded. "Dolores does have an eye, and I love what she did with her dining room."

"You two are here bright and early," Jaime called as he came through a side door.

"Lynn just had a great idea. She suggested we have the reception here."

Jaime looked around. "What about the customers?"

"We move the wedding up to the first of June and move the restaurant's opening back."

He nodded. "It would certainly give us a bit of breathing room," he agreed. "We'd save a lot of money by not having to rent a hall, the chairs and tablecloths—"

"The kitchen would be perfect for the caterer," Lynn said.

Jaime rubbed his hands together and smiled. "I like it. We have a hall, so that means I've already finished half of the things on my wedding to-do list."

Violet shook her head. "Isn't that just like a man?" She took his arm. "Well, don't worry. I'm certain I can find a few more things to add to your list."

He shook his head. "Isn't that just like a woman?"

"Where do you want me to start working?" Lynn asked.

Jaime pointed to the damaged wall. "I'm going to tear out that sheetrock. It'll be a lot easier than trying to patch all those holes."

Lynn pulled a pair of gloves from her pocket. "This is right up my alley. I'm good at tearing stuff up." It took her a couple of minutes to get the hang of swinging the large hammer at the proper angle to do the most damage while still avoiding the wall studs, but soon the sheetrock began to come down.

When they stopped for lunch she was surprised to notice that it was raining again. She started to call Crissy on the pretext of relaying her new cell phone number but realized Crissy would be in class, so she called Beulah Mae instead. When Beulah Mae didn't answer Lynn left a message with her new phone number.

The rain continued throughout the day and into the night. When Lynn woke up on Wednesday morning to hear the rain still slapping against the roof, she was tempted to pull the cover

over her head, but she had promised to help her mom and Jaime again. Wall demolition was harder than she had anticipated. As she eased her sore body from the bed, she realized that tonight's game would be cancelled. The ball field was undoubtedly flooded. She held on to a flimsy hope that by some miracle it wouldn't be cancelled. She could tolerate any amount of mud and muck for a chance to spend a few hours with Crissy.

Later, as she and her mom were driving to the restaurant, she was forced to turn the wipers on high. "Can you believe this rain?" she asked.

"I'm just glad we're working inside and that this won't delay us," her mom said.

"The game will be rained out tonight." She could no longer kid herself.

"Have you talked to Crissy since Monday?"

"No. I didn't want her to feel like I'm pressuring her."

Her mom was silent for a moment. "Be careful that you don't back off so much that she starts to think that you have no interest in making the relationship work."

The rain continued throughout the day. When Lynn and her mom got home that afternoon there was a message from the team captain informing Lynn that the game had indeed been cancelled. Tired from working, she took a hot shower and changed into sweats. After her mom left to have dinner with Jaime, Lynn stretched out on the couch and flipped on the television. A couple of hours later, the phone woke her. It was Crissy.

"The field is under about six inches of water," Crissy said. "It'll take days to dry out."

Lynn struggled with her conflicting emotions. She had really been looking forward to spending time with Crissy, but there was still a measure of relief in not having to see the gang. She knew she had to face them eventually.

"Have you heard anything from the Realtor?"

"No. He said he probably wouldn't know anything until the end of the week or later," Lynn said.

"What have you been doing now that you're not working?"

"I helped Mom and Jaime at the restaurant yesterday and today. Guess what? They're getting married."

"Wow! That was fast."

"Actually, I think it was a lot more serious before he left than she ever let on. If his dad hadn't died, I bet they would have been married years ago."

"You make sure I'm on the invitation list."

"Well . . . I sort of volunteered you to help with the decorating."

"Oh, did you now?"

Lynn thought it was best to air all her careless assumptions at once. "I volunteered your mom, too." She quickly explained how their names had been offered as unpaid labor. "If you'd rather not—"

"Stop it. I love your mom. Of course we'll help." She giggled. "Look at me. I'm as bad as you are. I just volunteered Mom. But we both know that she thrives on this sort of stuff."

The sweet sound of Crissy's laughter caused a physical pain deep within Lynn. She wouldn't be able to see her until Friday. It was almost more than she could bear. She made a quick decision. "Why don't we get the gang together for dinner tomorrow night?" She cringed when Crissy hesitated and then avoided the question.

"Everyone was asking about you at the barbecue on Sunday," Crissy said. "I had to tell them that we're . . . taking some time apart."

Lynn hadn't missed the fact that Crissy hadn't described their situation as being a breakup. She was heartened by the distinction. "I'm sorry I flaked out on you. I should've been there to help you tell everyone."

"They were really upset. I gave them your mom's number but told them I thought you might need a little time. I'm sorry if I misspoke."

Lynn hadn't realized her reluctance to face the group had been so obvious. On some level she knew she wasn't being rational. After all, these were her friends. "No. You were right."

"It might be better if I wasn't along for dinner," Crissy said. "If we both go, it'll only confuse the situation."

Any elation Lynn had been enjoying was crushed. She managed to mumble an agreement. She knew she wouldn't call them for dinner. The outing had been an excuse to see Crissy. She didn't think she could stand being around them without Crissy. It would be too painful.

Before she could say anything more, Crissy inadvertently gave her an out. "Karen and Deb probably won't be able to go. They both have papers due. The game being rained out helped both of them."

"I'll wait. Maybe we can get together after everyone is out of school. Speaking of which, how are you doing with your classes? I was surprised you were able to go Monday."

"Since I've quit working, I've managed to get caught up on everything. It feels strange not having to get up at four or five in the morning to study. I actually watched a movie Sunday night."

Lynn laughed. "The money is making us crazy. I got a cell phone."

"No! You?"

Lynn gave her the number. "I wanted to make sure the Realtor could find me."

"That place was beautiful. I'm glad you saw the potential the old house had. I could tell you really liked it."

"Crissy, everything about the place felt right." She wanted to add that it was everything they had ever dreamed of but decided not to push the point.

"I hope everything works out the way you want."

Lynn's breath caught. "I hope so too." If all her dreams came true, they would soon be living at and working the ranch together. After making sure they were still on for dinner at Kim's on Friday, she hung up.

CHAPTER THIRTY-TWO

The call from Nathan Bainbridge finally came late Friday afternoon. Lynn was at the restaurant helping her mom and Jaime and dreaming about her dinner date with Crissy. Nathan didn't pull any punches when he told her the bad news. Someone had outbid her on the property.

Lynn was stunned. She had been so certain she would get the land. "Is there anything else I can do?"

"No. Apparently, the other bid was quite a bit over the asking price. Naturally, the owner accepted that offer. The only possibility is that for some reason the buyer pulls out at the last minute or there's some sort of mortgage problem. Don't get your hopes up. That rarely happens." He cleared his throat. "But listen, don't let this discourage you. There are plenty of other places in the area that are just as nice. We'll find something for you. The only other listing I have now that's close to your needs is a little over three hundred acres."

"That's too big," she said. She still couldn't believe she hadn't gotten the ranch. She heard papers rustling.

"I don't have anything smaller at this time, but I'll start checking around. I'm sure something will come along." He promised to give her a call as soon as he had a promising lead and hung up.

Lynn turned to find Jaime and her mother standing behind her. "I didn't get the land. Someone outbid me."

Her mother hugged her. "I'm sorry. I know you really wanted it to work out."

"I'm sure something will come along," Jaime said. He took his gloves off. "I think it's time to call it a day."

"Amen," her mother replied.

"Why don't I take you two to dinner tonight?" Jaime said.

"I'm having dinner with Crissy," Lynn said, although she no longer felt like eating.

"I'll take you up on that offer of dinner." Her mom squeezed his arm.

They quickly put their tools away and dumped the garbage they had generated during the day before heading home to get cleaned up.

As her mom drove, Lynn closed her eyes and rested her head against the back of the seat. "I can't believe someone else is getting the place. I was so sure."

Before her mom could respond the cell phone rang again. Lynn snatched it off her belt, hoping it was Bainbridge calling her back to tell her that there had been some mistake, that her bid had been accepted after all. She was so positive it would be him that it took her a moment to recognize Beulah Mae's voice.

"I've been sprung," she announced.

"What?"

"I'm free to leave whenever I want. The psychiatrist and doctor found me both mentally competent and physically capable. I didn't even have to retake the physical since I did so well on the last one and it had been less than six months since I took it."

"I thought you weren't going to be able to talk to the psychiatrist until next week."

Beulah Mae laughed. "He had a cancellation, and by some miracle my name was moved up to fill it."

"How did you manage that?"

"Hey, I never tell my secrets."

"He said you could leave."

"There are a few stipulations."

"Such as?"

"I can't officially check out of here yet." She snorted. "I told you he would cover his butt. He sort of gave me a short leave of absence."

Lynn waited for her to explain.

"I told him I wanted to go back home. He agreed to let me leave on my own for two weeks. That should give me time to get home and see if there is any family around still. And if so, do I want to live with them or find a facility nearby? If not"—she hesitated slightly—"I come back here." She quickly reverted to her usual good humor. "Anyway, I'm calling to let you know where I'll be."

Lynn frowned. "How are you traveling?"

"Since I'm not sneaking off, I can take the bus."

Lynn didn't like the idea of her alone on a bus. "Why don't you fly?"

"I'm not very fond of airplanes."

"You're afraid to fly?" Lynn was amazed. She couldn't imagine Beulah Mae being afraid of anything.

"I didn't say I was afraid. I said I didn't like it."

Lynn knew she had to be careful with the way she presented the offer she was about to make. If Beulah Mae sensed that Lynn didn't think she was capable of making the trip alone she would get bullheaded stubborn and go alone just to prove Lynn wrong.

"After that last fiasco I guess you don't trust me to drive you."

"Hey, I didn't say that. I know you're busy helping your mom, and as soon as that land deal goes through you'll really be hopping."

Lynn didn't feel like talking about the land. She needed to get used to the idea first. "Mom and Jaime pretty much have everything covered. I think I'm getting in their way." She winked when her mom glanced at her.

Beulah Mae was quiet for a moment. "Well, if you want to take a ride up that way, I'd sure appreciate the company."

"It should be easier this time around, since I've got a vehicle that I can drive."

"Thank God for that. I wouldn't have the nerve to call Jay again."

"When do you want to leave?"

"The sooner the better. I'm sitting on go."

"How long should I plan on staying?" Lynn didn't want to be gone for two weeks.

"You can do it in two days of easy travel, less if you push hard. You don't have to hang around and wait for me. If it doesn't work out I can always take the bus back."

"Then let's take off early tomorrow morning. Is seven too early?"

"No, that's perfect. Can you go by that bakery and get some more of those little cinnamon rolls for the road?"

"Sure. I can stop by there on my way over." Lynn put the phone away. "That was Beulah Mae. She finagled her way in to see the psychiatrist early and he gave her a two-week leave."

"You're going with her?"

"I'm going to drive her up. She was intending to take the bus, but I'd rather she didn't." She rubbed her chin. "I sure hope she still has family around there. I hate the idea of leaving her alone, but I don't want to be gone that long."

"If you're saying that because of the restaurant, Jaime and I can handle it."

"I know you can. There are other things, too. As it is I'm going to miss practice on Sunday." She felt a little guilty for the relief she felt. "I need to find a place. I can't keep living with you forever."

Her mom patted Lynn's arm. "You know as long as I'm alive you'll always have a place to stay."

Tears burned Lynn's eyes. To cover the sudden rush of emotion, she turned to humor. "Thanks, Mom. How do you think Jaime will feel about me coming with you guys on your honeymoon?"

"Sweetie, I said you'd have a place to stay. I didn't necessarily mean that it would be with me."

"Ouch!"

CHAPTER THIRTY-THREE

After getting out of the shower, Lynn pulled on a robe and fell across the bed. She still couldn't believe she hadn't gotten the land. She cursed herself for not offering more. Then she cursed the Realtor. Why hadn't he told her to bid more? Shouldn't he have known that the bidding would be high? She flipped over and stared at the ceiling. The money was supposed to have made everything simpler, but nothing seemed easier. Her mom and Jaime still insisted on doing the repairs themselves. Crissy was still driving that same old battered car, and she was still looking for a place of her own.

A knock on the door woke her. She glanced around, unable to believe she had fallen asleep.

"Lynn," her mom called out. "I'm getting ready to leave for dinner. Are you awake? It's almost seven. Weren't you supposed to meet Crissy?"

Lynn sprang off the bed. "I'm up, Mom. Thanks." She yanked on her favorite jeans and polo shirt before grabbing her sneakers and pulling them on. She ran her fingers through her hair as she picked up her keys and wallet. She reached for the cell phone and stopped. It had been a silly, impulsive decision to get it. Nathan Bainbridge could have left the message on her mom's answering machine. She stared at the phone for a long moment before finally clipping it to her jeans. At least she could put it to use calling Crissy to let her know she was running late.

As she passed by the kitchen stove the clock indicated it was only six fifty. She could be at Crissy's in twenty minutes. Being ten minutes late was nothing to sweat over. She relaxed and took time to grab a soda from the refrigerator. As she bent over the cell phone twisted and dug into her side. How did people walk around with these things all day? she wondered as she removed it and set it on the counter.

Thirty minutes later she found herself stuck in the middle lane with no place to go. The radio announcer was making jokes about the eighteen-wheeler filled with chocolate bars that had caught on fire. The oozing mess was pouring onto the roadway six miles ahead of her. Emergency personnel had completely closed the road. The exit to Crissy's was a mile beyond the truck. When the wise-cracking announcer started talking about marshmallows and graham crackers, Lynn turned the radio off.

To make matters worse, one of the trucks stuck beside her was an oversized cattle truck filled with hot, frightened cattle. The idiotic honking of the guy behind her wasn't helping anything.

An hour later, things slowly began to improve when the police at the accident site managed to clear one shoulder of the road and started directing traffic onto it. By the time Lynn finally screeched to a stop in front of Crissy's house it was already a little after nine. She ran to the door and knocked. She was beginning to wonder if Crissy was going to answer when the porch light came on and the door opened. It didn't take a genius to see she was in deep trouble.

"I'm sorry." She was trying to pour the story out so quickly that most of what she was saying was incomprehensible even to her own ears.

Crissy finally held up a hand to stop her. "Why didn't you call?"

"I was stuck in traffic. I couldn't."

"I thought you had a cell phone."

Lynn wondered what had possessed her to tell Crissy about the phone. Now it would be nothing but trouble. She'd have to keep it with her all the time. "I'm not used to carrying it. I forgot it."

"You mean you didn't like having to keep up with it, so you left it at home," Crissy said.

Lynn slumped against the doorjamb. "I didn't think I'd need the damn phone."

Crissy sighed. "I'm starved. Let's get over to Kim's before they close." She quickly locked the door.

As they approached the truck she put her hand to her nose. "What is that smell? Have you been hauling manure?"

"No. I was stuck next to a cattle truck. It'll be a while before I'll want to eat beef again." Suddenly the last thing she wanted was a hamburger. She was on the verge of suggesting another place when she saw the flash of an almost sadistic smile cross Crissy's face and realized payback was on its way. They would definitely be eating at Kim's tonight.

Conversation on the ride to the restaurant could best be described as short and sporadic. She wanted to tell Crissy about Nathan's call but couldn't bring herself to talk about it. So she concentrated on driving.

At Kim's, Lynn quickly discovered that once she rejected all the menu's entrées that contained beef the only thing that remained was chicken nuggets. One bite of the rubbery, beige-colored mystery meat was all she could handle. She gobbled her fries and eyed Crissy's fries, hoping for a handout that never materialized.

She struggled for something to say that would make things better. "Would you like for me to go with you to pick out a new car?"

"No, thanks. I'll take my dad. He knows a lot about cars."

Lynn bit back her caustic reply. She wanted to talk about the ranch but was afraid Crissy would respond with another flippant remark. Instead, she stormed back to the counter and ordered a large serving of onion rings and another of chili fries. Crissy hated both.

By the time they made it back to Crissy's house, Lynn was certain she would die from the heartburn that had resulted from her childish impulse. Her misery didn't stop her from crawling out of the truck and walking Crissy to the door.

"I'm really sorry I was late," she said. "I promise I'll keep the phone with me from now on."

"You should keep it with you. You never know when the Realtor will call."

"I didn't get the land. He called this afternoon and—" To her embarrassment her voice broke. She turned to leave, but Crissy grabbed her arm.

"Why didn't you tell me sooner?"

Lynn brushed at the betraying tears that kept trying to slip down her cheek. "Why? It's just one more thing I fucked up."

"How did you mess it up?"

"My bid was too low. The other bid was above what the seller was asking." She pulled away. "I have to go."

"Lynn, please. Stay and talk to me."

"I'm tired and need to get home. I'm driving Beulah Mae to Arkansas tomorrow." She gave a quick wave as she headed toward the truck. As she drove off she noticed in her rearview mirror that Crissy was still standing on the porch watching her.

Why did everything have to be so complicated?

She stopped at a self-service car wash and cleaned her truck before she drove to a convenience store to top off the gas tank and buy a road atlas. On her way out she noticed an ATM and decided to get some extra cash. At least she would be prepared for her trip with Beulah Mae.

CHAPTER THIRTY-FOUR

The following morning Lynn threw a couple of changes of clothes into her duffel before she grabbed her keys and cell phone. Her mom was still sleeping so Lynn left a note on the table reminding her that she was leaving with Beulah Mae. She promised to call if she decided not to drive straight back. She put the note on the table where her mom always sat to have her morning coffee and placed a salt shaker on it to keep it in place. Then she quickly wrote a note for Mr. Greenberg and Mrs. Harmon telling them she would be by later in the week to visit. She was about to walk away when she noticed a stack of mail. The envelope on top had her name on it. She ripped it open and found the credit card she had applied for when she opened her new account. She quickly followed the instructions on how to activate the card, signed it and slipped it into her wallet. It might prove useful on the trip. At the last minute she grabbed a coffee thermos from beneath the counter. She would have it filled and buy a couple of travel mugs at the bakery.

Lynn pulled into the parking lot of the nursing home at five minutes before seven. She was about to park when she saw Beulah Mae coming out to meet her. After pulling alongside her, she got out and took her suitcase, opened the rear door and tossed it in with her own bag.

"Did you get the cinnamon rolls?" Beulah Mae asked as she scurried around to the other side of the truck.

"I told you I'd bring them, didn't I?"

"You're in one of your moods. I should have taken the bus."

"It's not too late. I can drop you off." She slammed the door and started around the truck to help Beulah Mae in. Once she had her passenger safely tucked away in the truck, she ran inside the nursing home and dropped off the notes for Mr. Greenberg and Mrs. Harmon at the front desk. When they were both settled inside the truck, she apologized. "I'm sorry. I guess I am in a pretty pissy mood."

"You need a long weekend with that hot girlfriend of yours."

After the awkward evening they had just shared, Lynn doubted Crissy would be very interested in spending any time with her and said as much.

"Let me guess. You two are fighting again." Beulah Mae tore into the box of cinnamon rolls while Lynn poured them each a cup of coffee. She set hers in the cup holder.

As she drove toward the interstate she recounted the events of the previous day. She started with Nathan Bainbridge's call and finished with her leaving Crissy's house without talking.

Beulah Mae seemed to be on the verge of saying something but must have thought better of it and turned her attention to a second cinnamon roll.

"Why do you like those things so much?" Lynn asked as she reached for her coffee.

"I like the way they make them small and the centers aren't so smushy. I don't like all that bread that you end up with when you get the bigger ones."

"What you really mean is you like the icing?"

Beulah Mae smiled and nodded. "That could be it too." After a minute, she added, "I'm really sorry about that property thing. I know how much it meant to you."

"I was just so sure I'd get it." She sat her coffee down and merged onto the interstate. "After I won that money I though all my major problems were over."

Beulah Mae polished off the cinnamon roll and wiped her fingers on a napkin. "As you get older you'll discover that money settles very little. It helps to keep the Man happy. Other than that, it's just something most people spend their whole lives chasing."

"So are you saying that no matter what I do, I'll always be miserable?"

"No." She stopped and stared out the window for a long moment.

Lynn had to concentrate on driving. Despite the early weekend hour, traffic was already heavy. She wondered if Beulah Mae had any intention of answering her. Maybe she hadn't heard the question.

"You're still young," Beulah Mae said suddenly. "I know you won't fully understand this right now, but there are so many things you still have to learn. It's the sort of stuff that you only learn by living it." She turned back toward Lynn. "I'm going to tell you something that's probably going to tick you off."

"Stop." Lynn shook her head. "We've got a long trip ahead of us. Can we please try to get through it without pissing each other off?"

Beulah Mae shifted around in the seat until she was more comfortable. "I guess we can try, but it's sure going to limit the conversation with you."

Lynn had to laugh. "Am I really that bad?"

"The last few weeks with you have been about as much fun as

a toothache."

"I promise I'll try to be less of a pain during the trip. Okay?"

"That would be a nice treat."

Lynn noticed that Beulah Mae had barely touched her coffee and suspected she might know why. "I thought I'd stop every couple of hours to stretch my legs, if that's okay with you."

"That sounds perfect." Beulah Mae picked up the coffee cup and sipped. "At least you know how to buy good coffee."

"How do you know I didn't make it?"

"I had your coffee once when you invited me over for dinner. I still haven't forgotten it."

"Well, enjoy your coffee. I'm planning on stopping in Austin, but if you need to stop before then just let me know."

"Did I ever tell you about the twins I dated when I lived in Austin? You talk about different personalities. One was an angel and the other was a devil. Oh, what a devil she was."

"How many girlfriends have you had anyway?"

Beulah Mae drummed her fingers on her leg. "Now that's an interesting question. Let me see. After Miss Rachel Rogers, there was Sally Jean. I haven't thought about her in years. Prettiest little thing you ever saw."

She launched into a long rendition about her previous girl-friends. She was only up to 1998 when they reached the city limits of Texarkana, Texas, seven hours later.

"I'm tired," she said without warning. "Why don't we stop here for the night?"

Although it was only a little after two in the afternoon, Lynn was actually grateful for the suggestion. She was exhausted. Plus, after listening all day to Beulah Mae's sexual exploits, she needed a cold shower.

They followed the signs to a Ramada Inn. Within a matter of minutes they had a room that, over Lynn's strong objections, Beulah Mae had insisted on paying for.

"Why don't we rest for a while and then we'll go somewhere

and have a nice dinner?" Lynn suggested. Beulah Mae looked as tired as Lynn felt.

"All right. I'll let you rest a while and then I'll take you around and show you some of the sights."

"I didn't know you had lived here."

Beulah Mae chuckled. "Haven't you figured it out yet? I'm like that old song. I've been everywhere."

Lynn unlocked the door and stepped into the room. She had barely set her bag down when she heard Beulah Mae give a loud sigh and collapse across the bed nearest the door.

"Lord, thank you for this wonderful bed," Beulah Mae said as she kicked off her shoes and almost instantly feel asleep.

Lynn shook her head in amazement and went to shower. As the hot water pounded down on her she considered calling Crissy. She missed talking to her. She missed their lazy Sunday mornings lying in bed rehashing all that had happened during the week. The talk would eventually end with them cuddling, which always led to lovemaking. A wave of desire struck her. She cursed Beulah Mae's stories and turned the cold water on higher. By the time she finally stepped out of the shower her teeth were practically chattering. She slipped on the old sweatshirt and pants she had brought along to sleep in and stretched across the other bed.

The sound of laughing children and rolling suitcases woke her. She sat up disoriented and blurry-eyed.

"Dang, if that's the way you normally look in the morning, it's no wonder that Crissy left you." Beulah Mae was sitting in the chair near the television, which was on but muted. The drapes were partially opened, allowing a bright strip of sunlight to shine through the gauzy sheers.

Lynn squinted and tried to speak. It took her a moment to regain her voice. "Do you lie awake at night thinking of ways to harass me?"

"No. It just comes to me." Beulah Mae flipped off the television. "It's after nine. We should probably get started."

Lynn looked back at the window. "Why is the sun still up?"

"We slept straight through the night."

"No wonder I feel like I've been lying here for hours."

Beulah Mae hopped up and began gathering her stuff. "That's the best night's sleep I've had in weeks."

"I guess we were more tired than we realized." Lynn eased herself off the bed and dug clean clothes from her bag. "I'll be ready to go in a minute."

When she stepped out of the bathroom a few minutes later, she was wearing her favorite jeans and polo short. The outer room was flooded with light. She noticed Beulah Mae looking her over.

"Why do you young people wear blue jeans all the time?"

"I don't wear them all the time. Sometimes I wear sweatpants." She held out the clothes she had just taken off as proof.

"I've seen cleaning rags in better shape than those pants you're wearing."

Lynn glanced down at her ancient jeans. Her car keys had long ago worn a hole through the right front pocket and the material had split just above the knee. The hem at the back of the legs had shredded away to a mangled knot of thread. After a long look she had to admit that they should probably be retired, but they were so comfortable she couldn't bear to part with them. She stuffed her sweats into the bag and zipped it closed.

"Don't you ever dress up?"

"Sometimes." Lynn was too groggy and hungry to argue. "I need some coffee."

"What do you wear when you go out to someplace nice?" Beulah Mae persisted.

"Black jeans." When she saw the older woman preparing for one of her tirades, she quickly stopped her. "I wear Dockers when I dress up." She picked up the bag. "I'm ready whenever you are."

Lynn ignored a long mumbled reply as she headed to the door.

CHAPTER THIRTY-FIVE

The closer they got to Little Rock the more nervous Beulah Mae became and the harder her fingers drummed on her knee.

"You're going to have a bruise on your leg if you don't stop pounding it," Lynn finally said.

"Sorry." Beulah Mae turned back to the window. Almost immediately the fingers began to dance again.

"It's going to be okay."

The person who turned to face her was no longer the feisty, self-assured woman Lynn had come to love. "What if they don't want me there?" The drumming increased. "Papa wouldn't want me back here after all I've done."

It seemed cruel to point out that her father had probably been dead for several years. Instead, she tried to reassure her. "A lot of things have changed since you left. They might surprise you."

Beulah Mae turned her attention back to the green meadows

and plowed fields that whipped past the windows. A long while later she motioned to a sign. "Take the next exit."

Lynn could feel the tension radiating from her friend. It was starting to take a toll on her. What should she do if there was a scene about Beulah Mae's return? Should she just sit in the truck and wait? Or drop her off and come back later?

Beulah Mae directed her through a series of turns. By the time they passed a battered and rust-encrusted sign announcing that they had arrived at Williamstown, they were both nervous wrecks.

The first building was an old gas station that had long since gone out of business. Grass and weeds had pushed their way through cracks in the foundation and now stood waist-high in spots. "Stop here," Beulah Mae ordered.

Lynn pulled into the empty driveway.

The older woman sat staring through the windshield.

As Lynn looked out over a short row of buildings that weren't in any better shape than the gas station, it became painfully obvious that whatever Williamstown had once been no longer existed. The place looked like a ghost town.

A strangled cry tore from Beulah Mae. "It's all gone. There's no one left here."

Lynn placed her hand on an arm that must have in years gone by been as solid as aged hickory. Now the muscles beneath the wrinkled skin seemed fragile. "Show me where you used to live. Let's find the house."

The snowy head bobbed.

Lynn pulled out and drove along a road that was in good enough shape to indicate it was still being maintained.

As they drove, Beulah Mae began to point things out. "There's the old store. That was the Hadleys' place. Turn here. There's the foundation to the school. Turn here. That's Mr. Albright's old barn. That chimney standing there was part of Emily Lou Taylor's house." On and on the memories and directions came until at last she pointed toward an empty overgrown lot. "That's where I lived."

The house was gone. The only clue that a building had ever been there was two faint lines of tire tracks carved in the driveway. The aggressive weeds hid anything else that might have survived.

Lynn parked on the street, but neither of them seemed to be in any hurry to leave the truck.

After a long silence, Beulah Mae turned away. "We can leave now. There's nothing left here."

Unwilling to give up, Lynn insisted that they keep looking. "Where was the church?"

"Back down the other way." She nodded in the opposite direction.

Lynn turned the truck around and headed back. When they reached the road where they had turned from earlier, she was directed to go straight ahead. A few moments later, they rounded a sharp curve and there sat a small wooden building.

"It's still standing," Beulah Mae said in awe.

Lynn parked on the street in front of the building and together they walked through the grass and weeds to the old structure. The closer they drew the worse it looked. The windows were all missing and most of the west wall had caved in. It was too dangerous to enter so they slowly made their way around it. On the east side they were able to get close enough to look through one of the windows, but the room was empty.

"It would break Papa's heart to see this place now," she said, her face wet with tears. "Maybe a part of him would have been proud of the old building's endurance."

"I think he would be proud of you too," Lynn said.

Beulah Mae lowered her head. "No, he wouldn't." After a moment she turned to her. "But thanks for saying so." She gave one final look at the old building. "I've seen enough. Let's go."

As they walked back to the truck, Lynn stubbed her toe on

something hard. When she looked down, the sun reflected off a shiny surface. She bent to examine it. Weeds and dirt had to be dug way, but eventually she pulled out a small brass plaque that was approximately six inches by eight inches.

"What is it?"

Lynn used her hands to wipe off the dirt. When that didn't work fast enough to please her, she grabbed the tail of her shirt and began to rub. Slowly the words emerged.

Mount Gideon Colored Church of Williamstown
Isaiah Johnson—Pastor 1922—1960
Billy Wayne Johnson—Pastor 1960—

There was no ending date for Billy Wayne. She handed the plaque to Beulah Mae.

She took it and gently ran a hand across its surface. "Billy Wayne was my brother. He was six years older than me." Suddenly she turned a slow circle before pointing toward a wooded area. "There." She took off before Lynn had time to ask her what was happening. They scrambled through a thicket of young saplings before coming to a quick stop.

It took Lynn a moment to pick out the tombstones among the weeds. Over the next two hours they waded through the overgrown cemetery. By the time they had finished searching, they had found the grave markers of Isaiah and Lizzie Johnson along with four of their children. Three of them had lived to adulthood. One was a child.

Beulah Mae stood over the grave of Sara Jane Johnson, who had died when she was four. "Poor Mama," she said, shaking her head.

Lynn noticed the date of birth on the marker. She had been born a year after Beulah Mae left.

"I have to clean this place before I leave," Beulah Mae said quietly.

Lynn nodded. "There's bound to be a town nearby where we can buy a hoe and a couple of other tools." She realized it was Sunday. "Do you think anything will be open today?"

"We'll probably find something," Beulah Mae said. "Not too many places close on Sunday anymore."

They walked to the truck in silence, Beulah Mae still clutching the plaque. Lynn's shirt was filthy. She dug into her bag for her last clean shirt and changed before they climbed into the truck and continued on the road out of town.

CHAPTER THIRTY-SIX

A few miles down the road they came to the town of Cedar Hill. As they drove in, Lynn noticed a boarded-up building that bore the faded sign of Hadley's Garments. Across the road stood a shoe factory that had also closed. There was sense of despair and hopelessness about the place that made her want to speed up and get away from it as quickly as she could. The town was small, but it had a hardware store. In the same block was a dollar store, a thrift shop and, sticking out like a sore thumb, a flashy Radio Shack. Lynn parked in front of the hardware store where several older trucks sat.

"I'm going to the dollar store," Beulah Mae said. "I'll meet you back here."

When Lynn stepped inside the dimly lit hardware store she felt as though she had stepped back in time. She heard a strange cheeping noise and turned to find a small area had been partitioned off. Inside were several baby chickens. Lights hung over the chicks to keep them warm.

"You interested in some chickens?"

She jumped at the unexpected appearance of a man who looked to be in his mid-forties.

"No, actually I'm looking for some tools."

"Well, we probably have 'em. What do you need?"

Lynn shrugged. "I guess a hoe, a rake, a pair of limb loppers and a couple of pairs of gloves should take care of it."

He nodded and started toward the back of the room.

It was then that she noticed three older men sitting around what she thought was an old woodburning stove. Two were Anglo, the third was African-American. They all wore overalls and faded work shirts. All three were whittling. When she saw them they nodded solemnly to her. Unsure of what to do she nodded back.

"I don't recognize you," the guy who was helping her said. "You movin' in around here somewhere?"

"No. I live in San Antonio. I'm just passing through."

He pulled a hoe from a rack and handed it to her. "Seems a far piece to drive for a hoe." He started to walk away.

"I need a rake also."

He nodded. "Well, a rake and hoe makes a lot more sense," he said as he reached over to pull one from a rack near the hoes. "Now let's see if we can't find you a tree saw. I don't have any of those fancy lopper things." As he headed toward the saws he pointed out a table covered with gloves. "Pick yourself out a pair that fits. The smaller ones are on the left-hand side." She found a pair that fit her pretty well and chose a slightly larger pair for Beulah Mae. As she started toward the register she grabbed a box of garbage bags. Then she noticed a rack of work shirts, and picked out two that would fit her and added them to the pile.

The guy was waiting for her at the register. "Anything else you'll be needin' today?"

"No, sir. That's it." As he began to ring up the items on a register that would have looked more at home in a museum, she asked him about Williamstown.

He shook his head. "Town just dried up and blew away. No jobs to speak of over that way. A lot of the folks moved over here to work at the factories. When they shut down, the young folks started leaving for the city as soon as they were old enough. Now, the rest of us are sittin' around here waitin' to die off, or until we have to move off to live with our kids in the city."

"Did you ever hear of a family named Johnson from over that way?" she asked.

He hesitated a moment. "Nope, can't say I did." He gave her the total of her purchases.

She paid and thanked him.

She was almost at the truck when she heard a step behind her and turned to find that one of the older men had followed her out of the store. The bright sunlight on snow-white hair seemed to glow against his dark skin. Lynn tried not to notice the almost halo effect it created.

"What's your interest in Williamstown?" he asked. "Not many white folks ever showed much interest in that old place."

"A friend of mine grew up there. Did you know any of the Johnson family?"

He looked her over. "Who is this friend of yours?"

"She's the oldest daughter of Isaiah and Lizzie Johnson."

He nodded slightly.

"Her name is Beulah Mae. Do you know her?" She held her breath.

He sucked on his upper plate for a moment. "As I recall it, their oldest girl died when she was fifteen."

"No, she didn't die. She ran away from home."

He worked on the upper plate some more. "No. She's dead." He walked away.

Lynn watched him get into a battered old Ford pickup and

drive off. She put the tools in the truck. Since Beulah Mae hadn't returned yet, she headed back to the hardware store.

"Need another hoe?" the man who had helped her earlier asked when she walked in. He had taken a chair by the stove now and was whittling along with the remaining two men.

She looked at the small mounds of wood shavings on the floor and wondered why they didn't sit outside. "No." She tore her gaze from the mess. "I was just wondering who that third man was who was sitting here earlier. I was talking to him outside, but I didn't catch his name."

"I'd imagine you didn't catch it 'cause he didn't give it," the same man replied. The other two didn't seem to notice that she was there.

Lynn made herself remain calm. "Then do you suppose you could tell me his name?"

"Yeah. I reckon I could."

She waited, but he continued to whittle. "Well?"

He looked up. "Well, what?"

She took a deep breath. "What's his name?"

"That was Pastor Johnson."

Lynn almost stomped her foot in frustration. "That was Billy Wayne Johnson from Williamstown?"

They at least had the courtesy to look surprised that she knew his full name.

She pointed toward the register. "I stood right there and asked you if you knew anyone named Johnson from that area and you said no."

"You surely did," he replied as he continued to shave thin slivers of wood from the strip.

She shook her head in defeat. "I guess this means you won't tell me where he lives either." The only sound that followed came from the baby chickens across the store. She wasn't about to give up without a last effort. She grabbed a flyer from the counter and wrote out her name, address and phone numbers on the back. Below that she added Beulah Mae's name. She remembered to use Johnson rather than her alias, Williams. "Will you at least give this to him the next time he comes in here?" She held out the paper to the man.

"Leave it on the counter," he said after a moment.

"Will you give it to him?"

He looked at her and frowned. "I told you to leave it on the counter."

She did as he said, but she didn't hold out much hope.

As she walked back out to the truck, she realized she couldn't tell Beulah Mae about what had just happened. It would break her heart to find a brother here who didn't want anything to do with her.

Beulah Mae was sitting on the tailgate waiting for her. Several large plastic bags were beside her. Through the thin plastic Lynn could see the cheap funeral sprays. One of the bags had a couple of bottles of water.

"It's all they had," Beulah Mae said as if she had read Lynn's mind. She ran a hand over one of the sprays. "I would have rather had real flowers."

"I'm sure your family would appreciate your effort."

"Maybe."

They put the bags inside the cab so they wouldn't blow out.

"I'm starving," Lynn said. "There's a Dairy Queen across the road. Let's go over and grab a burger."

Beulah Mae stared straight ahead. "I'm not hungry. I'll wait for you in the truck."

There was a rigid set to her back that Lynn hadn't noticed before. Her face revealed nothing. Something must have happened in the dollar store.

She did not intend to leave Beulah Mae sitting in the truck while she ate. She was about to suggest the drive-through window when she noticed the box of cinnamon rolls. "On second thought, I think I'll just have one of those cinnamon rolls. I can eat it while I'm driving back to the cemetery. I never could work on a full stomach."

Beulah Mae turned and stared into her eyes for a long moment before finally nodding.

For the first hour they worked without speaking. Lynn finally went to the truck for the water. She brought back a bottle for Beulah Mae.

After taking a couple of sips Beulah Mae cleared her throat. "It's a bad thing when pride gets in the way of letting someone know how much you care." She nodded toward her parents' graves. "I always intended to come back to see them, but I was too proud. I knew what Papa would say to me. I couldn't face it."

Lynn thought about the encounter with the older man in the parking lot and wondered if she would ever be able to tell Beulah Mae about him.

"My baby sister, Annie, was working in the dollar store."

The statement had been made so calmly that it took a moment for Lynn to comprehend its true meaning. At least two of Beulah Mae's siblings had moved to Cedar Hill. Maybe they had moved there to work in the factories too.

"How can you be sure it was her?"

"I recognized her."

"But she was only a tiny baby when you left." She thought about Billy Wayne. He hadn't looked like Beulah Mae at all.

"She looked so much like Mama I would have known her anywhere."

Lynn wondered how it must have felt to walk into that store and not only see but also recognize a person you hadn't seen in nearly seventy years. "What happened?"

She took a long drink of water before turning to Lynn. "I told her who I was. She told me that as far as the family was concerned, I died the day I took up with that woman."

"I'm sorry."

"I tried to explain to Annie that there was nothing else I could have done. I would have really died if I had stayed here and tried to live a lie." She looked down at the graves again. "I had to leave." She picked up the rake. "I just wish I had told everyone how much I loved them before I left."

Lynn suddenly had a vision of Crissy standing on the porch watching her drive away. She pulled the cell phone from her belt and stepped away a few feet before she could change her mind. When Crissy answered, Lynn didn't give her time to say anything beyond hello.

"I love you and I miss you," she announced without preamble. "I hate being away from you. We need to fix whatever's wrong between us."

"I agree completely."

Crissy's reply caught her off guard and for a moment she couldn't believe she had heard correctly. Finally, she found her voice. "Can we get together as soon as I get back?"

"When will that be?"

Lynn glanced at her watch and at the work left to be done at the cemetery. "I can't get back until at least late afternoon tomorrow, possibly even Tuesday morning."

"Let's have dinner on Tuesday night."

Lynn wanted it to be a special night. She struggled to recall a nice restaurant that Crissy would like. Then she remembered that a couple of years ago Crissy had gone to the Tower of the Americas restaurant with her parents and raved about it for days. "Let's go to the Tower. I'll pick you up at eight, and I promise to be on time."

There was a slight hesitation before Crissy agreed. "I'll see you at eight on Tuesday night."

Lynn practically danced a jig as she put the phone away.

"I hope you plan on wearing something besides those raggedy britches," Beulah Mae said as she raked a pile of weeds into a bag.

Lynn picked up the hoe. "I can probably find a decent pair of Dockers in my closet."

"Don't forget to shine your boots. They were looking a little rough the last time I saw them." She tied the bag. "While you're at it, you might try running an iron over your clothes, and a little starch wouldn't hurt."

Lynn smiled. "I promise to make you proud."

"You already do," Beulah Mae replied as she walked away with the trash bag.

It was almost dark by the time they made their way back to Little Rock and found a room. Neither felt like going out, so they ordered a pizza. By the time it arrived they had both showered. They ate in near silence, each lost in her own thoughts.

"I've been thinking," Lynn said. "When Crissy and I find a place, we want you to come live with us." In her heart, she knew Crissy wouldn't mind.

"I can stay at Morning Sunrise."

"I know you could, but I think you could help me a lot."

"How? I'm too old to be chasing after horses."

"But you know a lot about other things. More importantly"— she hesitated—"you make me want to be a better person. Nobody, not even Crissy, pushes me to grow and to be better the way you do."

Beulah Mae shifted and began to drum her fingers on the table. "I'm too old to be of any good to you."

Lynn cleared her throat. "I'm not offering you a job so much as a home. It's yours for as long as you want it." She picked at the edge of the pizza box. "There was just me and Mom until Crissy came along. Over the last year or so, I've come to think of you as family."

Beulah Mae blinked rapidly and began to examine a button

on her shirt. "Are you doing this because you feel sorry for me? Because I can take care of myself just fine."

"I'd be lying if I said I didn't feel bad about what happened today, but no, the idea has been growing ever since I won the money." She pushed her chair back. "I'm not fooling myself about the ranch and how much I don't know about running one. The truth is I'll need all the help I can get."

"I don't know how I can help you."

Lynn smiled. "You can keep me from being too much of a nimrod."

Beulah Mae rolled her eyes. "I'd have a better chance of walking on water."

They went to have a leisurely breakfast the following morning. Neither of them seemed to be in a rush to start the long drive back. Lynn had made two calls the previous evening. The first one was to her mother to let her know that they were spending the night in Little Rock and that she would be home Monday afternoon or Tuesday morning. The second one had been to Deon. She asked him to arrange a get-together with Sondra and Jose for later in the week. She didn't tell him what she had in mind. In truth, she wasn't really sure yet, but somehow she intended to help them. Later on she would see what she could do about paying off the college loans for the Sunday brunch group.

As they ate Lynn suddenly remembered the letter she had mailed for Beulah Mae. "You can tell me to mind my own business," she began, "but what was the deal with that letter you asked me to mail for you?"

Beulah Mae ate the last bite of her hotcakes before answering. "She's an old friend. I wrote to ask her if we could crash at her place if we needed to. I thought it would be safer than staying in a hotel."

Since they weren't in a hurry, Lynn had an idea. "Would you

like to see her while you're here?"

A look of sadness passed over Beulah Mae's face. "I got a call from her girl a few days after you mailed the letter. Celine died last year."

Lynn stared at her waffles. "I'm sorry."

"I try not to be sad. She had a good life. She and Ellie were together for fifty-two years."

"That's a long time." She thought about the struggles in her short, five-year relationship. "How did they do it?"

"They fought like cats and dogs."

"What?" Lynn was shocked. "How could the relationship survive for so long if they didn't like each other?"

"I never said they didn't like each other. Their love was strong. They were both very strong, opinionated women who always wanted to be right." She pushed her plate away. "In fact, they sort of remind me of this young couple I know."

"I don't have to always be right."

"Yes, you do."

"No, I don't." Lynn realized what she was doing and burst into laugher. "Let's go home." As she pulled cash from her pocket, her phone rang. "That's probably Mom wondering if I'll be there for supper." She tossed the money on the table and answered the phone.

"Lynn, this is Nathan Bainbridge."

"Oh, hi. Have you located another piece of property?"

"If you still want it, the Burton property is available."

Lynn almost dropped the phone. "You mean it? What happened to the other buyer?"

"You remember us talking about mineral rights?"

"Yes."

"Well, the buyer wanted all the rights and the seller wasn't willing to let them go."

"Why? Are they really that valuable?"

"Naw. I think that Burton is feeling guilty about selling the old place and just wants to hang on to a part of it. He called me this morning and said he'd accept your original bid if you were still interested."

"You bet I am."

"When can you come up and sign the paperwork?"

"I'm in Little Rock right now . . ." She glanced at her watch. It was a little before nine, and the trip back to San Antonio would take about nine hours. How much farther was it to Bandera? "I can't get back there until tonight."

He chuckled. "I'm sure Burton will be satisfied to accept your verbal agreement until you can get back. Tuesday or Wednesday would be fine." They made an appointment for Tuesday morning at ten.

When she got off the phone Beulah Mae had already paid the bill and was urging Lynn to hurry.

"Did you hear that?" Lynn asked as they headed for the parking lot.

"I heard what you said and saw your face light up like a kid's at Christmas. I figured it must be something to do with the property."

"The other deal fell through. They couldn't agree about the ownership of the mineral rights."

"The buyer was probably some greenhorn thinking he could buy a piece of Texas property and get rich with an oil well."

"I'm going up to sign the paperwork on Tuesday morning." She spun around in a circle, stomped her feet and started laughing like a fool. "It's really going to happen." Tuesday was shaping up to be a great day.

CHAPTER THIRTY-SEVEN

Finally satisfied with how her hair looked, Lynn slipped the blue-striped shirt that Crissy had always liked off the hanger and pulled it on. She had spent almost half an hour ironing it to perfection. After it was buttoned and carefully tucked into neatly pressed navy blue Dockers, she pulled on her newly polished boots. She checked her hair and made a few final touch-ups before she grabbed her wallet, keys and cell phone. She wasn't due at Crissy's for another hour, but she was too nervous to sit still. She hadn't told Crissy about the land yet. She wanted to surprise her tonight. She had gone up that morning, signed the necessary paperwork and put down the good-faith money. Nathan had told her that it normally took about a month to close on a property. Her wait time would be a little less since they didn't have to deal with a mortgage company. She rolled her shirt sleeves as she made her way to the kitchen.

"You look very nice," her mom said when she came into the kitchen.

"I'm taking Crissy to the Tower for dinner." She rubbed her chin nervously and glanced at her watch. "I'm a little early."

"Do you have enough time to stop for some flowers and maybe a nice bottle of wine?"

Lynn glanced up. "Why didn't I think of that?"

Her mom simply looked at her in amazement and shook her head.

"Thanks, Mom." Lynn gave her a quick peck on the cheek.

"Should I expect you home tonight?"

Stunned, Lynn stared at her mom. "I can't believe you asked that. Of course, I'll be home."

"Well, I won't be."

"I don't need to know any more." Lynn headed for the door.

On the way to Crissy's, she stopped and bought a dozen yellow roses and a bottle of Crissy's favorite chardonnay. Only then did she allow herself to entertain the idea that the night could possibly lead to more than dinner. *It's just dinner*, she reminded herself. She wasn't going to rush Crissy.

Despite the stops, she still had to circle the familiar block three times to keep from arriving early. She spent the time debating whether to tell Crissy about the property before, during or after dinner. Each time seemed to have it benefits and its drawbacks.

As she made her way up the sidewalk she finally decided it would have to be before or after dinner. She didn't want to tell her in the restaurant. When she reached the door she debated on whether to ring the doorbell or just walk in. After all, she had lived there for years. A serious case of nerves kicked in and she rang the bell. Her jaw nearly dropped when Crissy answered the door in a skimpy black dress held up by delicate spaghetti straps. Unable to find her voice, Lynn held out the wine and roses and sent a silent thank you to her mother.

"How nice," Crissy said as she took the gifts. "Come on in while I take care of these."

When she turned toward the kitchen Lynn drank in the view offered by the low-cut back. Her heart began to pound as her gaze traveled downward. The short dress showcased Crissy's long, shapely legs. By the time she reached the sexy black heels, her tongue was practically hanging out. She gave herself a swift mental slap and did a slow count to ten before trusting her voice. "That's a new outfit."

"I thought I'd wear something special for tonight."

Lynn glanced down at her own clothes and regretted not buying something new. Crissy had given her this shirt for Christmas two years ago. She brushed at the front, trying to smooth out the wrinkles caused by the seatbelt.

When Crissy returned a few minutes later she was carrying a white gift box. "I got a little something for you too." She held out the package.

Again Lynn praised her mom's foresight. She opened it and found a white silk shirt inside.

"I've always wanted to buy you one of these," Crissy said as she ran her hand across the shirt. "Would you mind trying it on? I want to see how it fits."

Lynn took the shirt from the box. "I'll only be a minute." Before she could move Crissy began to unbutton the shirt Lynn was wearing. She tried not to react to the touch of warm finger-tips against her skin, but it took everything she had to maintain her composure. It seemed to take an eternity for all the buttons to be released. When the teasing fingers reached her waistband, Lynn could no longer stand the agony and yanked the shirttail from her slacks. She fumbled with the final buttons, but Crissy pushed her hand away.

"Careful. You're going to rip the button off."

Lynn held her breath until Crissy stepped back with the new shirt and began to unbutton it. When she finally finished, Lynn quickly switched shirts. She had intended to step away and button it herself, but Crissy was quicker and she had to endure the entire process in reverse. When the tempting fingers released the button on her slacks, Lynn stepped away and took over the process of tucking the shirt in.

"How does it look?" Her voice shook slightly.

"I like it." Crissy's hand brushed across the shoulder and down Lynn's arm. "Turn around. Let me see the back."

Lynn gritted her teeth as gentle hands ran across her shoulders and then down to rest on her sides.

"Nice," Crissy murmured.

Lynn closed her eyes and began a slow count of ten. She had only gotten to seven when the warm hands disappeared from her side. When she turned Crissy was holding her old shirt. Lynn wasn't sure she could go through the entire ordeal again and still keep her hands to herself. "I'll wear this."

"You worked so hard to iron this one. I didn't mean to suggest that you needed to change."

"I want to wear this one. It feels nice." She felt warmed by the bright smile she received.

"We should probably get going," Crissy said as she removed a long black shawl that had been draped over the back of the chair.

Lynn experienced a mixture of relief and regret as the shawl covered the lovely bare shoulders.

"I thought I'd better take this. It might be a little cool in the restaurant."

Lynn nodded and tried to ignore her trembling legs. She longed for a cool breeze. At the moment, she felt certain that her own body's temperature was contributing to global warming.

On the way to the restaurant they discussed the renovations being done by her mom and Jaime. She suddenly remembered her news. When Crissy had opened the door wearing that dress, she had forgotten all about the land. They were almost at the restaurant. She decided to wait until afterward.

"How are the wedding plans going?" Crissy asked.

Lynn gave a loud sigh. "Right now, all of their time is being sucked up by that building. It's in horrible shape."

"I can help once school is out."

"Thanks. I know they would appreciate it."

She listened as Crissy began to talk about the ideas she and her mom had already been discussing about the wedding. As she drove toward the glowing warmth of city lights Lynn began to relax. There was no need to worry about the night; as long as she was with Crissy everything would be perfect.

After parking she made her way around the truck to help Crissy down.

"I like your truck. You look sexy driving it."

Lynn felt her neck growing warm. "You look pretty hot your-self. I'm surprised that dress doesn't burst into flames."

Crissy smiled coyly. "I didn't think you had noticed."

"I would've had to be blind not to." She offered her arm.

Crissy slipped her hand under Lynn's arm. "I was thinking about you when I bought it."

There was a huskiness to her voice that set Lynn's legs to trembling again. Before she could think of a response, Crissy moved closer. Her soft breast pressed Lynn's arm.

"After dinner, could we take a walk along the River Walk?"

"Sure." Lynn wanted to shout that she would walk to the moon if it meant Crissy would be walking beside her.

They ignored the occasional glance cast their way from the mostly tourist crowd as they crossed the plaza of HemisFair Park and into the glass-paneled elevator that would take them to the top. The distance from the ground to the tip of the antenna was seven-hundred and fifty feet. The Tower of the Americas, origi-nally built as the theme structure of the 1968 World's Fair, had held the distinction of being the tallest observation tower in the United States until the Stratosphere Tower was built in Las Vegas. At the top of it sat the recently renovated restaurant, which revolved to offer its patrons a three-hundred-and-sixty-degree view of the city.

A family with three young children and two older couples followed them onto the elevator.

"The view is wonderful," Crissy said as the elevator began to rise. "I had forgotten how far you can see from up here."

Lynn agreed, but in truth she had never been up in the tower. Until recently, the restaurant had been much too expensive for her to consider. She wasn't exactly afraid of heights, but she was much more comfortable being at ground level.

The father of the three kids began to explain to them that the tower revolved.

The oldest, who appeared to be about six, looked up at her dad, her face etched with concern. "Is it going to unscrew and fall off?"

The group chuckled softly at the child's concern as the father tried to explain the structure wouldn't unscrew and fall off.

The weekday crowd at the restaurant was much lighter than the weekend. When they arrived they were quickly seated. Their waiter appeared and took their drink orders. Crissy ordered a glass of Chardonnay; Lynn requested a dry vodka martini with an olive. She seldom drank, but tonight was a special occasion. They studied the menu while they waited for the drinks.

"Grandma Anderson loves the linguine *pescatore* here." Crissy closed the menu. "I think I'll try it." As she leaned forward the shawl slipped slightly from her shoulder. "What are you having?"

Lynn tried not to notice the smooth bare shoulder peeking out but found it hard not to. She focused her attention back to the menu. "I think I'll have the cedar-planked salmon with lemon butter sauce."

After their drinks arrived and Lynn ordered, they settled into a relaxed conversation. They talked about the softball league and the upcoming playoffs. Then Lynn asked about Crissy's classes.

"I'm really looking forward to a few weeks off," Crissy said. "I'm embarrassed to admit that I enjoy not having to work."

"I think most people would consider a full course load as working."

"I don't want the money to become a crutch."

Lynn looked at her and hoped they weren't treading on dangerous ground. She tried to think of something neutral to say.

Crissy lay her hand on Lynn's arm. "Don't look so scared. I'm not going to start ranting again." She sipped her wine. "In fact, I've wanted to tell you that I was proud of the way you went to see Stoner and offered to share the ticket. It wasn't fair of me to verbally attack you as I did that day in the car. I've thought about it a lot. I know you came to the Taco Hut to surprise me. I'm sorry I was such a butt."

Lynn shook her head. "No. You were right. Stoner and his family needed that money. Maybe even more than we did." She took a deep breath. "I was being greedy. I'm sorry."

"Why did you give me half of the money?"

"It was the right thing to do. Besides, I certainly didn't need all of it."

"I invested most of it." Crissy hesitated a moment. "It's still in both of our names."

"You didn't have to do that."

"I wanted to. Lynn, I hope I haven't given you the idea that I'm no longer interested in trying to make this relationship work."

"I get confused sometimes," Lynn admitted. "It seems like you run hot and cold on the subject."

Crissy set her wine aside and leaned forward slightly. "I've been doing a lot of soul-searching and I think I'm feeling guilty. I don't want to like having the money, but I do." She looked into

Lynn's eyes. "Does that make me a bad person?"

"No. Why do you feel like you have to struggle so hard?"

"I don't know, unless it's because my parents and grandparents did. I watched them working hard and saving to get what they have. I guess I just feel as though I should be doing the same."

"Try thinking about it as you would a washing machine."

"What?" She glanced at the martini in Lynn's hand.

Lynn chuckled. "I'm not drunk. Look, you wash your clothes in an automatic washer. Your grandmother tells those stories about how she used to have to wash clothes in a tub with a scrub board. Yet you don't feel guilty about using a washing machine. So why should the money be any different?"

"It's a big leap from a washing machine to three million dollars."

"Why does it have to be? If you think of both as tools to help you live a better, more enriched life." Lynn wondered how she could make her point more clearly. She finally gave up and added, "I don't want the money to change my life. I want it to enhance my life."

There was a slight nod from Crissy.

"If I can buy the ranch now rather than ten or fifteen years from now," Lynn began, "then that's ten or fifteen years more I'll have to do what I like."

"But will anything ever mean as much if you don't work for it?"

"I think what you spend the money on will determine that. I don't care what you purchase. It'll mean more to you if you buy it because it's something you really want and not just something that you picked up because you can afford it."

Crissy nodded. "I think I see your point. The money can symbolize whatever I choose to make it mean."

"Exactly. It's a tool, not a burden."

The waiter arrived with the food. Their attention turned to

the wonderful-smelling fare. The food was every bit as delicious as it was touted. When they finished a waitress with a dessert tray appeared to tempt them. Crissy succumbed to the temptation and ordered a rich slice of chocolate cake, but Lynn passed and settled for coffee. But then she ended up eating most of the cake when Crissy couldn't finish it. By the time they left, they were both stuffed.

CHAPTER THIRTY-EIGHT

When they stepped out of the elevator the night air was still warm. Several people were strolling around the plaza.

"I can't believe we've had such a long spring," Crissy said. "I could get used to this."

"It's nice to not go from winter to summer," Lynn agreed.

"Is it okay if I've changed my mind about the River Walk? I'm not ready to go home yet, but I don't want the hassle of a crowd."

"Sure. It's fine. Why don't we walk around here in the plaza?" She couldn't remain quiet about the land any longer. "I signed an agreement to buy the Burton property."

Crissy stopped and stared at her. "The place we saw?"

Lynn nodded.

"But I thought someone else was buying that."

"The deal fell through." She quickly recounted the story.

When she finished Crissy hugged her tightly. "When can you

start working on it?"

"He said it would take a while for them to get the survey done, title search and all that stuff. So I guess about a month."

"Are you going to try to do the renovations on the house yourself?"

"Heck, no. I'm just tearing out things at Mom's restaurant and it's hard work. I can't imagine how difficult it would be to have to put it back together. I'll hire someone."

Crissy hugged her again. "I'm so happy for you. I know how much it means to you."

Lynn was about to ask her what the land would mean to her, but just then a large group of tourists came rushing by.

"Let's find someplace where we can talk." Crissy slipped her hand back beneath Lynn's arm.

They strolled in silence for a long while. Crissy seemed lost in her own thoughts, as was Lynn. They left the tourists behind as they wandered toward the far side of the plaza. Soft strains of music could be heard coming from one of the distant buildings.

Crissy pointed to a park bench. "Let's sit here and listen to the music for a while."

Lynn glanced around. The area was in deep shadows. She wasn't sure they should be so far away from the crowd. She visually checked the entire area, but there didn't seem to be anyone around to bother them. Once they were seated Crissy rested her head on Lynn's shoulder.

"I'm such a hypocrite," Crissy said. "I whine about the money, but I sure have enjoyed tonight."

"We certainly couldn't have done this a month ago."

"I've missed you."

Lynn's heart skipped a beat. "I've missed you too."

Crissy raised her head slightly and Lynn kissed her. The kiss slowly intensified until their frantic breathing filled Lynn's ears. She tried to pull away, but Crissy grabbed her and pulled her back.

Lynn's hand seemed to move on its own as it slowly caressed the side of Crissy's full breast. The sensuous sighs of pleasure made Lynn bolder. Her thumb circled the bulge of nipple straining through the dress. Lost in the driving desire of the moment, her lips left Crissy's demanding mouth and kissed the length of the soft neck. There was no protest when her hand eased inside the low-scooped top and closed over the warm breast. The need for more drove her to free the soft mound. Her mouth trailed a path to the nipple. Hands entwined in her hair urged her on. Hot breath burned the back of her neck. The low lush cries of desire drove her almost to the point of frenzy.

Her tongue and mouth continued their exploration of the wonderful breast as her hand moved downward to start its journey home. Soon it moved along the length of a smooth supple thigh. With each stroke it rose higher. Her fingertips skimmed the edge of a garter belt. The knowledge that nothing but the thin layer of Crissy's panties lay between her and her quest was nearly too much. She made herself slow down to regain control. The arching body urging her on didn't help.

Desperate hands pulled her head away from the breast and back up to full hungry lips. Her hand could no longer be denied. As it made its way upward, thighs parted, granting her access. Almost too quickly she arrived at her destination. The smooth satiny material of Crissy's panties was damp with desire. Lynn tried to restrain herself, but the writhing body beneath her hand drove her beyond control. Her finger slipped beneath the material and pushed it aside. The warm breeze carried her own sighs of pleasure as her fingers slipped into the warm wet folds. She wanted to prolong the moment, but the need was too great. There was a brief time of near-frantic thrusting followed by the heart-stopping instant when everything teetered on the edge . . . then ecstasy as Crissy came in her hand.

Neither woman moved as they struggled to regain their breath. The memory of where they were finally snapped Lynn back to reality. She eased her hand from between Crissy's legs.

"I'm sorry. I guess I got a little carried away," she said as she helped Crissy readjust her clothing.

Crissy kissed her. "Don't ever apologize for something so wonderful. Just hurry up and get me home so we can start over."

They ran to the truck laughing and giggling like teenagers. As soon as they were in the truck Crissy slid across the seat and snuggled next to her.

"Crissy, I know you have another semester of school and all, but I was wondering if maybe after you graduated . . . if . . . maybe."

Crissy kissed her. "Move back home with me. We can live here until the house is renovated and then we'll move out there together."

Lynn hugged her close "There's nothing that would please me more."

Publications from
BELLA BOOKS, INC.
The best in contemporary lesbian fiction

P.O. Box 10543, Tallahassee, FL 32302
Phone: 800-729-4992
www.bellabooks.com

ASPEN'S EMBERS by Diane Tremain Braund. Will Aspen choose the woman she loves . . . or the forest she hopes to preserve . . .   978-1-59493-102-4 $14.95

THE COTTAGE by Gerri Hill. The Cottage is the heartbreaking story of two women who meet by chance . . . or did they? A love so destined it couldn't be denied . . . stolen moments to be cherished forever.   978-1-59493-096-6 $13.95

FANTASY: Untrue Stories of Lesbian Passion edited by Barbara Johnson and Therese Szymanski. Lie back and let Bella's bad girls take you on an erotic journey through the greatest bedtime stories never told.   978-1-59493-101-7 $15.95

SISTERS' FLIGHT by Jeanne G'Fellers. *SISTERS' FLIGHT* is the highly anticipated sequel to NO SISTER OF MINE and *SISTER LOST SISTER FOUND*.
          978-1-59493-116-1 $13.95

BRAGGIN RIGHTS by Kenna White. Taylor Fleming is a thirty-six year old Texas rancher who covets her independence. She finds her cowgirl independence tested by neighboring rancher Jen Holland.   978-1-59493-095-9 $13.95

BRILLIANT by Ann Roberts. Respected sociology professor, Diane Cole finds her views on love challenged by her own heart, as she fights the attraction she feels for a woman half her age.   978-1-59493-115-4 $13.95

THE EDUCATION OF ELLIE by Jackie Calhoun. When Ellie sees her childhood friend for the first time in thirty years she is tempted to resume their long lost friend-ship. But with the years come a lot of baggage and the two women struggle with who they are now while fighting the painful memories of their first parting. Will they be able to move past their history to start again?   978-1-59493-092-8 $13.95

DATE NIGHT CLUB by Saxon Bennett. *Date Night Club* is a dark romantic comedy about the pitfalls of dating in your thirties . . .   978-1-59493-094-2 $13.95

PLEASE FORGIVE ME by Megan Carter. Laurel Becker is on the verge of losing the two most important things in her life—her current lover, Elaine Alexander, and the Lavender Page bookstore. Will Elaine and Laurel manage to work through their mis-understandings and rebuild their life together?   978-1-59493-091-1 $13.95

WHISKEY AND OAK LEAVES by Jaime Clevenger. Meg meets June, a single woman running a horse ranch in the California Sierra foothills. The two become quick friends and it isn't long before Meg is looking for more than just a friendship. But June has no interest in developing a deeper relationship with Meg. She is, after all, not the least bit interested in women . . . or is she? Neither of these two women is prepared for what lies ahead . . .   978-1-59493-093-5 $13.95

SUMTER POINT by KG MacGregor. As Audie surrenders her heart to Beth, she begins to distance herself from the reckless habits of her youth. Just as they're ready to meet in the middle, their future is thrown into doubt by a duty Beth can't ignore. It all comes to a head on the river at Sumter Point.   978-1-59493-089-8 $13.95

THE TARGET by Gerri Hill. Sara Michaels is the daughter of a prominent senator who has been receiving death threats against his family. In an effort to protect Sara, the FBI recruits homicide detective Jaime Hutchinson to secretly provide the protection they are so certain Sara will need. Will Sara finally figure out who is behind the death threats? And will Jaime realize the truth—and be able to save Sara before it's too late?
978-1-59493-082-9 $13.95

REALITY BYTES by Jane Frances. In this sequel to Reunion, follow the lives of four friends in a romantic tale that spans the globe and proves that you can cross the whole of cyberspace only to find love a few suburbs away . . . 978-1-59493-079-9 $13.95

MURDER CAME SECOND by Jessica Thomas. Broadway's bad-boy genius, Paul Carlucci, has chosen Hamlet for his latest production. To the delight of some and despair of others, he has selected Provincetown's amphitheatre for his opening gala. But suddenly Alex Peres realizes that the wrong people are falling down. And the moaning is all too realistic. Someone must not be shooting blanks . . .
978-1-59493-081-2 $13.95

SKIN DEEP by Kenna White. Jordan Griffin has been given a new assignment: Track down and interview one-time nationally renowned broadcast journalist Reece McAllister. Much to her surprise, Jordan comes away with far more than just a story . . .
978-1-59493-78-2 $13.95

FINDERS KEEPERS by Karin Kallmaker. *Finders Keepers*, the quest for the perfect mate in the 21st Century, joins Karin Kallmaker's *Just Like That* and her other incomparable novels about lesbian love, lust and laughter.   1-59493-072-4 $13.95

OUT OF THE FIRE by Beth Moore. Author Ann Covington feels at the top of the world when told her book is being made into a movie. Then in walks Casey Duncan the actress who is playing the lead in her movie. Will Casey turn Ann's world upside down?
1-59493-088-0 $13.95

STAKE THROUGH THE HEART: NEW EXPLOITS OF TWILIGHT LES-BIANS by Karin Kallmaker, Julia Watts, Barbara Johnson and Therese Szymanski. The playful quartet that penned the acclaimed *Once Upon A Dyke* are dimming the lights for journeys into worlds of breathless seduction.   1-59493-071-6 $15.95

THE HOUSE ON SANDSTONE by KG MacGregor. Carly Griffin returns home to Leland and finds that her old high school friend Justine is awakening more than just old memories.   1-59493-076-7 $13.95

WILD NIGHTS: MOSTLY TRUE STORIES OF WOMEN LOVING WOMEN
edited by Therese Szymanski. 264 pp. 23 new stories from today's hottest erotic writers
are sure to give you your wildest night ever!   1-59493-069-4 $15.95

COYOTE SKY by Gerri Hill. 248 pp. Sheriff Lee Foxx is trying to cope with the realization that she has fallen in love for the first time. And fallen for author Kate Winters,
who is technically unavailable. Will Lee fight to keep Kate in Coyote?
                                                        1-59493-065-1 $13.95

VOICES OF THE HEART by Frankie J. Jones. 264 pp. A series of events force Erin
to swear off love as she tries to break away from the woman of her dreams. Will Erin
ever find the key to her future happiness?   1-59493-068-6 $13.95

SHELTER FROM THE STORM by Peggy J. Herring. 296 pp. A story about family
and getting reacquainted with one's past that shows that sometimes you don't appreciate what you have until you almost lose it.   1-59493-064-3 $13.95

WRITING MY LOVE by Claire McNab. 192 pp. Romance writer Vonny Smith
believes she will be able to woo her editor Diana through her writing.
                                                        1-59493-063-5 $13.95

PAID IN FULL by Ann Roberts. 200 pp. Ari Adams will need to choose between the
debts of the past and the promise of a happy future.   1-59493-059-7 $13.95

ROMANCING THE ZONE by Kenna White. 272 pp. Liz's world begins to crumble
when a secret from her past returns to Ashton.   1-59493-060-0 $13.95

SIGN ON THE LINE by Jaime Clevenger. 204 pp. Alexis Getty, a flirtatious delivery
driver is committed to finding the rightful owner of a mysterious package.
                                                        1-59493-052-X $13.95

END OF WATCH by Clare Baxter. 256 pp. LAPD Lieutenant L.A Franco Frank fol-
lows the lone clue down the unlit steps of memory to a final, unthinkable resolution.
                                                        1-59493-064-4 $13.95

BEHIND THE PINE CURTAIN by Gerri Hill. 280 pp. Jacqueline returns home
after her father's death and comes face-to-face with her first crush.
                                                        1-59493-057-0 $13.95

18TH & CASTRO by Karin Kallmaker. 200 pp. First-time couplings and couples who
know how to mix lust and love make 18th & Castro the hottest address in the city by
the bay.   1-59493-066-X $13.95

JUST THIS ONCE by KG MacGregor. 200 pp. Mindful of the obligations back home
that she must honor, Wynne Connelly struggles to resist the fascination and allure that
a particular woman she meets on her business trip represents.
                                                        1-59493-087-2 $13.95

ANTICIPATION by Terri Breneman. 240 pp. Two women struggle to remain professional as they work together to find a serial killer.   1-59493-055-4 $13.95

OBSESSION by Jackie Calhoun. Lindsey's life is turned upside down when Sarah comes
into the family nursery in search of perennials.   1-59493-058-9 $13.95

BENEATH THE WILLOW by Kenna White. 240 pp. A torch that still burns
brightly even after twenty-five years threatens to consume two childhood friends.
                                                        1-59493-053-8 $13.95

SISTER LOST, SISTER FOUND by Jeanne G'Fellers. 224 pp. The highly anticipated sequel to *No Sister of Mine.*   1-59493-056-2 $13.95

THE WEEKEND VISITOR by Jessica Thomas. 240 pp. In this latest Alex Peres mystery, Alex is asked to investigate an assault on a local woman but finds that her client may have more secrets than she lets on.   1-59493-054-6 $13.95

THE KILLING ROOM by Gerri Hill. 392 pp. How can two women forget and go their separate ways?   1-59493-050-3 $12.95

PASSIONATE KISSES by Megan Carter. 240 pp. Will two old friends run from love?
                    1-59493-051-1 $12.95

ALWAYS AND FOREVER by Lyn Denison. 224 pp. The girl next door turns Shannon's world upside down.   1-59493-049-X $12.95

BACK TALK by Saxon Bennett. 200 pp. Can a talk show host find love after heartbreak?
                    1-59493-028-7 $12.95

THE PERFECT VALENTINE: EROTIC LESBIAN VALENTINE STORIES edited by Barbara Johnson and Therese Szymanski—from Bella After Dark. 328 pp. Stories from the hottest writers around.   1-59493-061-9 $14.95

MURDER AT RANDOM by Claire McNab. 200 pp. The Sixth Denise Cleever Thriller. Denise realizes the fate of thousands is in her hands.
                    1-59493-047-3 $12.95

THE TIDES OF PASSION by Diana Tremain Braund. 240 pp. Will Susan be able to hold it all together and find the one woman who touches her soul?
                    1-59493-048-1 $12.95

JUST LIKE THAT by Karin Kallmaker. 240 pp. Disliking each other—and everything they stand for—even before they meet, Toni and Syrah find feelings can change, just like that.   1-59493-025-2 $12.95

WHEN FIRST WE PRACTICE by Therese Szymanski. 200 pp. Brett and Allie are once again caught in the middle of murder and intrigue.
                    1-59493-045-7 $12.95

REUNION by Jane Frances. 240 pp. Cathy Braithwaite seems to have it all: good looks, money and a thriving accounting practice . . .   1-59493-046-5 $12.95

BELL, BOOK & DYKE: NEW EXPLOITS OF MAGICAL LESBIANS by Kallmaker, Watts, Johnson and Szymanski. 360 pp. Reluctant witches, tempting spells and skyclad beauties—delve into the mysteries of love, lust and power in this quartet of novellas.
                    1-59493-023-6 $14.95

ARTIST'S DREAM by Gerri Hill. 320 pp. When Cassie meets Luke Winston, she can no longer deny her attraction to women . . .   1-59493-042-2 $12.95

NO EVIDENCE by Nancy Sanra. 240 pp. Private investigator Tally McGinnis once again returns to the horror-filled world of a serial killer.
                    1-59493-043-04 $12.95

WHEN LOVE FINDS A HOME by Megan Carter. 280 pp. What will it take for Anna and Rona to find their way back to each other again?   1-59493-041-4 $12.95

MEMORIES TO DIE FOR by Adrian Gold. 240 pp. Rachel attempts to avoid her attraction to the charms of Anna Sigurdson . . .   1-59493-038-4 $12.95

SILENT HEART by Claire McNab. 280 pp. Exotic lesbian romance.
                                                1-59493-044-9 $12.95

MIDNIGHT RAIN by Peggy J. Herring. 240 pp. Bridget McBee is determined to find the woman who saved her life.   1-59493-021-X $12.95

THE MISSING PAGE A Brenda Strange Mystery by Patty G. Henderson. 240 pp. Brenda investigates her client's murder . . .   1-59493-004-X $12.95

WHISPERS ON THE WIND by Frankie J. Jones. 240 pp. Dixon thinks she and her best friend, Elizabeth Colter, would make the perfect couple . . .
                                                1-59493-037-6 $12.95

CALL OF THE DARK: EROTIC LESBIAN TALES OF THE SUPERNATURAL edited by Therese Szymanski—from Bella After Dark. 320 pp.
                                                1-59493-040-6 $14.95

A TIME TO CAST AWAY A Helen Black Mystery by Pat Welch. 240 pp. Helen stops by Alice's apartment—only to find the woman dead . . .   1-59493-036-8 $12.95

DESERT OF THE HEART by Jane Rule. 224 pp. The book that launched the most popular lesbian movie of all time is back.   1-1-59493-035-X $12.95

THE NEXT WORLD by Ursula Steck. 240 pp. Anna's friend Mido is threatened and eventually disappears . . .   1-59493-024-4 $12.95

CALL SHOTGUN by Jaime Clevenger. 240 pp. Kelly gets pulled back into the world of private investigation . . .   1-59493-016-3 $12.95

52 PICKUP by Bonnie J. Morris and E.B. Casey. 240 pp. 52 hot, romantic tales—one for every Saturday night of the year.   1-59493-026-0 $12.95

GOLD FEVER by Lyn Denison. 240 pp. Kate's first love, Ashley, returns to their home town, where Kate now lives . . .   1-1-59493-039-2 $12.95

RISKY INVESTMENT by Beth Moore. 240 pp. Lynn's best friend and roommate needs her to pretend Chris is his fiancé. But nothing is ever easy.   1-59493-019-8 $12.95

HUNTER'S WAY by Gerri Hill. 240 pp. Homicide detective Tori Hunter is forced to team up with the hot-tempered Samantha Kennedy.   1-59493-018-X $12.95

CAR POOL by Karin Kallmaker. 240 pp. Soft shoulders, merging traffic and slippery when wet . . . Anthea and Shay find love in the car pool.   1-59493-013-9 $12.95

NO SISTER OF MINE by Jeanne G'Fellers. 240 pp. Telepathic women fight to coexist with a patriarchal society that wishes their eradication.   1-59493-017-1 $12.95

ON THE WINGS OF LOVE by Megan Carter. 240 pp. Stacie's reporting career is on the rocks. She has to interview bestselling author Cheryl, or else!
                                                1-59493-027-9 $12.95

WICKED GOOD TIME by Diana Tremain Braund. 224 pp. Does Christina need Miki as a protector . . . or want her as a lover?   1-59493-031-7 $12.95

THOSE WHO WAIT by Peggy J. Herring. 240 pp. Two brilliant sisters—in love with the same woman!   1-59493-032-5 $12.95